Red Hot Summer

By

Elaine Nolan

Other Publications by Elaine Nolan

Evolved
Of Heroes and Kings

Available from Amazon and Kindle

Soundtracks available on Spotify and iTunes

New titles coming soon

Evolved (rerelease)
Evolved 2.0
Crossing Lives

Red Hot Summer Original Soundtrack available to listen online:
      https://bit.ly/RedHotSummer-spotify
      https://bit.ly/RedHotSummer-iTunes
      https://bit.ly/RedHotSummer-Deezer

To connect on social media, and keep up to date with all new releases and events:

    www.elainenolan.net

    facebook.com/Elnolan40FromNow

    twitter.com/elainenolan2

    instragram.com/elnolan_40fromnow

    pinterest.com/elno40FromNow

    youtube.com/elainenolan1001

    soundcloud.com/elaine-nolan-3

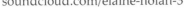

ISBN-13:978-0993002687
ISBN-10:0993002684

A catalogue record for this book is available from all National Libraries of Ireland and from the British Library.

Cover designed by © Paramita Bhattacharjee
www.creativeparamita.com

40 From Now Logo by © Ninja Kitten Studios

A *40 From Now* Publication
© 2015 Elaine Nolan

Acknowledgements

Siobhán Hayden
Tuen Mantodea
Tony Murray
Rim Aad Quinn
Orla Stafford

Table of Contents

Revenge is an act of passion; vengeance of justice.
Injuries are revenged; crimes are avenged.

~ Samuel Johnson ~

Prologues

Fifteen years ago
Blackwater Point, Wexford, Ireland

The 1954 Mercedes-Benz 300SL Gullwing was Lee's dream car, and although now tired, he drove with pleasure. The setting summer's sun glowed on the long, silver-grey bonnet, turning it silver-pink. Beneath the sun's caress, the reconditioned engine purred as he drove, her maiden voyage since her resurrection and restoration, receiving admiring and appreciative looks along the route. Now, he drove her home.

After the day at the beach, his wife slept in the seat beside him. He knew how she felt. The cool sea breeze affected him in the same way, clearing the cobwebs from his mind, yet leaving him tired from the experience. Still, it had been a wonderful day. His only regret was the absence of his daughter. With the national state exams two weeks away, his little girl opted to stay home to study. She was right, but they were only intermediary exams, and no reason to worry. Not with another two years of school ahead of her. She was a bright kid, quiet and studious by nature, a worrier too, and to a fourteen year old, he supposed, these exams seemed like life and death.

A casual glance in the rear-view mirror showed a car gaining on them. Not a difficult achievement as the Gullwing cruised below the speed limit. Another quick glance saw the car closing the gap, and he shook his head as he calculated what their speed could be, almost double his own. He eased onto the road's hard shoulder to give them room to pass and the car whizzed by, tinted glass obstructing his view of the driver.

The passing car did not continue with the velocity at which it had approached. The brake lights flashed ahead of Lee, and he slammed on his own brakes. What the hell was this asshole doing? The car ahead came to an abrupt stop, and Lee spun the Gullwing onto the grassy verge to avoid a collision. The jolt woke his wife, and she looked at him in dazed surprise. He gave her knee a gentle, reassuring squeeze, before jumping out to confront the other driver. As he stepped out, the other driver emerged.

"You?" Lee growled at the approaching figure. "Why?"

The other man levelled a gun.

"You should have stayed out of my business," he replied.

"Your business?" Lee roared at him, moving his hand to his own gun, secured in the side holster, inside his jacket. "What you're doing is illegal. Do you think these tactics will scare me?"

"Who said anything about scaring you?" he said, squeezing the trigger.

A second shot silenced Anna's scream as she watched her husband's body fall to the ground.

Five years ago

University of Honolulu, Meteorological Research Station, Hawaii, USA

Dan placed his putter back into his golf bag, and stretched in the warm, late evening sun, before hoisting the bag onto his shoulder. The day was too good to waste stuck inside the Meteorological building, and his putting needed the practice. As head of the research team on the island, he had others to step in should a problem arise.

Postgraduates, eager to complete their thesis, made up the majority of the team. Dan offered advice and hands-on technical training on Pacific airflows, and active weather monitoring of rainstorms. At this point in his life, he could tell the weather in his sleep. Still, the Pacific was capricious, and her unpredictability continued to hold his fascination. To study her was a life-long commitment, a calling.

The faculty changed its policy this year, and Dan now had to deal with volcanologists at the base. One or two a year were not uncommon, but this year saw an upsurge in the number of students, stretching resources to their limits. They pitched in with the day-to-day chores, and everything ran like clockwork. Just how Dan liked it. As for the volcanoes, Dan knew a link existed between the Pacific weather and the fiery eruptions on the seabed, but something caused a stir with these new arrivals.

He returned to the main research centre, a routine check-in with his kids. The centre was buzzing as he entered. Ah, the thrill of scientific discovery, he thought. It had been a while since he'd felt its tingle. Dumping the golf bag in his office, he wandered back into the hubbub, the Volcans mingling with the Met students. It was a strange sight, but one Dan was getting accustomed to. The two scientific streams never worked this closely before and he noted the mood. Not excitement about a discovery, but a solemn intensity. Everyone huddled together, their attention focused on a large overhead screen, no one wanting to miss a single detail. Dan muscled his way in.

"What have we got?" he asked. The kid at the console looked up.

"We've just downloaded the latest data from the two teams, and I'm running future projections based on the readings," she answered. Dan didn't like what he saw on the screen.

"This is a mistake," Dan reasoned. The student shook her head.

"I've also correlated weather readings from over the last twelve months, and included seismic and volcanic emission data taken last year," she answered.

"But, these readings are way off scale," he replied. "This projects an upcoming disaster."

Kenny, head of the volcano research, nodded.

"That's not the worst of it," he said.

"There's more?" Dan said, with uncharacteristic sarcasm. Kenny nodded again.

"The Pacific region is the most active volcanic chain in the world. Last year the sulphur emissions increased at an unprecedented, and alarming rate, as did the CO_2 levels," he explained.

"I'm aware of the volcanic status in this region," Dan replied, "but can the emission readings be wrong?"

Kenny shook his head, and Dan glanced at the red swirls on the screen.

"This is bad," he said. "This is showing impending heat waves, an increase in tornado and hurricane intensities, and God knows what else."

Kenny nodded.

"That's not the worst of it," he said. Everyone looked at Kenny, expectant but fearing the news.

"Tectonic activity also increased on this plate, stresses were recorded at a new high," he said.

"What kind of activity are we talking about?" Dan asked.

"A three centimetre shift in two years. If the volcanoes continue at their present level of activity, we're looking at a major shift from the plate."

"A significant earthquake," Dan whispered. Kenny nodded.

"At least a magnitude seven, if not eight," he said. "And resulting tsunamis."

"Do we have a timescale?" Dan asked.

"We'll be lucky to get away with another two or three years," came the answer.

The room went quiet at this revelation. They understood the consequences – earthquakes, floods and whatever else Mother Nature thought of throwing at them.

Two years ago
Los Angeles, California, USA

The prediction that the sea would find its way into the divide, turning California into an island, proved wrong. What no one expected was the chain of volcanoes along the fault line. Magma erupted through fissures in the thin crust, and grew at an alarming rate, proving to be as active as the Pacific Ocean chain.

On a human scale, the cost of complacency was high, making it one of the deadliest natural disasters. The death toll was even higher than the last tsunami that hit Indonesia the year before. Tsunamis were becoming a common occurrence within the Pacific, and the resulting backlash wave from the Andreas Fault shift caused devastation, reaching as far as the shores of Eastern Europe. Europe hadn't escaped the Earth's destructive rampage either. Extensive and unprecedented levels of rainfall caused severe flooding in Switzerland, including parts of France, Germany, the United Kingdom and Ireland.

The States now walked on an economic knife-edge. The added cost of economic aid to the southern states most affected by hurricanes and tornadoes, put a severe strain on America's financial resources. America would have to swallow her pride and seek help from her allies across the Atlantic.

Only time would tell who her friends and who her foes were.

Chapter 1

Ten months ago
Carlow, Ireland

The early autumn dawn was cool and grey as the solitary figure lengthened her stride on the empty road. She preferred running in the early morning, fewer cars passed, and the air was fresher. Linkin Park played at a low volume on her iPod, the throbbing bass of their songs always good to run to, and it blocked everything else out. A light mist descended, a precursor to the heavy rain predicted for later in the day. Her baseball cap shielded her face from the dampness, but she still raised her head to feel the mist on her burning cheeks. Her hot and ragged breath made little swirls ahead of her as she neared her destination.

Turning off the road, she slowed to a jog up her driveway, her breathing returning to normal as she reached her home, a two-storey house situated just off the N9, on the Kilkenny side of the town. Jessie ran out to meet her, a West-Highland pup, with a tendency to go for the legs of her tracksuit as she walked. He followed her around to the back of the house, the entrance she always used. The front door was for sales people, and those who didn't know her well. Preparing breakfast, she threw titbits to the hound sitting by her side, a daily ritual for both of them. While she ate, she skimmed the headlines of the news on her e-pad, arriving in her inbox while out on her run.

Putting the e-pad aside, she picked up and reread the enigmatic letter from her solicitor, rechecking the date and time she'd noted at the bottom. Not that she needed to. Due to her meticulous nature she also wrote it into her day diary and her electronic scheduler. The old man wouldn't tell her what it was about over the phone, only adding to the mystery.

Jessie slept at the foot of her bed as she showered and dressed, choosing a dark pinstripe suit and a burgundy shirt. While meticulous by nature, paying great attention to detail, she resorted to scrunch drying her hair, having always had unmanageable kinks and waves. An unruly mop completed the picture of otherwise neat perfection. She scratched Jessie on the head as he tried following her out, but she threw him a doggy biscuit, and he knew he wouldn't be going with her.

Driving into town and parking behind the courthouse, she walked the short distance to the solicitor's office, surprised to find a removals van parked illegally in front of the building. Sidestepping stacked boxes, she entered and spoke to the receptionist, following her into the building, where Gerald Morris met her at the door to his office. The old man greeted her with a hug more suited to a grandfather than her legal adviser, and invited her in, offering her a seat and a cup of tea. She sat down, but declined on the tea.

"Never touch the stuff," she said.

"Coffee then?" Gerald asked, to which she accepted. He relayed the order to the receptionist still waiting by the door.

"You must excuse the appearance," he said, waving a hand at the stacks of boxes and papers, "but we're moving to bigger premises."

"To where?" she asked.

"That new office block on the Dublin Road. We're expanding at a phenomenal rate, and it's getting tight for space here," he answered. "And how are you doing? The last time we spoke you were investing in a hotel, but I've seen you working behind the bar once or twice, so can I assume the venture wasn't a success?" he asked.

She laughed.

"Quite the opposite," she answered. "Being a silent partner has its advantages. I help behind the bar, or as security on the door, whenever they're short staffed, and I get to see what's going on."

He chuckled.

"So like your father. He was devious in his business dealings too. And your own venture?" he asked.

"Wise Light?" she asked, and he nodded. She grinned, remembering the hours she'd spent quizzing him on company law.

"I can be selective about my clients now," she answered.

"That is good news, but my dear, you didn't come here for a chat or to listen to me prattling on," he said. Leigh smiled, but held her tongue. The old man continued. "I'm also on the verge of retirement, and I wanted to clear out all of my old cases, and in inventorying all my old files in storage, we came upon these." He laid a hand on two strong boxes, sitting on his desk.

"And they are?" she asked.

"Yours," he replied. "Or, to be more precise, they were left in my possession, and to be given to you. One of them, your father gave me before that tragic car crash. The second arrived soon afterwards. I presumed your father arranged for it to be delivered here."

"But the accident was over a decade ago. You gave me everything when I turned eighteen, why am I finding out about these now?" she asked keeping her voice level. Gerald frowned, and she held up a hand. "Mr Morris, I'm not questioning your integrity, but why now?"

"To be honest my dear, they only came to light during the inventory. My old memory is not as good as it used to be, but I remember a strange incident." He paused as the coffee arrived, and he poured a cup for her.

"If I recall, your father gave me specific instructions regarding the first box. No one but you was to have access to it. He didn't elaborate on its contents, and I didn't pry. As you can see, they've never been opened, or even tampered with. But that does not explain the delay." He paused again, taking a sip of his coffee. "Soon after the accident, as I left the office, a man approached me. A tall man, as I recall, who demanded I hand over the box to him. I denied its existence, but he insisted, became threatening, so I called the Gardaí. After what just happened, I locked the box in the vault in the basement for safekeeping. It turned out my instincts were right. During the night someone broke into the building, and only my office was ransacked, but nothing was missing. The vault hadn't been touched. When the second box arrived, I placed it with the first for safekeeping. I suppose it's the old axiom of 'out of sight, out of mind', and these boxes resurfaced with the impending move. I apologise for the delay."

She shook her head as she stood.

"No, it's understandable, given the circumstances." She placed a trembling hand on the boxes. These were her dad's. How odd that something of his should re-emerge now.

"And you don't know what's in them?" she asked.

He shook his head.

"As I've said, he never told me."

"Keys?" she asked.

"I'm sorry, also mislaid," he answered. "I'll get one of the younger, more able-bodied men to help carry them out. Are you parked nearby?"

"Courthouse," she replied.

With the boxes stored in the boot she drove home. Carrying them in, she placed them on the table and sat down, examining both the boxes and their locks. She looked at Jessie, and the Westie cocked an ear at her, a quizzical grin on his face.

"Let's find out what we got, pooch," she said to him, and she went to the garage, a separate structure at the rear of the premises. It was her dad's old workshop, the place where he'd indulged in his favourite pastime of car restoration, and she retrieved the bolt cutters from the tool rack. The locks snapped as the cutters bit through the metal, making the dog scamper away, and hide behind the door until the ruckus ended.

"Coward," she called after him, a single ear cocked as his little head peered around the door.

Opening the larger of the two boxes she found two thick notebooks, papers and photographs. Lots of old photographs, tied together in small bundles. She took the items out one by one, placing them beside each other on the table, until she reached a single envelope.

Her hand stilled. The envelope was addressed to her, in her dad's handwriting, and she pulled her hand back, as though hearing her father calling her. After all these years, it still made her feel like a little girl. She reached in for it, her name written in his flowing script and in ink, from the fountain pen he used to love writing with, but it chilled her.

Giving herself a little shake, she scolded herself for being silly and superstitious, not two areas she suffered from. Lee taught her to be practical and scientific. Nothing in life happened without a reason. Looking at the envelope she thought there must be a one hell of a reason for him to have written to her all those years ago, one damn good explanation for this letter. She glanced at the dog, but Jessie watched her with intent, without a whimper. Leigh turned over the envelope, finding it sealed, and using a knife from the wooden knife block, she slipped it between the fold, cutting the paper open before pulling out the folded page. She opened it and read her father's words.

Dearest Leigh.

If you are reading this, it means I am dead, probably your mother too, and my purpose in writing this is to warn you. All is not what it seems, and as much as it pains me to tell you, neither am I. Forces greater than myself work in the world, and it is all I can do to keep the wicked at bay. For years I've lived and worked a double life. Your mother knew and understood the dangers. You're too young, and I hope you are not so by the time you have to read this.

Leigh, there are people in the world bent upon its destruction, but please believe me, I am not one of them. It is my duty to protect, it always has been, and in writing to you I'm striving to protect you too. Arming you with knowledge is my only defence. If you are reading this, then my actions have put you are in danger, and my darling I am sorry.

I've left you my journals to uncover the truth, but please, I beg you not to pursue it, unless your own life is threatened.

*I love you so much, my little princess. Please forgive me for
this. Don't hate me for what I thought was the right thing to do.*

Your loving father

Leigh let the page fall from her hands as they trembled. She stood
up, and ran her fingers through her hair, breathing hard. The words were
hard to digest. The implications were immense. Something about a
double life? No! She didn't want to believe it.

Putting the letter aside for the moment, she thumbed through one
notebook, but it made no sense. Most likely it was written with some
form of encryption, and if her father wrote them over a decade ago, he
would have done so with limited technology, unlike now, with the
myriad of software decryption programs she had available to her.
Glancing at her watch she realised she was running late, and swore to
herself as she ran up the stairs to get dressed for work.

A rare occasion, the hotel found themselves short staffed, and she
stepped in to help behind the bar. The function turned out to be a Garda
retirement party. A large party at that, and Leigh just smiled as those she
served looked at her, as though trying to figure out why she seemed
familiar to them. One cop stared at her incredulously.

"Jaysus child, why didn't you tell me things were this bad? I
thought your old man left you a little something to live on," he said.
Leigh laughed at him.

"They needed help, so I'm helping," she answered.

Tom shook his head.

"This is no place for a little girl like you," he said.

"I'm not a little girl anymore, Tom," she replied.

He huffed and turned to the Gardaí standing nearby.

"Fellas," he roared at them. "You remember a Detective Garda by
the name of Lee Harte?" The older ones nodded, murmuring recollections

amongst themselves, while those newer to the Force looked on with interest; they'd heard the name. "Well, we have the pleasure of being served by his little one," Tom continued. For the next while Leigh endured introduction after introduction, and anecdotes from those who remembered the man. Owen watched with amusement while Jamie was stunned.

"You know these people?" Jamie asked, in awed tones.

"My dad was a Garda. Some of these people worked with him," Leigh answered.

"You actually had a dad?" he said.

"Yeah, contrary to popular belief I wasn't hatched in an evil science project," she answered

"How come you never talk about him?" Jamie inquired.

"He's dead. Not much to talk about," she said, sharper than she'd intended. To avoid any more questions she took another order.

"Don't go there. She's touchy about family stuff," Owen whispered to him.

And so the night wore on, but a moment or two got stuck, and lengthened, and Leigh listened to more stories about her dad. Jamie listened with keen interest as Tom revealed more about a young Leigh than she liked. The younger, newer guards asked for her number. Anyone who could stand up to a man like Tom, and who could give back as good as Tom gave, deserved a date. Leigh refused them all. No coyness, no palming off with maybes, but with definite no's. The braver ones sought Tom's help, but he laughed at them. They were big enough men to fight their own battles.

The night wore on, the chatter growing louder despite people dwindling away, and the clean-up was fast and furious. Tom remained the sole survivor of the party, and he watched Leigh, sipping the last of his pint.

"Haven't seen your head on many wanted posters, so you must be doing something right," he commented as she approached him.

"Just haven't gotten caught, that's all," she answered.

"No bigger crime than getting caught," he said. "Looks like you straightened yourself out."

Her dad's oldest and closest friend, he'd dealt with her anti-social behaviour after her parents' deaths. He gave her a good fright, and saved her from a juvenile criminal record, and probably a more senior, permanent one. She nodded and sat beside him.

"I'm doing all right. Couple of ventures, all legal," she told him.

"And working here is?" he asked.

"Protecting an investment," she answered, and glanced about to make sure the boys didn't overhear. Tom looked at her in surprise. "I'm one of the owners, but that's not common knowledge," she told him.

"You've done good, kiddo," he told her, and her smile turned into a soft laugh. "But you look like there's something on your mind," he said, and it was her turn to look surprised. Going back to the bar, she returned with two bottles of American beer, and handed one to him.

"To your old man," he said, raising the bottle. She gave him a haunted half smile, not unlike Lee senior, and chinked her bottle against his. "Spit it out, kid," he said to her. "I know you better than you think I do." She sighed and sat.

"The weirdest thing happened today," she started, "I was with my solicitor, and he came across some of dad's stuff they'd misplaced. I guess I'm just a little rattled by it, and then seeing you here."

"A lot of old memories," he concluded, and she nodded before taking a long drink.

"Tom, did dad ever keep a journal?"

Tom shrugged.

"We all kept a work log, cases we were working on. Is that what you mean?"

"To be honest, I'm not sure what I'm talking about. There was an old notebook, but I couldn't make sense of it," she replied.

"I could take a look at it, if you like." Before Leigh could answer him, Jamie interrupted them.

"You order a taxi?" he asked the Garda. The big man nodded and finished his drink.

"Can I drop you off along the way?" he asked Leigh. She shook her head.

"I'm staying awhile, maybe have a pint with the lads," she answered.

"That's after-hours drinking, and illegal," Tom scolded.

"So what are you still doing here?" she fired back.

"Just leaving, just leaving," he answered.

He paused at the door, half-turning to look at her, but found her lost in thought at the table.

Chapter 2

Leigh returned home early in the morning, the taxi rolling up the drive, the pint or two turning into three or four at the very least. While the hotel was an investment, Leigh paid little attention to the financial end of it. Accountants did the worrying, and the other two owners were more involved in the day-to-day running of the business. Leigh just liked to keep her hand in on occasion, and she liked the social aspect to it.

A solitary creature by nature, sometimes she found other human interaction comforting, and after the shock of the afternoon, last night was one of those times. Fortified with alcohol, Owen suggested going home with her, but she smiled and walking away, invoking her dad's old sayings of never visiting the same place twice. Like the old cliché of 'never returning to the scene of a crime', and Leigh applied that to most areas in her life, especially former partners, no matter how brief, or fun, it may have been.

Jessie's bark changed from low and menacing to a higher pitch of excitement as Leigh entered, disgusted to find she'd left the metal boxes on the table and in plain sight. Uneasiness grew as she approached them, knowing the reason lay in the information they contained, the revelations she wasn't sure she wanted to know.

The smaller of the two boxes disturbed her most, where she'd found another two notebooks, a set of keys and a gun. Now she opened that box again, taking out the contents, allowing the keys to fall from its envelope. She flipped the attached label over, reading the address scribbled on it, the ink fading on the card. Pushing the keys to one side, she retrieved the two journals, finding they too contained the same nonsensical writing. She paused, thinking about the decryption programs available to her, before loading everything into the smaller box, including the remaining contents of the first, and carried it to her office.

Leigh inherited this four bedroom house, the only home she'd ever known, but over the years she toyed with the notion of selling up, as much for downsizing as for getting away from the past. These notions never lasted long, only reared its ugly head whenever a bout of melancholy took hold. Such bouts never lasted, and she wouldn't dream of leaving. It held her past, and where would she go? Having travelled around the world, spending considerable time in Germany, she always returned home. Besides, she'd argue with herself, where else would find the same space to work on her cars?

Originally her father's office, Leigh used it for her own business, using the concealed safe, a reinforced steel box, hidden behind the converted fireplace, its disguise complete with cast iron façade and cedar mantelpiece. Over the years she'd made upgrades to the security, including an electronic keypad, and after entering the code, the entire ornate front section opened out. Removing the four notebooks and letter, she placed the box and its remaining contents into the safe and shut everything, the mantelpiece clicking closed.

To an outsider, the excessive level of security would seem overkill, but her business demanded it. As an IT consultant and developer, specialising in high-end security and encryption systems, she'd secured several government and international business contracts. Ensuring the safety, security and integrity of those systems was the reason for her success. That vault contained database prototypes, sensitive information, and where she now placed the box and gun. That's all she could say about it, having no idea as to the make or model. She knew her dad possessed a gun, a necessity for his job, but he never brought it into the house. Adamant she have nothing to do with them, she sat through many a stern lecture from him on their dangers.

Locked away, she put it out of her mind, and concentrated on the journals, sitting in silence as she studied them. She leafed through them, paying attention to the first few pages, trying to determine their sequence, until she noticed an oddity inside the front covers. Each contained a musical symbol, a clef, the musical notation that showed the pitch of the music. The journal she held in her hand had the bass or the 'F' clef, like a backward 'C'. She opened the cover of the next notebook, surprised to find an alto clef. Not one of the usual clefs, and it resembled a 'IK' on the five lines of the stave, the central stave line going through the centre of the 'K'. A quick check of the inside of the other two covers revealed another two symbols, the treble or 'G' clef, the most recognisable of all musical symbols, and the tenor clef, same in shape to the alto clef but with the centre of the 'K' sitting a line higher on the stave. She put the books in order - treble, alto, tenor and bass and smirked to herself. That much figured out, at least.

The scanning process was slow and laborious, each page having writing on both sides, and dawn peeped through a gap in the blinds by the time Leigh finished the first journal. Using the letter for comparison, and a reference point, she typed in her father's words before also scanning that in, matching the text up with the handwriting. She chose one of her own decryption programs, but it would take time, and tiredness now claimed her. She stretched, trying to loosen tight and weary muscles in her shoulders and thought about scanning the other journals, but there was no point, not until knowing the first one contained something of importance.

Right now hunger and tiredness gnawed at her. Curled up on the floor, Jessie's snores were soft and low, but at the slightest movement from her his ears cocked and he opened one eye. Springing up, he followed her to the kitchen as fast as his little legs would allow, and she made a small snack, feeding the pooch more than she ate herself. Giving into the need for sleep she climbed the stairs, and fell into bed, taking her boots off before crawling under the covers.

Waking to rain pounding against the window, she groaned as she rolled over to check the time, finding it to be just past midday, disturbing Jessie as she arose. She could never figure out how he got up onto the bed while she slept, and he gave a throaty yawn and a puppyish yap. A long hot shower relieved the stiffness from her shoulders before she remembered what she'd been doing.

Back in the office she brought the screen to life, checking the deciphering progress, finding it still incomplete. A frown crossed her forehead as she opened the report log, her expression changing to one of surprise as she read the results. The program completed its job but returned four possible results, and now depended on a key to give a single, definitive solution. A key, she thought and checked the four options. A small smile formed as she looked at them on the screen. She'd scanned in the notebook with the treble clef, better known as the 'G' clef because the line the inner scroll started on. Could it be that simple, she asked herself, but the results report showed 'G' as one of the potential keys. She chose that, and the program started.

She gave it more thought. If the journals all showed a different clef, then no two journals would be coded the same, firing her curiosity. What was so important that her father went to such lengths? While she waited for the program to run and recompile based on the new key given, she checked her mail and scheduler, noting that the deadlines for two projects were looming, but both were well in hand. A beep from the other screen drew her attention, and she opened the file, the opening words grabbing her attention but she printed it out, then sprawled on the sofa with the paper copy.

It read like a novel, a boy's action adventure story, but she reminded herself she was reading about her own father. Or perhaps a Walter Mitty fantasy? And no way it could be true, right? It would've given any spy thriller author a run for their money, except she recognised the names. Some of the names at least. Tom, her self-appointed godfather and the Garda from last night, who'd straightened her out in her wayward teens, warranted a mention in this story. But the jovial, sometimes tough man, was a far cry from how her dad described him. Instead, he used the words cold and merciless. Not the stern giant she remembered. Her dad's version of him was far more ominous, much more sinister.

She flipped ahead a couple of pages, but her recollection of her father was of an exacting man, a meticulous planner who left little to chance. She smirked, recognising that same trait in herself. Turning to the back page she found details of her mother entering into his life and what he wrote astounded Leigh, embarrassed her. Returning to the start of this tale she jotted down names and places as she went along. Reading the entire document didn't take long, and she skimmed back over her notes. That her dad wrote about his training while in Templemore, the Garda Training College, came as no surprise, but his life before then fascinated her. He called it a conscription, dragged into a secret society of spies, if his notes were to be believed, by the then Garda Sergeant Tom Barnett. Was Tom's manner so bad, so sinister?

She sat back and rubbed her tired eyes, recalling several times when Tom hauled her underage ass from some nightclub or other. To make matters worse, she'd been high most of the time, having taken E's and god knew what else. She now considered herself lucky to have survived, but at the time it dulled the pain and hurt, blocked out how alone she felt in the world. Tom hadn't been gentle about it either, waiting until she sobered up before giving her hell. She remembered a rough slap that split her lip, the bruises on her arm where he'd grabbed her and dragged her into a squad car, bruises that lasted weeks. In hindsight Tom could have been as her father described him, hard and taking no bullshit. Perhaps he'd just been easier on Leigh than on her dad. She returned from musing on her own past and concentrated on her father's instead. The vehemence with which he wrote surprised her. She always remembered him as a man of few words, but the few he used said everything. What became clear was his hatred and loathing for Garda Sergeant Barnett who, by the end of this journal, made it to detective.

But why did her father write these? To purge his soul, his conscience? Who knew? The only person who could answer that lay in a grave about two kilometres away, and no point looking there for answers.

Chapter 3

Her idea of getting away from it all involved a car, usually one in distress or in need of repair. As a child she spent weekends and holidays either under a car, or inside it. To earn pocket money, Lee put her to work cleaning the interior of a 1959 Morris Minor 1000 that he'd spent months restoring. As she grew older, her responsibilities also grew, and she progressed to checking tyre pressure as part of her regular duties. When she was old enough to lift a bonnet, Lee explained the entire internal workings to her, adding oil and washer bottle checking to the list.

Tom smirked at the memories when he found her in the garage, head buried in the engine bay of a car, the bonnet propped against a nearby wall. As he stepped inside, his presence registered with that four-legged ball of fur she called a dog, and it jumped up to bark at him. Leigh looked up, surprised, but said nothing. With her hair tied back, she looked younger than her twenty nine years, looking almost as young as the last time he'd needed to sort her out.

"You're as bad as your old man, tinkering around with toy cars." Tom's deep voice echoed within the garage walls.

"Toy cars, huh?" Leigh said. "Should've got you to put the gearbox bell housing back in. See how well you play with toys."

"Your old man used to bandy technical jargon like that at me. Meant nothing then, means nothing now," he confessed, no hint of it being an apology. "So what's this one then?" he gestured to the car.

"'69 Triumph Spitfire, Mk 3," she answered, wiping her hands. "Just needs an oil change, then put back on the bonnet." She turned around, and took her time selecting a tool from the bench.

"So where's the other fella?" Tom asked.

"What other fella?" she asked back.

"The redhead you were going out with. Into his cars as well," Tom said. The tool in her hand clanged against the nut.

"He was an arsehole," she answered. Tom scratched his chin, stepping further into the garage. Something beyond Leigh caught his eye. He stepped around her, and let out a low whistle.

"Now what is that?" he asked of the long sleek form before him, with two white racing stripes up the dark blue bonnet.

"AC Cobra," she answered, and Tom shook his head.

"Looks like a licence loser," he said. "You and your old man, and your fast cars."

She laughed.

"She's a kit. Put her together myself. Took about a year," she said, and Tom turned to frown at her.

"She legal?" he asked, and she gave him a flat stare.

"And risk an encounter with the local constabulary? I shudder at the thought," she answered. "She's legal. Garage certified, registered and taxed. Want to see her papers, Garda?" Tom picked up the slight sharpness in her voice, but knew her better than that. He knew she'd have the legal stuff sorted out. Not that she had always been compliant with the authorities, but that was a long time ago. Yet a hint of her teenage rebellion lurked beneath the surface. Contained, but still there.

"Top speed?" he asked, and a slow smile spread across her face.

"She hit a hundred and fifty."

"Miles or kilometres?" he asked.

"Miles," she answered, and he shook his head.

"How the hell did you find that out? There aren't decent enough stretches of road to hit that speed on," he said, but held up his hand. "No, don't tell me. I don't want to know."

She chuckled to herself, but said nothing, again waiting him out, using his own tricks against him.

"I was thinking about that journal you talked about the other night," he said. Leigh's stance stiffened. She thought on it, long enough to cause him concern.

"Why the interest in it?" she answered.

"Nature of the beast," he answered. "When I hear of a Garda's notebook lying around I get nervous, no matter how much time has passed. The information in them could still be sensitive," he said, and she nodded. He knew she would grasp the severity of the situation. Her livelihood depended on it.

"I understand what you're saying, Tom, but it's just gibberish. Probably dad just playing about with encryptions, and you know how good he was at that stuff. I wouldn't even know where to start working it out," she lied with conviction. Tom fell silent, and Leigh knew from experience the cogs were spinning fast in his head. Tom liked to give the impression he was a slow and deliberate thinker, but Leigh learned a long time ago that nothing could be further from the truth.

"Still, I should look at it," he pressed. Tom now pushed too much for her liking.

"Why waste your time," she answered.

"Well if you're sure they're nothing to do with his work," he said, sensing he wasn't getting anywhere.

"Fairly sure."

"Just to be on the safe side," he began, stopping as her jaw set, just like Lee used to do, and he knew he'd stepped onto thin ice with her.

"Some security software consultant I'd make if I couldn't keep my own stuff safe," she said.

"A fair point," he conceded. "I'll leave you to your toys, but if you change your mind or if anything should happen…"

"Like what?" she threw back at him.

"Who knows," he answered. "You know where I am."

She nodded and followed behind him as he walked out. About to round the house and disappear out of view, he gave a quick glance back and found her at the threshold of the garage still watching him, a hostile look on her face and he wondered why, wondered if she told the truth about Lee's notebook, about not deciphering it. That worried him as he got into his car. No longer the shy little bookworm, she'd grown into an indifferent young woman. The only things to stir her were computers and cars. Just like Lee. Her teenage rebellion was a knee-jerk reaction to their deaths, but her subsequent detachment to everything became more than mere teenage angst. His gut told him she lied about the journal, and that barefaced lie amazed him.

Finishing with the car, reinstalling the bonnet, Leigh returned to the journal and her notes. One name popped up over and over again throughout the document, referring to a place, and she resorted to the web to search for it. Despite all her safeguards, a firewall tweaked to her technical specification, the attempted breach in her security caused her concern. She broke the connection and opened the log file, but it raised more questions than it provided answers. The tracer program attempting to attach itself to her systems used a complex and enhanced encryption process reserved for government departments. It got her thinking. More than thinking, it became a fixation for the moment, more from the technology used than for any other reason, using a newer configuration, and it intrigued her. More than intrigued, it fascinated her. Not an insurmountable problem, she mused, computer systems were a product of logic, and therefore had a solution, which just eluded her at present. It needed time to fester on her brain, allowing her subconscious to mull over the problem and present the answer, or at the very least, the next logical step to be taken. She needed another distraction, something else to divert her attention, and that logical solution was the next journal.

She went to the safe to retrieve the next notebook, and her fingers brushed against the set of keys. She took them out with the book, curiosity about the journal battling curiosity about what the keys would unlock. No point in wasting time, and again, all things in logical order, while the computer decrypted the journal, she could investigate the address on the key tag. Preprograming the code for this journal meant the next instalment of the story would be ready and waiting for her when she returned. With that plan, she dedicated the next hour to scanning the second notebook. She drove into town, taking the left slip road down

Burrin Street, then turned on to Pembroke. The rundown wooden gates seemed familiar, a memory itching at the back of her mind as she parked, noting in the growing evening light the peeling paint and the general state of disrepair. She grasped the old, but sturdy, padlock then looked to the keys in her hand, selecting the most likely one. At first she thought she'd made a foolish mistake, but lack of use over the years made the lock slow to give way.

She unbolted the gate, opening it inwards, uneasy at every groan and creak the wood made. With the diminishing light from outside, the interior was gloomy, but a vague recollection told her she'd find a light switch on the wall where the gate ended. That memory proved correct though not as high as she thought. As the single bulb overhead sprang to life, she remembered this was her dad's second garage, the overflow garage when there'd been too many car bits strewn about back at home.

All completed projects ended up here to make room for the next labour of love. Much bigger than she remembered, the last time she'd stepped foot in here was about fifteen years ago, conscripted into waxing and polishing Lee's last completed project, the Gullwing. She frowned at the covered bulky object before her, not recalling any other car in the garage at the time, unless someone returned the crashed Mercedes to its home. Pulling the tarpaulin off she inhaled sharply, finding the Gullwing, its undented and perfect silver bonnet gleaming under the naked light bulb. Trying the driver's door handle she found it locked, but selected the one most likely key from the set, and it unlocked with ease, trying one of the remaining keys in the ignition. The engine roared to life, sounding loud in the confined space. She killed the engine and got back out, surveying her surroundings before returning her attention to the car.

It only raised more questions. If the keys were in the second box, arriving at the solicitor's office after the so-called crash, then who sent them? No way had her father posted them from beyond the grave. Tom, she wondered, but dismissed that idea. Tom would have given her the keys a long time ago, and would've known about the journals, but they seemed to be as big a mystery to him. She took a step back, and her head brushed against something, startling her. Looking up she saw a plastic knob attached to the end of a thick cord and caught hold of it, the trap door groaning on its hinges as she pulled it open, an extendible ladder folded on the hidden side. She straightened it out, and climbed.

The street lights illuminated the space through the half opened blinds of the attic windows, and Leigh scanned along the wall, finding the outline of a light switch, and the florescent tube glowed and hummed for a moment before flickering to life. Even with the dust, the place was neat with a living area and office space, complete with a mini cooker and refrigerator, a large desk with two old fashioned wheeled chairs, and a filing cabinet. An old couch sat against the remaining wall. She scanned the book-lined shelves, surprised to find paperback novels mixed in with technical manuals. The car manuals didn't come as a surprise, as she picked out the makes and models she'd helped her dad work on, but the other manuals grabbed her attention, adding credence to her father's fanciful tale, books ranging in subject matters as the latest surveillance techniques in the early 1980s, to military manuals from several countries.

She turned her attention to the filing cabinet and found it locked. One key remained unused on the set and she tried it, and it fit. She opened it, finding old photos, papers, a gun with ammo, and camping equipment. The sleeping bag looked well used, and she wondered if her dad spent nights here. She took the papers and photos out, skimming through them, figuring them to be case and assignment notes and in her dad's handwriting. She hesitated in reaching for the weapon, wondering about talking it, but left it where it was.

Taking the pictures and documents with her, she retreated to the ground floor but thought on what to do with the Gullwing. Without giving the old car a check over, she wouldn't consider driving it, and with a final glance at the relocked garage doors, she returned home.

Chapter 4

The job didn't come through the usual channels, and the second journal put Leigh on edge. Not one to suffer from the jitters, the journal still rattled her. Her father outlined in meticulous detail his assigned operations and assassinations, noting his methods of execution, his tricks for extracting information, often in an innocent fashion. The disgust and loathing he had towards himself was clear in his writings, but paled compared to the loathing he held towards his handler, a name she'd not heard before.

The list of names and places noted from his journals grew, but her computer systems came under attack each time she searched the references. And now this offer to meet with a new client. She didn't believe in coincidences, there was no such thing. Her father taught her that. So why'd she agree to a meeting? The caller sounded kosher, mentioned all the right names in the initial telephone conversation, names of people she'd worked for exclusively. But again, why? She didn't need the money, or the challenge, but it piqued her curiosity, as did the meeting's location. Yet another coincidence, she wondered, the client choosing the lobby of her hotel.

Designed to cater for business meetings and quiet get-togethers, the lobby offered comfortable surroundings while maintaining a level of discretion, without it seeming clandestine. Leigh found him easily enough, sitting reading the paper, or at least giving that impression. Christopher Lantry.

That name put her on edge, but tried not to let it show as she walked towards him, slowing her stride as he looked up and spotted her. She wanted to appear relaxed, that this was what it was supposed to be, a meeting with a potential client.

"Mr Lantry?" she asked, and he smiled.

"Miss Harte," he replied, standing to greet her and offering a handshake, his grip firm and warm. She sat opposite him, surprised to find he'd already ordered coffee for her. He poured her a cup.

"So Mr Lantry, what can I do for you?" she asked with no preamble. He studied her from over the rim of his own cup and found her scrutinizing him in return, sizing him up. He held back on answering her, surprised when she didn't fall for the ploy and try filling the silence between them. After what he'd learned of her, should he be surprised? She reminded him very much of her father, a keen penetrating gaze, but on her it seemed softer, or perhaps time distorted the memory of Lee. He put down his cup.

"I'm afraid I've resorted to a ruse to get you here Miss Harte, or may I call you Leigh?" he asked, a twinge of annoyance arising as she shrugged, seemingly unperturbed by his admission. "What do you know of Huntington?" He saw her mouth tighten and her features harden.

"It's just off Anglesea road, Dublin 4," she answered.

"I believe that's Haddington road," he answered.

"Oops, my bad," she replied, unapologetic. He let silence reign again as they sized each other up.

"I knew your father," he said, expecting her to react, and again was disappointed. Instead, Leigh settled back into her seat, resting her elbows on the armrests, her fingers interlaced in front of her, leaving her coffee untouched as she watched him, a closed book to him. Too much like her father, he concluded. This time she broke the silence.

"So why am I here?" she asked, her directness not unexpected, but still surprising him a little.

"You don't seem to be a person easily intimidated, so I'll be blunt and give you some advice, and that is to back off."

"I have no idea what you're talking about," she lied, and he almost believed her, but the coldness in her eyes betrayed her.

"I don't know how you came across Huntington, but I'm telling you to stop." While his tone didn't alter, she heard a sharpness to it.

36

"Stop what?" she asked, sounding innocent.

"Huntington. How did you find out about it?"

"I'm sure I overheard the women in the gym mention it, some trendy little health spa, isn't it?"

He held back a smirk at her smart remark, at her challenge. If he denied it would it fuel her curiosity all the more? That was a dangerous trait in her father, that curiosity, that inability to let go and just walk away. How much like him would she prove to be?

"If that's all it is, then you have nothing to worry about."

"If that's all it is, then why try breaking into my systems?" she asked, imitating his sharp tone. Again, her direct challenge took him by surprise.

"I like to know who I'm dealing with," he answered. She replied with a slight raise of an eyebrow that said likewise.

This young woman before him was a far cry from the child she'd been, the child he'd known before their deaths. It was obvious she didn't remember him but she was young the last time she'd seen him. While the profile he'd read on her was accurate in terms of her history and her associates, her personality profile proved not so accurate. Nowhere did it mention her as being this much of a hard ass. He decided on a tactical retreat and he stood.

"Heed me well Miss Harte. Huntington is none of your concern, but it could prove detrimental to your health if you persist on delving into areas you don't belong."

He left her, and she glanced about to see him enter the lift. Only when the doors closed, and he disappeared from sight did she breathe, her hands and arms shaking. Now she understood why she came, to get the measure of the man who controlled her father. But more than that. By meeting the man, it proved the journals were true, confirming everything her dad wrote. Lantry existed, Huntington existed and her dad was an agent, an assassin, a spy of some sort.

That's why she'd come, to disprove the journals, not wanting to believe the person her dad was, not wanting to believe he'd been capable of such acts and actions. For the first time in her life, she hated him.

Lantry used the elevator as a ploy to make good his exit. Getting out at the fourth floor, he walked to the stairwell and descended again, taking his time until informed by his agents when Leigh left. Re-emerging in the lobby he joined Barnett who took Leigh's vacated seat.

"Well?" Lantry demanded.

"Hard to know," Barnett confessed.

"And this alleged notebook?"

"They found nothing in her house," Barnett answered. "If it exists she must have locked it away."

"So Lee kept a record," Lantry mused. "I refuse to believe she mentioned it to you, and then out of the blue searched for me and Huntington. Do you think she'll heed the warning?"

"I don't know."

"Why not? You assignment was to watch her."

"It didn't seem necessary. After she straightened herself out, it looked like she reverted back to being the quiet little bookworm."

"And where did this journal come from?"

"She mentioned her solicitor coming across them in their old files," Tom answered. "She said they looked like gibberish. But you knew Lee, always messing about with encryptions."

Lantry nodded.

"But she specializes in high-end security systems and encryptions, how difficult would it be for her to work out his cyphers?"

"Not very," Tom admitted.

"Keep a better eye on her. If it looks like she's not taking the hint, a stronger warning will be necessary." Tom nodded as he stood and left, knowing too well what Lantry meant.

Dozing off, Jessie's low growling woke her. He jumped up, his little body taut, staring at the door. Someone's in the house, she thought and looked towards a display console on the wall near the bed. One internal light flashed, yet the alarm didn't sound, and that worried her. Easing herself out of bed, praying the floorboards didn't creak, she crept to the door, peeking through the thin gap.

Nothing seemed out of the ordinary. No shadows moved in the gloom yet Jessie continued to growl, lower and quieter now that Leigh was up and prepared to defend him. She moved to the wardrobe, sliding a door open wide enough to retrieve a hurley, then returned to the door. She glanced back to her phone, but estimated it would take too long to call for reinforcements. What if she was wrong, and Jessie was reacting to a bat or a mouse?

Feeling more secure with the weighty ash club in her hand she moved barefoot to the stairs and hunkered to a crouch, scanning the lower floor. Staying close to the wall she descended but froze halfway as something fell in her office. A surge of anger rose within her, and she descended the remaining steps quicker than before.

A shadow jumped across the doorstep of her office and she stiffened for a moment, questioning her decision not to call the Gardaí, but she knew by the time she got through and explained herself, the element of surprise would be gone. She had no idea who or what she was up against, but she had a hunch. The journals, the panicked thought ran through her mind. Had she left any of them out? She didn't think so.

She spun around at movement behind her, one intruder advancing on her, and he didn't expect her to be armed as she swung the club at his knee first and then his head. He went down, but lay still.

The door of her office opened, a beam from a flashlight blinding her and she turned to run. A hand grabbed her ankle, and she fell forward, hitting the ground hard but she rolled over and kicked her assailant in the face with her free foot. He yelled, but she didn't hang about for apologies and scrambled up, grabbing the hurley again and swinging at the next guy. It missed, and he stepped inside the arc of her swing, grabbing her, locking her arms at her sides.

At a disadvantage with no shoes, her heel still managed to inflict pain as she kicked back at his shin. Not hard enough though, and he pushed her hard against the wall. She got an arm free and reversed elbowed him, catching him in the ear. In pain, he loosened his grip on her, but the moment of freedom was short lived and she was tackled to the ground again, her hands pinned behind her. No amount of struggling worked in freeing herself.

"Miss Harte," she heard a familiar drawl, and twisted around to look up at the speaker. She felt no comfort in knowing her assumptions were correct as Lantry leered down at her.

"I warned you to stay out of my affairs but you wouldn't listen. As you've chosen to ignore my warning, you leave me with two choices; to shoot you or recruit you. Which will it be?" She answered by struggling against her bonds.

"Have it your way," he replied, and she felt a sharp pain before blackness overtook her.

Chapter 5
Present Day
Malone, New York, USA

The German experienced few difficulties escaping the so-called watchful eyes in Washington. The sloppiness of US Agents both pleased and irritated him in equal measures; pleased for it enabled him to run his enterprises freely, but irritated by the lack of standards, offering him no challenge. He refocused his attention to the people in the factory yard climbing aboard trailers, floodlights adding much needed illumination in the dim evening light.

Three trailers sat side by side, enough to hold everyone, with space to spare. Tonight would be his last night to play ferryman across the Canadian border, his sources informed him. And his sources were never wrong. As one of the trailer doors closed, a woman screamed in the claustrophobic gloom. Someone shouted at her to shut up, or they'd leave her behind. The threat worked. She feared staying more than she feared the dark. And why not? She'd sold everything she owned to make a new start in Canada, and the German's services hadn't come cheap, but it came with visas and new IDs, credit ratings, financial scores and credible employment records. By the time the trucks rolled out of the factory yard, the German had disappeared.

Jake crouched low against the wall of the trucking depot, watching the shadowy form of his long-time nemesis, having followed Karl Gouderhoff here from Washington. The dark hid him well as the German's hired hands completed their task of loading the trucks, and the German left. Jake followed him, hanging back should Gouderhoff turn around and see him. After getting this close Jake didn't want to lose the element of surprise. It had taken time to get close to his adversary again, and he didn't want the opportunity to slip through his fingers because he got careless and fucked up.

Gouderhoff disappeared around a murky corner and Jake tailed him, plunged into darkness when the surrounding buildings blocked out the light. He stopped, and pressed his back against the wall, straining for any sound, any hint of movement, but the alley was dead. No sound, no light, no footsteps echoed in the night. He tensed, experience and a sixth sense telling him his prey was close. He eased his gun from its holster and controlled his breathing.

"Hello Jake," came a deep voice, sounding a metre or two away from him. "I wondered when you'd show up."

"It's over, Karl," Jake growled, preparing to move, knowing the other man already pinpointed his location.

"Let it go, Jake. This country is already in turmoil, economically and environmentally. Where's the point in arresting me now?" Karl asked, surprising Jake. Gouderhoff hadn't moved.

"Call it the fulfilment of a lifelong dream."

"You should consider raising your standards. I could make it very profitable for you to have other dreams," Karl answered.

"Don't you know it's still a federal offence to bribe an officer of the law," Jake replied.

"You haven't identified yourself, that's entrapment. I know the law too," Karl answered with a tight laugh.

Tiring of the verbal combat Jake lunged, but only found air. Gouderhoff ran in the darkness. Jake swore and took off after him.

The alley ended with a wall and Karl jumped without pausing, making a grab for the top, mustering all his strength to pull himself up and over as he heard Jake approaching fast. Being taller, Jake clambered over without difficulty, but lay flat at the sound of a single gunshot. He heard the bullet strike the wall behind him, but jumped up and resumed his pursuit.

Karl was fast, but Jake was younger, and gained on him in the maze of alleys that Karl led him through, footsteps giving away the direction in which to turn at each junction. Until no sound came. Not even the heavy,

42

breathless gasping of air. Karl was fit. Jake knew that, but as fit as Jake was, his own lungs were burning in protest.

His eyes adjusted to the gloom, and he did a quick 180-degree turn to scan his surroundings. With his back turned, Karl attacked, knocking Jake to the ground. Karl turned to run again, but Jake twisted to grab the other man's leg, also pulling him down. Jake's revolver lay out of reach where it fell and he left it there, grabbing for it would leave him open to attack. Besides, a bullet was too good for Karl, too quick a death. Both men scrambled to their feet, but Jake threw the first punch, and the fight began.

Karl sensed it coming, and rolled with it, as Jake's punch landed on his jaw, but swung back. He missed Jake's head, pounding into Jake's damaged shoulder instead, the pain making Jake gasp for air. Karl knew it was his bad shoulder; he'd shot him there some time ago. Intending it as a warning shot, Karl miscalculated Jake's reaction, and the wounding served to inflame Jake, making him more determined to bring Karl down. With his opponent in agony, Karl threw more punches and kicks, catching Jake in the ribs and midriff, winding him before Karl made another run for it. Jake recovered much quicker than Karl expected, grabbing his gun as he ran after Karl. Annoyed to find him still dogging his heels, Karl turned and fired another shot, but his aim was off, posing no danger to his pursuer.

He heard return fire and turned again, running for his life, sucking in more air and willing his legs to pump faster, breaking into a sprint, feeling an exhilaration he hadn't felt since his youth, and found himself back at the loading bay now devoid of trucks or people. Reaching his car, he jumped in, started the engine and drove away without turning the lights on.

He spotted Jake emerging from the alley. A constant thorn in his side, Jake's determination defied logic or reason, and it baffled Karl. Constant, but challenging, helping Karl keep his edge. And contrary to what he had told the man, Jake's appearance tonight surprised him. It annoyed Karl; he'd underestimated his adversary, again.

Jake burst from the maze of buildings and opened fire on the vehicle, knowing he had no other hope of catching Gouderhoff. The screech of tyres told him Karl got away. And not a damn thing he could do. He wasn't even supposed to be here, and now he'd let the bastard get away, again.

"Fuck," he roared into the night sky.

Chapter 6
Washington, USA

In a furious mood, Senator Wilma Swayne stormed through the halls of power. She'd started the ball rolling for aid negotiations with the Europeans, arranging meetings with the Ambassadors and Consuls from the major European countries. She and her staff did all of this, and now they denied her a seat on the negotiating committee. How dare they? She didn't do all this work just to be left on the side lines, unable to fight for the rights of those she knew would be left behind. That would include any race of people not of European descent, and the poor, the ones always forgotten, left behind to fend for themselves, and unable to flee back to the relative safety of Europe. She, however would not forget them, could not forget them. Their votes secured her a place within these walls, she owed those people, she was their representative, and by God, she would represent them. She made her way to Senator John Perry's office, not knocking, but barged through to the Senator's office.

"You bastard," she growled at him. Perry looked up from the papers on his desk, not surprised by her outburst. He'd been expecting her, just not this soon. Nor did he like this woman, he never did. He found her policies and politics too radical and considered this woman a bully. Perry preferred a more conservative approach, and he preferred his women a hell of a lot less aggressive.

Swayne glared at him, clenching her jaw, but biting her tongue to stop herself from saying too much, or saying anything that would keep her off the committee. This man represented everything she hated, his election funds donated by wealthy folks and large corporations that exploited the poor, her poor.

"You need me on this committee," she said, reining her temper in and bringing her voice back to normal. "I've already contacted most of the European Ambassadors."

"And?" Perry answered in his low southern drawl. He sat back in his chair, awaiting another outburst from her, but she surprised him. She took a deep breath and folded her arms.

"What do you want?" Perry asked.

"To be part of the team," she answered, with no trace of anger.

"And why should *I* allow *you* to be part of *my* team?" he asked, stressing his supremacy in this decision-making process. Swayne decided on a different approach.

"You need me," she stated. Perry waved his hand.

"Yes, yes, so you've said. You already started the negotiations." Swayne shook her head.

"No," she answered. "You need someone who will appear to campaign for civil rights with the Europeans, and who better person to have on your team? I have every intention of fighting for those basic rights, for all Americans. Having me fighting in your corner will improve your own standing and image. Just think about it. Not only do you have the mega big corporations sitting in your pocket on this one, but you will also have put together a team that cares about the little people, the grass roots people. You will become the man who can bridge the great divide between the rich and the poor. And you won't even have to lower your standards to do it, just meet me half way."

"An interesting proposition but why should I listen to it, much less heed it?" he sneered.

"Because if you don't you'll have countrywide riots on your hands," she answered.

"Is that a threat, Senator," he demanded.

"No, Senator, a fact," she threw back at him. "It's already beginning, by hungry and desolate people, regardless of race or colour. The people you pretend not to see on your way here every day, the homeless, the displaced, everyone affected by these natural disasters. They are sleeping in the streets, or in shelters, if they're lucky. Most have lost everything, their homes, their jobs, their livelihoods, but it disgusts you to think that you need to help these people, doesn't it?"

"If these people wanted to better themselves they would do something about their situation. They'd find themselves other jobs, apply to Social Services," he replied.

"Jobs? How can they? The companies that buy you off are laying people off, and outsourcing their work to European, Indian and Asian labour forces. Or don't you read the papers? Is the money enough to pretend the problem doesn't exist? As for Social Services, they're so overwhelmed in the wake of these disasters they're scarcely coping, and people are slipping through the cracks in the system all the time. With the current situation, the department cannot provide an adequate service. They're understaffed, and the federal budget is just not enough to help everyone. So what the hell are you doing about it?" she demanded.

Perry sat back in his seat.

"That's why you need me," she added "I've negotiated tougher deals than this, overcome bigger obstacles than this, achieved results that benefited everyone. You know I can do this."

"I'll think about it, and discuss it with the other committee members," he answered.

"Thank you," she replied, departing with less force than she arrived with.

The meeting lasted less than twenty minutes, but judging by Perry's less aggressive tone she knew she'd given him something to think about. He'd want to come out of those negotiations looking as good as he could to the American public. Public image and money drove the man; she knew that the moment she met him. After fifteen years in a violent marriage, predicting what the man would do next, reading postures, gestures and expressions became second nature to her; an uncanny talent she used when working with people. She recognised those who were in deep pain and sorrow, but her compassion for those who suffered did not blind her to every sob story she heard.

John Perry looked out of his office window, leaning against the large wooden frame, and watched the Washington evening bustle, little though it was. His mind went back to Swayne and their confrontation earlier. God damn that woman, he thought. Too shrewd, and far too clever for his liking, and not a damn thing he could do about it.

When cracks appeared in the fabric of society and widespread panic started, several senior members of the House approached him, proposing a committee to oversee a possible solution to the upheaval, a measure to deal with the mass migration and emigration caused by the climatic and geological crisis. He accepted of course, getting on committees always a wise move, and the other members were people he'd worked with on other ventures, most of them profitable.

Several options sat on the table, including the prospect of systematic and controlled emigration of Americans across the Atlantic to Europe. It was still only an option, a contingency plan in case the whole country sank into the seas. Perhaps that was Mother Nature's plan. And the latest reports warned of more severe flooding in the mid-western areas from torrential storms. The shift in the San Andreas Fault, and the resultant backlash wave, caused considerable damage to the Californian coastline and beyond, and as for the growing number of volcanoes…

Estimates for the damage now ran into trillions of dollars. Although from experience, estimates never came close to the actual cost. In Perry's mind reducing the number of people to claim aid would reduce the final cost. It was a harsh measure, but perhaps the best and most economical one. A lot was at stake here, including a large profit up for grabs in the sale of illegal visas to Europe.

A leading politician with a plan approached Perry, sent an aide to represent him, but Perry had no problem dealing with anyone wishing to do business at a handsome price. As for this Eurocrat, Perry was content in not knowing his identity, and only the aide knew who they both were. On this Perry had no choice but to trust him, as far as trust went in this business. Still, it was an innovative plan, a short-term scheme with a high yield.

The original idea included Perry's retirement to a quiet and picturesque European city, supported by his percentage from the proposed black market visa sales, but with including Senator Swayne on the team, the possibilities opened for Perry, personal advancement in power his next favourite occupation, after money making.

With including Swayne on his team, he could negotiate for greater numbers of Americans in Europe, and increase his profit in the long run. If Perry engineered this emigration as the only salvation, something he'd secured, he would become a modern day American Messiah. This could be his springboard into European politics. After all, someone needed to take care of the needs and considerations of the new Euro-Americans. By putting Swayne on the committee perhaps the Eurocrat would not suspect Perry's amendment to the scheme.

He returned to his desk, picked up the phone and dialled Swayne's extension, knowing she'd already left for the evening. His message to her assistant was curt but direct, informing her of a meeting scheduled for the following morning with the other committee members. He'd waited until he saw Swayne from his window, and she was a creature of habit. The surveillance and investigative report he'd requested on her revealed that, and he opened the folder, skimming through the opening pages that contained personal and family information. She'd married at fifteen years of age, but by the time she turned thirty, she'd set up her first 'Breakaway' Shelter, a scheme she started over twenty years ago to support victims of domestic violence.

The next section and accompanying medical file gave a detailed account on her, telling a sorry tale; broken bones and miscarriages from excessive beatings were among the well documented list. Even Perry had to admit, the beatings were excessive, and he begrudgingly admired her courage to leave and make herself a better life. The report hinted at a darker side to this 'women's saviour', her election shrouded in quiet controversy. Rumours of vote rigging and bullying for votes ran riot throughout these halls, but a thorough investigation into the matter proved otherwise. Still the rumours wouldn't die, despite the mounting evidence to the contrary. Swayne was an outspoken black and women's rights lobbyist in Washington. With those issues, votes had been easy to find. There was no need for Swayne to vote rig. Perry believed those not wishing to see another woman in the House, especially a black one, started the rumours. The rest of her file gave a detailed outline of her political career, that did not make her any more endearing.

After spending five years establishing her centres, which offered counselling and rehousing assistance, Swayne then ran for local public office and won. Whilst there, she implemented long-term solutions for unemployment and housing, and while many other local politicians disliked her, despite their resentment, they went along with her plans. Not that they had much choice. Swayne put her plans into action before they were approved, moves that hadn't earned her brownie points, but most of her strategies were still in place to this day.

Her obvious altruistic nature shone through the report, infuriating Perry all the more. Nowhere did it hint she helped others for a fee, skimmed from election funds or received unaccountable donations as funding. There was no scent of bribability about her, and in spite of numerous threats on her life, she refused to back down.

As for scandal, there was none, with perhaps the exception of a loud-mouthed ex son-in-law who wanted to make a fast buck by trying to sell his story of what it was like to live with this woman. The respectable papers didn't buy it. Not in Washington anyway. Some of the trashier tabloids tried to outbid each other for the tale, but it proved not worth the effort.

After Public Office came Governorship but Swayne only lasted a single term. She stepped down to spend more time with her family and support her eldest daughter going through a nasty divorce with the aforementioned son-in-law. Supporting her family when they needed her most won her respect within her community, considering her family support policies. Here was a politician practicing what she claimed to hold dear. It made him feel nauseous.

He sighed and turned to stare out of his window again. He'd need a different approach to handle this woman. Perhaps the way to get what he wanted was to let her believe she got what she wanted, a better deal for her so-called poor. The people Perry believed not profitable enough to worry about. If Swayne wanted to campaign for these people, then she was welcome to it. So long as he achieved his goals, he didn't care how he got there.

Chapter 7

Apartment 502, Bancroft Place, Washington, USA

The naked form asleep in his bed surprised Jake, as he returned to his apartment early the next morning. Women had always been a mystery to him, but Caroline proved more so, coming around more often of late, despite the minor detail that her husband was on leave from the Air Corp. How she gained access to his apartment puzzled him. No matter how many times he changed the locks, she always found a way in. Maybe she plied her charms on the building manager and it irritated Jake, this invasion of his space. The only thing to annoy him more was letting Gouderhoff slip through his fingers again. Too tired to give a shit about either of them, he eased himself into bed but despite his weariness, sleep evaded him, his mind raced on earlier events, inventing options that hadn't come to mind, and that annoyed him even more. Beside him, Caroline stirred, sensing the warmth of his body and she moved to him, curling her arm around him before settling back again.

He drifted off to sleep, but it seemed an instant later that he awoke to Caroline's soft caresses and he glanced at the clock beside his bed, dismayed to find that five hours passed, feeling like five minutes. He turned to look at Caroline, her deep brown eyes wide with lustful anticipation.

"Where were you last night?" she asked, using her pout to its full potential. "I waited for ages for you." She may have been pouting, but her hands belied her sulkiness.

"Working," he answered. "Why are you here? I thought Warren was on leave?" he demanded. She pouted more.

"We had a fight," she answered.

"So you thought you could come here?" he sighed. "Why didn't you go somewhere else?"

"When you didn't come home, I almost did. But they don't make me feel the way you do," she replied, confirming his suspicions he wasn't her only extramarital lover. Irrational envy rushed through him, counteracting her touches. Pushing her aside, he got out of bed leaving her to sulk at his abrupt manner. She wanted him, her pride wounded that her manipulative talents weren't working on him. On hearing the shower she thought of joining him, but the water stopped and sounds of the TV came to life.

Jake secured the towel around his damp waist while pictures exploded onto the TV screen. Glancing up, he caught his reflection in the window opposite, and he thought of the sorry sight he made. His short, dark hair already drying, curling a little at the ends, and falling onto his broad forehead. Beneath well-defined eyebrows, his hazel eyes appeared dull and lifeless. Lack of restful sleep and the demands of the job took its toll on him. Creases appeared under his eyes. Tilting his head, the two features he disliked the most came into profile. His nose suffered the most damage in all his years on the job, and after numerous operations to fix it, it now appeared, to Jake anyway, too straight. In his opinion, it added to his too-square jaw. Again, the result of reconstructive surgery. He tore his eyes away, hating when he caught himself scrutinising his face. Sometimes it seemed as though he looked at the face of a stranger. Even the expression in his eyes changed over the years.

The TV screen distracted him, and he listened with half an ear as a reporter listed off the latest natural disasters around the world. Earth tremors in California and rioting dominated the list. News of violent demonstrations outside the Canadian and Mexican Embassies grabbed his full attention. He knew negotiations were still going nowhere with both nations, Mexico sticking to its guns on keeping its borders closed to North America. The US were hit by an economic and social crisis, and to the South Americans, it was payback time. Jake knew it wasn't that simple. Mexico also suffered with earthquakes, their losses as heavy as their northern counterparts. He knew, in reality, they were worse off economically. As for Canada, they closed their borders three months earlier, after mass migration northwards, and Canadian Officials estimated somewhere between thirteen and fifteen million Americans had entered. Jake guessed the number to be closer to fifty million, especially if Gouderhoff had anything to do with it.

With the closure of the Canadian border, anger erupted at the neighbouring countries, and mass demonstrations had started outside both Embassies. Lack of progress with negotiations resulted in larger demonstrations while the drastic and dramatic climate changes affected more and more people. So focused on the television, Jake didn't notice Caroline emerging from the bathroom and move towards him. She wrapped her arms around him, startling him, and he pulled loose from her embrace, disappearing into the bedroom to get dressed, slamming the door behind him.

Washington was hot and overcast. Thunder threatened to roll, lending an angry look to the sky, yet gave no assurances that if the heavens opened, it would take the oppressive heat away. Jake left his apartment for the office, surveying the previous night's destruction and mayhem en route. His office was quiet, with half the workforce present. Most left in search for cooler climates. Others stayed away from the chaos and the stifling heat of the city.

Jake stepped out from the elevator, and headed for his desk though he had no time to sit and rest. A yellow post-it note stuck to his PC screen summoned him to the boss's office. He sighed, taking his jacket off, throwing it over the back of his chair. It was going to be one of those days, he thought. He could feel it in his aching, thirty four year old bones.

Upon entering the office of the Head of the Criminal and Domestic Investigation Bureau, that feeling nestled into the pit of his stomach. Myers glared at him.

"What the hell were you doing in New York?" he demanded. Jake wasn't surprised the boss found out.

"Chasing a lead," he answered.

"From what I hear it wasn't the only thing you were chasing last night. You went without informing anyone of your whereabouts or getting approval, or even getting back up! What the hell did we teach you?" Myers lectured him. "You think you're immortal? You think you're Superman? Well, you're neither. This personal vendetta of yours against Gouderhoff is ending. As of now the case is closed."

"What?" Jake exploded.

"Gouderhoff's gone," Myers stated. "A team carried out a search on all his premises last night. They were wiped clean. A check-in clerk at Newark airport ID'd his mug shot this morning. I suspect he's run back to Europe."

"Shit!" Jake said, running a hand through his hair. "Why didn't someone call me? This was my case, god damn it! Why wasn't I told?"

"You weren't there *to* call. You must've switched your cell phone off. Why? So we couldn't pinpoint your location?" Myers roared back at him. "We lost him Jake, no thanks to you."

"Didn't you find anything?" he asked. Myers shook his head.

"Nothing. The Canadians were onto his ID scam, as much as we were, they were waiting to grab him when he crossed the border, if we couldn't catch him first."

Jake looked at him, puzzled.

"I didn't realise we were working with the Canadians on this one," he said, a hint of suspicion creeping into his voice.

"A token gesture. We fed them bits and pieces, just to keep them happy. But that's it."

"That's it," Jake exploded again. "Two years I've been on this, working my ass off on it, and that's all you can say, 'that's it!'"

"Jake, you fucked up last night, big time. This case is now closed. There's nothing more you can do, nothing short of following him to Europe, and that you aren't doing. Now get the hell out of my office, file a report on what you were up to last night, and you'd better make it a convincing one. Then, if there's a bar still open and stocked in this goddamned city, get drunk. Now get out of my office."

Jake left, slamming the door behind him. Yep, one of those days.

He lay in bed, having followed Myers' orders to the letter. He filed a report on his activities in New York and found a liquor store. His apartment was quiet and empty. Caroline was gone by the time he got back and he didn't care where. It felt good to be alone, to wallow in his misery and defeat. Just him, and a bottle of bourbon. He rarely drank, but he made up for it that night, and had a hangover to prove it.

As he stood under the shower, the hot water pounding against him, waiting for the painkillers to kick in, the telephone rang and he ignored it, letting the machine pick it up. He was still furious at letting that bastard get away. How many times did that make now? He'd lost count over the years. He knew this obsession had to end before it ended him, but this latest failure sickened him, leaving him with nothing else to give a shit about.

Until the bomb exploded a few blocks away.

The explosion sobered him up as his apartment block rocked from the blast. He went to the trembling windows, seeing a thick plume of black smoke rising into the sky. The telephone beside him rang again, and he snatched it up.

"Did you hear it?" Myers roared at him.

"Hear it? It damn near blew my windows out," Jake snapped back.

"Canadian Embassy. Get your ass here, now," Myers barked at him and hung up without waiting for any kind of response. Jake sighed and looked at the smoke, now spreading across the sky as the wind caught it, and dispersed it around the city.

When he arrived at the embassy a few blocks away, fire fighters still battled the blaze. He stopped cops on his approach, flashing his ID to get answers but found out little. No one seemed sure of what happened. A thorough investigation couldn't take place until the fire was out, and the fire marshals secured the site. There was nothing Jake could do but wait.

He spotted Myers just inside the embassy gates, deep in a heated conversation with a bunch of other suits, and as one of them shifted out of the way, Senator Wilma Swayne came into view, surprising Jake. Black civil rights were more her domain, not possible bombings, and he wondered why she was there. The meeting broke up, and Myers spotted him. He made a beeline for him, bringing the formidable force of the Senator with him. Myers introduced his agent to her who shook Jake's hand. Her strength surprised him.

"Agent Mann," the Senator greeted him. She stood a good few inches shorter, but with an authoritative manner. Jake guessed she hadn't gotten into the Senate without crushing a few balls along the way.

"This is a despicable act," she said, her voice shaking with unvented anger. "No warning given, and no one claiming responsibility. God knows the death toll. I've given my personal assurance to the Canadian Ambassador, and the Canadian Government that we'll find who's responsible for this. I want this investigated, and that's where you come in Agent Mann. Mr Myers tells me you're one of his best, and that's what I want. Is that understood?" Jake nodded in response, and the Senator looked satisfied. Grim, but satisfied.

"I've given instructions that you're to get full cooperation in this," she continued. Jake heard the calmness return to her voice as she spoke. She caught him sizing her up but said nothing, used to that by now from so-called strong men who wanted to know what they were up against. This man's assessment of her was cool, methodical and systematic. All part of his job, she concluded.

"Gentlemen, if you will excuse me, the press are waiting." The Senator left them and Jake turned to Myers.

"Wanna fill me in?" he asked. Myers shrugged.

"I got called to a meeting this morning with the Senator and Canadian Ambassador about the demonstration last night. It seems the party got a little wild. On the way back to the Bureau, the bomb went off. Swayne tried chewing my balls off about lack of surveillance and all that crap. I explained about the lack of manpower since the heat wave hit, but it cut no ice with her, and with no history of threats, there was no reason to set up surveillance."

He caught hold of Jake's arm and walked, pulling the younger man with him past the gathered crowd. He let Myers pull him away from the commotion and media circus. Out of earshot, Myers stopped.

"She's pissed off because it happened on her turf, in her constituency. That's why she is so damn adamant about getting results."

"And what do we have?" Jake asked.

"Fuck all," Myers spat. "We've got nothing. What we hope to have in a couple of hours, when the fire's out, is the security surveillance disk from the embassy itself. All their security stuff is in a vaulted basement."

He got breathless, as he always did when he got frustrated, but he resumed his walking again, moving away from the destruction. Jake caught up with him.

"The Senator wants us to work the disk," Myers huffed. "If we're lucky we might pick out any known terrorist who were part of the assemblage." Jake grunted at the idea and Myers nodded in agreement as he huffed and wheezed his way along the street.

They made their way back to the office on the still-operating Metro, and reached the shady cool interior of the office. Jake stared at the brown padded envelope on his desk, a white address label with his name typed upon it, but no other details, no postage marks. Protocol procedures kicked in and before touching the package he donned a latex glove. Picking up the envelope he peered inside, finding a CD case sitting in the bubbled padding. Careful not to compromise any evidence on the case, he pulled it out, checking behind it for any nasty surprises. Opening the case, he found a disk inside, and again no markings on the silvered surface, no manufacturers imprint. He turned to his PC and inserted the disk, aborting the auto play program. He ran an antivirus protection program against it first and it appeared to be clean. Accessing the drive he found a single media file, and a video image sprang to life on his screen. A date appeared on the bottom of the image, yesterday's date, and it faded in to show people chanting. The picture panned across the screen and the embassy came into view, text streaming across the bottom of the screen.

"We, the People, find Canada guilty of infringing America's most basic civil rights - The right to freedom and the right to life. This crime will not go unpunished."

~ A.L.L. - *Americans for Life and Liberty* ~

The text ended as dawn approached and the image came to a spectacular conclusion. The program closed, but Jake caught and stopped the auto delete programme. He sat back in his chair and sighed. Great. Now what was he supposed to do? Arrest the entire population of Washington? Ejecting the disk, he popped it back into its case and envelope, and took them down to forensics, hoping they could give him answers, but none were forthcoming. There were no prints on the disk, case, or envelope. No trace evidence. Whoever sent it knew forensics. Frustrated, Jake returned to his desk, deciding to hold off on talking to Myers for the moment.

He replayed the video, this time concentrating on the people chanting but all he saw was the back of people's heads or side views that showed little of anyone's face. The images shot by at speed and he restarted it, slowing it to a frame-by-frame mode. Nothing ominous stood out. Even still, he continued to replay it, freezing the frames and scanning the edges, and stopped. Something was out of place. He peered at the screen. A face caught his attention. Not a side view or partial glimpse, but a full face, staring at the camera. Jake swore at himself for having missed it before. He highlighted the area, using the best software available to D.C.I.B. to refocus and clean up the image each time he enlarged it. His breath caught in his chest. The face smiled at the camera, smiled at him, taunting him, and Jake glared at the screen, at the smiling face of Gouderhoff.

Chapter 8

Swayne was nervous, more nervous than she should've been. She'd withstood tougher ordeals than this one, sitting at the oval conference table in Senator Perry's office, awaiting the last two Senators to arrive. Fear and uneasiness filled her. To feel any different meant she shouldn't be there. Fear, because she didn't trust the motives of these people, especially not Perry, who sat opposite her at the table. The uneasiness stemmed from thinking she was out of her league on this one.

Yet there lay the challenge, to be the little fish that rippled the great big pond, and that sensation excited her, drove her on. The fear came from an irrational place, but instead of allowing it to dominate her, to control her, she turned it around and used it as her guide, her driving force. Whether she won or lost was nothing compared to taking action.

She reread the documents Perry sent her the previous night, and knew the documents well, but Swayne wanted him to think she needed time to get up to speed. Why, she wondered to herself, but this was the best tactic to take with Perry, allow him to think she struggled. She half listened to his small talk conversation with California's Senator, Jason Michaels, but Perry turned to her.

"How's your daughter?" he asked. The question took her by surprise.

"She's fine," Swayne replied.

"Georgia just had another baby not too long ago, isn't that right? A difficult birth, I heard," he went on.

"Twenty-two months ago," she corrected. "There were a few problems, but Georgia and Dylan are doing just fine." She wondered what all this led to.

"Good. Give them my best, won't you," he said giving her a little smile. "My own son and his wife are expecting again. They're on their fourth."

"Congratulations," Swayne offered, and Michaels echoed her good wishes. Why tell her this, she wondered. To win her over? A 'there's a woman present, talk babies' approach? She didn't fall for it, Perry never discussed his personal life. Her bullshit detector was set on full alert with this man. Years of abuse honed this skill, sharpened her ability to read people. But Perry proved difficult to read. There were no cracks in that pompous façade that she could see, and that unsettled her more than her nervousness. No one was without a crack, or two. Not even those who came to her for help and put on solid, and brave, faces.

The arrival of the other two Senators interrupted her thoughts, Larry Whitney from Chicago and Thad Gerrard who represented Ohio. Their respective States, along with Michaels', suffered high death tolls from the climatic upheaval. In Chicago, ground temperatures soared to 56°C, too hot for most people, and the death toll from heat exhaustion was high.

In Ohio, the story was the opposite, yet with the same deadly results. Farmlands, destroyed by the heat, were now being washed away by sudden torrential rain and mudslides. The ongoing devastation in California continued to be a headline on most news channels. Each Senator at this table had people to take care for; the desperate and destitute people who'd lost everything. Swayne knew of the reputations of these men, and unselfish acts were not in their nature.

"Now we're all here, we'll begin," Perry kicked the meeting off. "Have you come up with anything? Jason?" Michaels pulled papers from his folder and passed them out to the others.

"These are the proposals and terms from both Asia and India," he said, in a soft voice that seemed out of place with his large frame. "They've enough problems of their own," he went on. "Korea and Japan have tough laws about allowing foreigners in. They're also in the middle of their own economic crisis and, as you may have seen in the news, another earthquake hit Kōbe yesterday. The resulting tsunami almost destroyed the city. They considered approaching us for help, especially as there's a notion yesterday's earthquake resulted from aftershocks of the one that hit California a few days ago. It's a possibility scientists haven't knocked on the head yet. China still won't open negotiations. As for India, they've got so many rules and terms we'd have to agree to just to get aid from them. We'd have to sell our souls to them if we wanted to evacuate there."

"Whoa," Swayne burst in. "Evacuate?"

"Yes, evacuate," Perry answered. "You don't think people would continue to live in these turbulent conditions, do you? Where would we put them all?"

"What about rehousing schemes, shelters?" she demanded.

"Where?" Perry asked. He picked up a file and hurled it across the table at her. "Perhaps you would care to go through these reports and find a suitable location, somewhere large enough to accommodate over a hundred million people. Somewhere that's not likely to be blown away, washed away or shaken to pieces," he added. He sat back while she glanced through the documents.

"These are only estimates. They'll come nowhere near what you think," she answered.

"Since when did estimates ever represent the actual total? You of all people should know how much initial figures are 'tip-of-the-iceberg' predictions," he said. Swayne backed off. She had no returning argument. But Trans-Pacific or Trans-Atlantic relocation? The thought of it made her head spin. She fell silent and Perry knew he'd dropped the bomb into her lap, and it weighed her down. Perhaps she would be easier to manage than he thought. He turned back to the others.

"Thad, what about you?" he asked.

"I've had lengthy discussions with the Russian Federation Consulate, and their help also comes with a high price," he answered.

"What kind of price?" Swayne asked.

"Large investments into their economies, and help with their flagging social reforms," Thad answered.

"Not to mention suffering their cold, harsh winters," Michaels quipped. The other men chuckled but Swayne remained quiet. She didn't like this one bit. These men appeared to have all this planned out. All except where to go. Did the American public have any inkling what these men were up to? She doubted it.

Yet, in a way it made perfect sense. The land here no longer provided enough support for everyone, and international aid could only do so much. A drastic short-term solution was needed to ease the current crisis, but what of the long-term implications?

Swayne listened as Senator Whitney gave a detailed report of his meeting with the Australian Ambassador, and the Consulars from several African states. Whitney considered Africa too unsettled, differing nations with their own individual policies, and varying degrees of stability. Dictatorships demanded too high a price for the resettlement of Americans, and the poorer nations needed too much investment capital. As for Australia, their immigration laws were too strict.

"Well, at least I have something more promising," Perry announced. "Initial contact with the EU looks encouraging. The majority of people leaving are first and second generation Europeans, and the EU appear to be anxious about the numbers migrating back. They're afraid it will put a strain on their own resources, so they're open to talking with us."

The other men murmured approval at this development, but Perry looked to Swayne.

"Well?" he asked.

"First and second generation Europeans? What about those of non-European descent?" she demanded. Perry smiled at her.

"That my dear, is where you come in."

Chapter 9

Jake glared at the screen, at the face of Gouderhoff, his adversary, taunting him. The bastard! This was all a game to him, but Jake needed evidence to connect the German to the bomb and A.L.L. This political group hadn't existed before now. It didn't show up on any of the law enforcement databases he accessed. This puzzled Jake, it wasn't Gouderhoff's style to get involved in a political group. Yet it didn't prevent him from setting it up, or supplying the firepower.

Jake allowed the smile that twitched at the corner of his mouth to grow. So Gouderhoff hadn't left the country. Now Jake could reopen the case, and resume the hunt for his prey. Armed with both disk and hard copies, he invaded Myers sanctuary, finding his boss on the phone, still flushed in the face, offering assurances to the person on the other end of the call. With a sigh, the conversation ended, and he looked at Jake.

"This better be a development, and it better be good," he growled at him. Jake handed him the printouts, and Myers studied them for a moment before looking up.

"Gouderhoff!"

Jake nodded.

"It looks like he's still here," he said. Myers dropped the sheets onto his desk.

"Guess you'd better find him then," he said. "Who, or what, is A.L.L.?" Jake shrugged his shoulders.

"I've run the name through every database in the country, and the ones I can access in Europe. There's no reference to A.L.L. anywhere. It looks like Gouderhoff's behind it though. Somehow I don't think he was there for the party atmosphere. Anarchy is his speciality," he answered. Myers glared at him.

"Destroying a neighbouring country's embassy is not anarchy, it's terrorism," he snapped. Jake shrugged again.

"I'll wait for the surveillance disks to arrive from the embassy, and see who else I can find. Gouderhoff's known and suspected associates are on file, and use that for comparison, but if others were involved, I can't see them staying around to watch the fireworks," Jake said.

"Really?" Myers tone grew angry and sarcastic. "Then explain why I'm looking at Gouderhoff's mug on this page," he demanded.

"He likes games. We both know that. It's his way of saying he can come and go as he pleases. That he's smarter than us."

"I'm starting to think he's right," Myers growled. "After two fucking years you couldn't even catch him, and you came out of the Academy as one of the best. So what does that tell you?"

"He doesn't give a shit about rules, regulations or civil rights," Jake shot back. He grabbed the printouts and opened the door.

"Now where the hell are you going?" Myers demanded.

"To put my god-damn restricted talents to some use." He slammed the door shut behind him, relieving some of his frustration. Gouderhoff played by his own rules, while procedures and regulations hampered Jake.

Official procedure stopped him eighteen months ago, when he came face-to-face with Gouderhoff, though it wasn't their first direct encounter. This cat and mouse game began many years prior to Jake's return home, before he entered the Academy for training, or retraining if the real truth was known. Something he went to great lengths to keep hidden.

Now, late in the evening, eight hours passed since the explosion, and Jake was no closer to answers. Sure, he had one answer, but until an hour ago Gouderhoff was filed as an unsolved case. Still waiting for the embassy to send their disks in, Jake called it a night, but before leaving, he made a quick call to forensics. This time there was encouraging news. The lab boys found what they thought were traces of the explosive used. The tall, wiry, and nervous type, Dave Winebeck only sat still when something required his complete concentration. This evening he was restless.

"Hey Dave, what's up," Jake greeted him as he stepped into the room.

"The end of the world," was the short reply.

"That good, huh? Lab said you'd found something." Dave nodded, and pulled a file from the mound of stacked papers on his desk, handing it to Jake. The information on the page made no sense to Jake, containing strings of broken binary code, gaps here and there, and on the bottom half, a chemical configuration, but that too was incomplete.

"This caused the explosion?" he asked. Dave sat down.

"I think so."

"Meaning?"

"I can't be sure." Troubling news, Dave never guessed. Dave probed. Dave took things apart, and then he probed and studied more. This time it was clear, Dave didn't have a solid answer.

"Any theories?" Jake nudged for more, and Dave sighed.

"No theories, just a hunch. I talked to a friend in EATA, the European Anti-Terrorism Agency. I emailed him everything I had and then he emailed back. EATA discovered it about four months ago, but they haven't figured it out yet either. They suspect it's a three-step device." He took a sheet of paper from the top of the paper pile, and handed it to Jake. "They think a starting agent creates a volatile gas, that explodes when it reaches a critical density and mass."

"Enough to destroy an embassy?" Jake asked, and Dave shook his head. "So something else blew up that embassy?" Jake ventured.

"Who knows," Dave answered. "EATA think they've found something. It's a silicon-based gel, odourless and colourless. It seems to be everything-less, except fire power, and far more stable than using nitro, so maybe it combines with other elements to create the explosions. Then it seems to burn itself out, leaving no trace."

"Oh shit!" Jake whispered and Dave nodded.

"We are talking major big shit. EATA think this thing could be programmed to ignite."

"What do you mean by programmed?" Jake asked.

"Just remember, all we've gotten from EATA are preliminary findings, and even then my buddy wasn't keen on sharing, but they seem to think it's a so-called 'smart bomb'. They were lucky enough to find a partial chip and sensor when they raided a warehouse along the Romanian-Hungary border."

"Dave, I don't mind telling you, all these 'seem to think' phrases are scaring me. Does anyone know anything definite?" Dave shook his head. Jake didn't like this at all, and he sat forward in the chair.

"Do we even know who owns the damn stuff, where it came from, how the hell it got into the US?" he asked.

"Getting it into the country is the easy part. We don't know what it is so we don't know what to look for. We know it's Eastern European, but EATA think it may have originated in the Middle East. From the sounds of it, it could belong to anyone. EATA have named it GS1, as in Global Strike. We need to find out more about it, what it is. Then we might have a hope of figuring out how to deal with it. This stuff could be anywhere in the country. Sniffer dogs are useless. What we're dealing with is a designer bomb, chemically engineered. Jake, if this thing is in the country, in large quantities, then we've got a problem. A big problem."

It took another two days for the security disk from the now ruined Canadian Embassy to arrive, and by the time Jake looked through people's faces and partial images, he lost more days. Myers failed to show as the weather grew more oppressive, leaving Jake on his own. Just how he liked it. As for any leads, none of the faces on the disk matched anyone on any felony list, either domestic or international. The most heinous crimes he uncovered within the mob were outstanding parking tickets.

Nothing more, and he was back to square one.

Chapter 10
Senate Buildings

Senator Swayne sat in stony silence as the arguments grew louder on both sides of the table. Yes, her demands were outrageous, and she expected the uproar, but the Eurocrats were fuming. Perry played along with her, allowing her to do most of the talking, the demanding. He'd made enquiries about her negotiating skills and liked what he heard, and over the past few days liked what he saw.

It seemed the other Senators missed the memo on Perry's plans, and Swayne sensed waves of anger emanating from those supposed to be on her side, supporting her. A few words from Perry after the initial meeting quietened most objections. For Swayne, the strategy was simple, haggling, starting with an unobtainable demand, or a list of demands, allowing the other side to haggle it down, whittling away the more unreasonable, ludicrous requests, allowing the other side to think they'd achieved success while leaving the important issues on the table. That strategy worked well for her in the past; she saw no reason not to believe it wouldn't work for her again.

Now into day three, it saw no change to the flaring tempers, yet in the midst of all this angst, Swayne sat with calm assurance she would get what she wanted, impressing Perry further. Little wonder she achieved so much with this level of commitment and belief in the greater good. He turned his attention back to the heated discussion. All that remained on today's agenda was obtaining European visas and Swayne had avoided that minefield, for in it lay the real heart of these negotiations. Such a pity the other Senators had so little faith in their colleague when she was about to secure them the biggest pay deal of their careers. Swayne turned towards Perry and looked at him. He shrugged, playing his side of the game.

"I suppose," he began, exaggerating his southern drawl. "So long as US citizens can be integrated and supported within European societies, we could forego the need to establish independent American towns in every European country."

It had been a tough morning negotiating that one, and the Eurocrats sighed in relief. Establishing an American town in every country was a ludicrous idea, but the Americans hung onto it like a lifebuoy. A stroke of genius on Swayne's behalf, but her comrades regarded her request in a similar fashion to the Europeans.

"Well, that's it," Swayne continued from Perry. "That's all the ground we're prepared to give, and to be fair, we've given into a lot of your demands by dropping most of ours. However, we are not prepared to give up on our request for visas, or redeployment of our citizens."

She sat back, but still had to tread carefully. It wouldn't do to lose the European support. America had its own bargaining chips, manufacturing industries and other businesses that could relocate and establish bases throughout Europe. Perry dealt with that issue, and if the rumours were to be believed, was paid by those companies he now claimed to speak on behalf of.

The Eurocrats looked weary, and bewildered. They came here to help and negotiate an aid package with these people, not argue with them, or be accused of making unreasonable demands. Just what the hell were these people playing at? Could Americans be that arrogant to think they had the right to go anywhere they pleased? All the ridiculous demands were rejected, including making the US dollar the new major currency, and giving them a dozen seats in the European Parliament. A dozen? What were these people thinking? It took three long days to get to the heart of the matter, to the real issue on the table; allowing Americans access to Europe.

The Europeans came here with the intention of agreeing initial trade terms, but they had wasted three of the allocated four days arguing over nonsensical issues, and this day was not over yet. Perry looked at the Europeans, knowing they were nothing more than high ranking civil servants, and not in a position to come to full and binding terms between

Europe and the US. They would need time to consult with Europe on the latest developments and return with a reply.

Perry looked at his watch and saw it was well past noon, making it evening time in Brussels. It seemed like a natural time for a recess for all of them and he suggested so. If that surprised Swayne or the others they didn't show it. Neither did the Europeans who nodded in agreement, and departed.

Chapter 11
European Union Commission Buildings, Brussels, Belgium

In the south east of the city, the iconic headquarters of the European Union, the Commission Buildings, housed EU Commissioners and delegates. Policies made within its walls, affected the whole of Europe, the older established nations and the emerging ones. Europe secured its place as a super State, one powerful multi-nation, with most member states united under a single currency and single treaties.

On the ninth floor of the building, a briefing put Europe's rosy and bright future into jeopardy. Sir Jonathan Medlington, Britain's EU Commissioner and one of the longest serving commissioners present, sat in stony silence. In his time in politics he'd never faced a problem like this. The rest of the delegation sat just as subdued. Grumblings of climatic upheaval had always been muttered within these halls of power, and the EU got proactive about tackling the problem, but the devastation to hit America served as a timely warning, a wake-up call to the EU member states.

While people migrating from one member state to another remained an economic fact of life, the current influx from the US took the EU by surprise. No one could have estimated the number of people fleeing America and returning home, to Europe. The numbers were staggering, overwhelming, and this created problems, the least of which was space. Where would everyone go? Would they find jobs, if jobs were available?

Unemployment created its own set of problems, how to support everyone within current social policies? No solutions were forthcoming, and with no reliable information to depend on, no definitive solution could be drafted. Now the US sought aid. Aid wasn't a problem. The EU contained the financial resources to bail the US out, unless the returning Europeans required help from the social and welfare systems within each member state. That burden would drain and strain the resources available to the EU.

The returning Europeans aside, it now seemed that Americans wanted to come to Europe. The number of visa applications rocketed during the last few weeks at all the European embassies in the US. These people wanted to relocate here. Relocate? What were they thinking of? There was barely enough room for the existing Europeans to live without allowing Americans all over the place. This was the nature of the report, and the cause of their concern. Medlington looked around at the team he'd pulled together from the member states most affected by this looming crisis.

"Any thoughts?" Medlington asked, his tone heavy and sombre.

"Do we have any policy regarding returning migration?" Dolf Janssen, the Dutch delegate asked. Dieter Thiel sifted through his notes.

"The only legislation we have refers to Article 7a but refers to third party non-EU countries, that entry, residence and movement of those non-nationals are a matter of common concern. There's no restriction on our own nationals coming back," he answered.

"It's also looking like the Americans may apply as asylum seekers," Padraig Brennan added. Several voices raised a shout of protest but Medlington soon quietened them down.

"Why do you say that?" he asked.

"The Irish embassy has been bombarded with queries about claiming asylum."

"And is it possible?" Maria Esprey asked.

Brennan shrugged.

"It's hard to tell. The UN guidelines about asylum seekers refer to conditions of hardship, torture or the threat of death if they stay in their own country. Someone's will be clever enough to argue that their lives are at risk, and from the elements. Who's going to argue with the forces of nature? If we don't act, we'll be inundated with asylum claims that we'll be powerless to stop."

"A disturbing point," Medlington mused. He knew Brennan researched the problem, along with other immigration regulations.

Ireland would be the hardest hit with returning immigrants; most Americans could claim descent to the small European country. No wonder Brennan was worried. However, this wasn't just an Irish concern, it impacted the whole of Europe. If people got hold of valid Irish visas and passports, they wouldn't be restricted to just Ireland. The whole of the EU would be open to them. A daunting and frightening prospect.

"Ladies and gentlemen, we have a very serious decision to make, and quickly," Medlington began. "Mr Janssen, you said we were powerless to stop our own nationals from returning?" Janssen nodded.

"But we could restrict that to valid passport holders," he replied. For the first time that day Medlington smiled.

"And what about the visas?" Esprey asked.

"Tell our team in Washington to come home," Medlington answered. "With the Americans playing games, they haven't achieved much. Let the Yanks come over here and fight their corner. They might be less cocky if they're not on their home turf."

Chapter 12
Brussels, Belgium

Day four of the American conference proved more successful. The only item needing agreement on was a date for a Euro conference, and it was how the five Senators came to be in the European City a week later. From now on the Senators would deal with the Commissioners, and other parliamentary members. Perry judged this a significant step forward. They would now deal with the real power brokers of the EU, not their underlings, and here the fate and future of millions of Americans would be decided.

The Senators sat in a large conference room. On the opposing team sat the Chairman of this committee, the British Commissioner, Sir Jonathan Medlington. Perry heard of this guy, reputed to be one of the toughest European officials around. One associate referred to him in less than polite terms, calling Medlington a 'ball-breaking bastard'.

An ominous start to any negotiation, and Medlington lived up to his reputation from the beginning, opening with a simple question; he asked them why. Californian Jason Michaels rose to the challenge. He may not have a State left to argue for, but millions of displaced Californians relied on him to make things better for them, somehow.

"Many citizens in the United States are of European descent and can trace their origins back to Europe, whether it is to Britain, Ireland, France or Spain. These people believe, as I do, in the right to return to these roots."

Medlington stared at him with piercing eyes, his gaunt narrow face giving no hint to what lay beneath the surface. Then he smiled, but the grin looked vicious and predatory. He'd expected the Yanks to pull this one, and was surprised they'd waited this long.

"You are quite correct," he answered. "Most of America was populated by European explorers, but whatever belief you maintain regarding the return to your ancestral roots, I believe you gave up that right in 1775 when you fought to be free of King and Country."

With his clipped accent, he spoke with precision, not wasting time on words. Yet he maintained a sense of control and authority. Wilma Swayne made a mental note of it. It helped to know your adversary before leaping into battle.

"There is an alternative," Medlington went on, that predatory smile growing. "The United States could relinquish its independence and return to the Commonwealth, to British rule, and swear allegiance to the Crown, again."

Perry's eyes almost popped out of his head in fury, but he held himself in check. Medlington's smile was vicious, and it reminded Swayne of a cat playing with a mouse. She concluded this man could be as dangerous to deal with as Perry, but she had yet to decide whether the Englishman played for personal gain or for the good of Europe. She still needed to get a full measure of her opponent.

During this initial US-Euro encounter Swayne remained quiet and observant. Strangely quiet, in Perry's opinion, and he voiced his disapproval later that evening. She shrugged him off. When she was ready to negotiate then she'd step up to the plate. Before concluding for the evening they approached the delicate subject of European admission. Medlington and the others aired their concerns on the potential numbers involved, and the Eurocrats insisted on pinning Perry down on this. Medlington proved to be a shrewd operator, often using Perry's tactics against him, while Swayne continued to assess what they were up against, and figure if there were any chinks in this man's armour.

Haggling would get them nowhere, and Perry's often evasive tactics seemed to irritate the Commissioner more and more. At least Perry cottoned onto that fact, the consequences of annoying these people would see all hope lost. They would return as failures, not the saviours Perry wanted to be portrayed as, and as the head of this team, he found himself unable to offload the blame. Medlington continued on, not giving them a moment's respite, demanding to know what the American's settlement strategy was in relation to housing and employment. The rapid fire questioning threw Perry, allowing Medlington the opportunity to question Perry's qualifications to even be in this room, or if he even understood what a strategy was. His dislike of Perry soon became evident, and having suitably insulted the US delegation, he then called a halt to the day's proceedings. In anger Perry turned to Swayne.

"Any ideas?" he asked, in a sarcastic tone.

"A few," she answered, packing away her notes.

A day later Swayne took the lead and Medlington wondered if this was yet another stunt of Perry's, using a woman, thinking Medlington would be easier on her. Within a short space of time he dismissed that notion. This woman was clearly an independent thinker, and it seemed, independent of Perry, who barely concealed his snide comments. Medlington liked her, despite his initial reluctance.

Many Americans applied to embassies for visas based on their grandparents' and great grandparents' nationalities, and if granted, the visas would give them access to anywhere in Europe. Naturally, the EU had a vested interest in controlling this process. After all, they would inherit the resultant housing, welfare and employment problems and Swayne tackled these issues head on, quoting accurate application figures to him. She'd done her homework and even implied the EU faced the same problems as the US. She then proposed combining resources. Intrigued, Medlington allowed her to expand on her proposal taking perverse pleasure, not in the proposal itself, which he conceded bore greater consideration, but because it was obvious she had not run this by the head of her delegation, if Perry's infuriated reaction was anything to go by.

"Wasn't it one of your own presidents, Kennedy perhaps, who said that drastic problems often required drastic measures?" Medlington said to her.

"And?" she asked in return.

"America is rather short on useable land at the moment for such a large population, or simply put, you have too many people. Why not introduce euthanasia? Eliminate the unnecessary elements, the homeless, the hopelessly unemployed or the old and the sick," he suggested, sounding almost amiable. They were all the categories this Senator worked with, and he knew that. He was eager to see how she rose to this latest challenge. Did she 'walk her talk'?

"A drastic measure indeed," she replied, holding her temper well. "We could even invite you to be the first participant, as you fall into both the old and sick category."

"Oh, I'm not that old, nor am I unwell," he replied.

"Anyone capable of making such an appalling suggestion is a god-damned sick bastard," she replied. Perry was livid, convinced she would blow the whole deal, but Medlington smiled.

"What do you propose, Senator?" he asked her and to Swayne, his smile seemed warm.

Chapter 13

Jonathan Medlington asked her to repeat the question.

"My question is regarding black Americans," she stated again. "Your own EU charter claims you cannot discriminate on the grounds of race or colour, but that's what's happening here. We can't claim European descent, but by the guidelines you've issued this morning, these people will once again be discriminated against. And not just blacks, but Native American Indians. They have no voice here, no place in your perfectly typed up guidelines, even though they're the ones most affected by what's happening. If these so-called guidelines apply to one aspect of America, then they should apply to all."

Silence followed her little speech. Medlington stroked his moustache, resembling a vulture waiting to swoop on a dying carcass. Swayne straightened in her seat, a hint of defiance, and from the corner of her eye saw Michaels nodding in agreement, California having one of the largest black populations in the US, and the largest population group displaced by the disasters. Medlington lowered his hand, and hinted at a smile.

"Thank you Senator. You've raised an important issue that will require a deeper discussion. I suggest we adjourn for lunch now and continue this in the afternoon. How does that sound to you?"

"That sounds just fine," she answered.

Perry rounded on her as they exited the building.

"Just what the hell are you playing at?" he demanded.

"All you're concerned about is your precious white ass, and how you can save yourself a nice soft landing, and that's your prerogative, but we are supposed to be here negotiating for every American," she answered, walking away from him.

Outside, police cars screeched to a halt at the end of the street, sirens blaring. A sense of urgency hung about the place. Police officers in protective gear ran towards them, urging them back to the security barriers of the building. Swayne understood the situation and ran back to the security gate, the guards ushering everyone back inside. Perry, always one to save his own ass, followed right behind her. Jason Michaels stood rooted to the spot. Panic and indecision racked his brain, making his body unable to move. A cop attempted to move him, but it was too late. They were both too close, and the blast from the car bomb lifted both men from the ground, slamming them into the security defences surrounding the EU building. Inside, sheltered behind the boundary wall, Swayne and Perry sought protection as far away from the windows as possible. The security defences bore the brunt of the blast but the building still shook.

Swayne moved first, ignoring the cops trying to hold her back. Oblivious to the dangers, Swayne's concern was for the injured. She was no medic, but she would do what she could. The stench of charred flesh overwhelmed her as she made her way to the street, finding the mangled body of Michaels. She ran to him, knowing she could do nothing for the man, but she knelt beside him, closing his sightless eyes.

Medlington appeared behind her, overheard her short prayer for her fellow compatriot. Medlington put his hand on her shoulder, but she didn't acknowledge him, so he cupped his hand under her elbow and lifted her to her feet. She stared around at the wreckage that lay before them, angry and confused, not understanding the viciousness behind such an act. More sirens registered, and she refocused, noticing Medlington beside her. Paramedics worked on those they thought they had a chance of saving. She saw the remains of a car, and her body shook, betraying her efforts to remain calm. Medlington put his arm around her and called over his aide, giving instructions to the man. Within moments his private car pulled up, and he guided Swayne towards it, helping her in which she did without protest, and allowed herself to be taken away from the awful sight.

Back at her hotel room Swayne still trembled, but the large glass of brandy Medlington gave her helped calm her, restoring heat and feeling back into her. Camera crews arrived within moments of the blast, and several of the clips broadcasted showed her kneeling by Michaels' body, and Medlington leading her away. The horrific scenes replayed on screen, no matter which channel she turned to, and Medlington decided she'd tortured herself enough, and turned the damn thing off as her phone rang. The news had hit the States by now, and Swayne smiled at the caller ID before answering, one of her daughters, frantic to know she was all right. She reassured them all, gathered at the other end of the connection, and the familiar voices helped calm her more than the brandy did. Food Medlington ordered went untouched, and she didn't engage in his attempts at conversation but she was grateful for his presence.

A knock on the door broke her from her thoughts, but didn't motivate her to move. Medlington answered it instead, unimpressed to find Perry on the other side of the door. The unexpected presence of the Englishman annoyed Perry. Swayne not only stole the limelight with her attempt to play Florence Nightingale, but now he found the Brit in her room. He barged in, pushing past Medlington, brandishing a sheet of paper, but seemed reluctant to relinquish it to either of them.

"Someone's just claimed responsibility," he said, holding the note up. Medlington snatched it from Perry's grasp before he could react.

"We demand the right to return to Europe," Medlington read, his brow furrowing. "Signed A.L.L. Who, or what, is A.L.L.?"

Swayne stood up.

"*Americans for Life and Liberty*," she told him. "They're the group who claimed responsibility for the Canadian Embassy bombing." Medlington seemed furious.

"I don't appreciate you bringing your problems with you, and these terror tactics are not going to advance your cause," he told them both. "The EU will not be held to ransom."

"Why send the note to you?" Swayne asked Perry.

"Obviously because I'm the delegation leader," he answered.

"But why you?" she pressed. "Why not Medlington, or one of the other Eurocrats?"

Medlington raised his eyebrows at the title, but Swayne didn't notice. "We're here negotiating for America, why target the ones who are working at getting a solution. These bastards are going to ruin any chance we have of securing those visas, of helping everyone we can." Perry looked at the page still in Medlington's hand.

"I trust you know the appropriate authorities to forward that onto," he said instead. Medlington didn't answer him, but turned back to Swayne.

"You seem to know more about this. Any ideas on how best to proceed?" he asked her.

"I know the agent working on the A.L.L. bombing in Washington. He seems to know who's behind it. As this is of concern for the both of us, I propose pooling intelligence, and resources," she said.

"Are you suggesting he works with the investigative team here?" Medlington asked, and she nodded. "A wise move. With due respect to the dead, we'll suspend all discussions for the next few days. It would be inappropriate to continue, given the circumstances. We'll speak about this later." He addressed Swayne, infuriating Perry to the point of outrage, and as the Eurocrat left, Perry rounded on Swayne.

"What in the hell is going on?" he demanded.

"Going on?"

"With you and that ... that man."

She stiffened, her jaw jutting out a little more as she squared up to him.

"There is nothing going on, except I'm doing what you came here to do, and are failing at," she taunted him. His attempt at a reply came out as an outraged squawk. "You have done nothing but bitch this whole time, while treating these people with utter disdain and contempt. Why would they deal with you when they can have a reasonable, and normal, discussion with me? If I didn't know better, I'd swear you were deliberately trying to have these talks break down, you pompous shit."

Her attack was ferocious, and it unnerved him, but he attributed her outburst as an emotional reaction to Michaels' death. Yet he didn't dare give this woman a slap to calm her down. He estimated his chances of surviving that action as slim. Leaving his desire to hit her unfulfilled, he turned and left, slamming the door behind him. Not as satisfying as his hand striking flesh, but the resounding bang compensated for that.

He hurried back to his own room, having his own reasons to be unsettled. The note was found in his room, left on the bedside locker, and addressed to 'Dallas'. They were in his room. And what of the bomb, he wondered. Was it meant for him? Was it a warning? Bringing Swayne along wasn't part of the plan. Was that the cause of the threat?

He locked the door to his room, and lay down to think out his next move.

Chapter 14
Washington

The persistent pounding on the door woke Jake. Mumbling obscenities at the late night caller, he trundled to the door, checking through the spyhole, before sighing and undoing the various locks and latches. Myers barged through.

"About time," he growled. Jake rubbed sleep from his eyes and checked the clock on the nearby bookshelf. It read 4:27am.

"And you interrupted my beauty sleep for …?" he asked, not caring to hide his hostility. Myers didn't answer him but headed for the kitchen and the coffee machine.

"There's been another bombing," he said, as the machine started.

"And?"

"A.L.L. claimed responsibility."

"Where?"

"Outside the European Commission building in Brussels."

"And outside our jurisdiction," Jake reminded him, but his shoulders sagged as Myers shook his head.

"Senator Michaels is dead. Blast got him. According to Swayne, the Europeans are threatening to end talks."

"Unless?" Jake asked. Myers turned his attention back to the brewing coffee.

"Swayne suggested a joint investigation," he answered, still not looking at Jake.

"A what?"

"You heard me. Swayne offered them our expert on A.L.L. to work with their top investigators."

"Fuck, no! I'm not an expert on A.L.L. and I'm not going back to Europe." Myers looked at him with curiosity.

"Back? You've been there before?" Jake mentally kicked himself for the slip-up.

"Vacation. Hated it."

Myers didn't question it, but poured himself a cup of coffee. As an afterthought, he poured one for Jake.

"So this A.L.L. is new, but you already suspect Gouderhoff is behind it, and you are the resident expert on him," Myers said, handing over the cup. Jake ignored it.

"Do I have a choice?"

Myers pulled papers from his inside jacket pocket, and threw them on the breakfast bar.

"You fly out of Dulles in three hours, so you'd best get packing."

The plane took off as scheduled, but Jake found the journey long and tedious. He never liked tight and confined spaces. To take his mind off his discomfort he occupied himself with work, rereading the files, not that he needed to, with his almost eidetic memory he could quote most of the documents verbatim, but still, he delved for any scrap he may have missed, any sudden revelation in the text. Someone from the US Embassy met him when he landed, a high up enough Official to brief him on what happened, handing him a copy of the note.

"That's it?" Jake asked, and the man nodded.

"Delivered during the talks. No one saw anything."

"And delivered before the bomb detonated?" Jake concluded, and the man nodded again. "Delivered to Senator Perry's room?" he asked, receiving another nod. God, this man was a fountain of information, he thought, but guessed he was CIA; certain mannerisms were far too familiar for Jake to ignore. He concentrated instead on the other details of the situation, but when he looked up was surprised to find they were headed for the EU Commission.

"I thought negotiations were suspended," he said.

"Talks on the visas are, but not the investigation."

"No rest for the wicked," Jake muttered, and the other man chuckled.

"Hope you don't suffer from jetlag," he commented. Jake gave him a sour look, knowing it would hit him later. Swayne waited for him at reception.

"Sorry to drag you all the way over here," she said.

"Why me?" he asked, surprising her with his aggressive tone.

"You investigated the Canadian bombing. With that connection you were the obvious choice, and if we cooperate with the EU ..."

"They'll cooperate with us," he finished. Swayne's smile was brief, but warm.

"That's what we're hoping for," she answered. An honest and upfront politician, he mused, wondering if he should check the weather forecast for Hell. Senator Perry, however, restored his lack of faith in statesmen when they met outside the conference room. The man's grip on Jake's arm tightened as he pulled him to one side, while trying to avoid Swayne's watchful and penetrating gaze.

"Agent Mann, I know you don't appreciate being here anymore than the rest of us do, so I'll make this easy for you, just consider yourself a token gesture," Perry said.

"What do you mean by token gesture?"

Unused to being talked back to, Perry glared at him.

"The Eurocrats have given into *some* of our demands, out of respect for Michaels' death. I just need you to do enough to ensure we get the rest of what we want," he said. Jake gritted his teeth, holding back a snippy comment.

"It sounds as though you don't expect results from this investigation," he said instead.

"I don't," Perry snapped back. "You failed to find or apprehend this group after the Canadian Embassy bombing, I want the same results here, but make it look convincing. Just enough to keep these Eurocrats from pulling out. Is that understood?"

"Yes sir, it is," Jake answered, catching Swayne's concerned look from the corner of his eye.

A receptionist guided the three Americans to Sir Medlington's offices.

"Well now, this is cosy," Perry commented. Medlington gave Perry a disdainful look, but approached Swayne instead, taking her hands in his.

"Feeling better?" he asked her.

"Yes, much better," she answered, smiling. She turned towards Jake. "This is the agent I told you about," and Jake found himself under scrutiny from piercing blue eyes. The Englishman stood almost as tall as him, with a moustache and goatee as clipped as his accent. He turned to Swayne.

"EATA have also sent one of their best to work with your agent," he told her, turning to the only other woman in the room. "This is Bianca Monteray, explosives expert with the European Anti-Terrorist Agency. But Wilma tells me you already know who's behind this?" That hard stare returned to Jake.

"Ah, yes, I believe I do," Jake answered.

"Then please enlighten us," he said. It took a moment for everyone to be seated, and Medlington returned to the other side of the table. The Senators took their seats first, leaving Jake the seat at the end.

"His name is Karl Gouderhoff," he began. "Born in Düsseldorf, his mother died there when he was three, and he lived with his father's sister in Frankfurt, while his father, an army engineer, was stationed there. Details about his teenage years are sketchy, but he popped up on record when he attended University in Ireland. After graduation, he returned to Germany and joined the army, but after an incident involving a suspected terrorist bomb, where a cadet died, Gouderhoff disappeared. He showed up on Interpol's radar two years later as a suspected assassin, but that remains unconfirmed. He's also been linked to arms smuggling and identity forgery."

"Drugs?" the man to Medlington's right asked. There were no introductions, nor did he volunteer his name, but his manner screamed of a military past. Jake shook his head.

"There's no evidence to suggest he's gone down that route," he answered.

"A terrorist with a conscience," the man commented. "Anything else?"

"His latest enterprise involved forging and selling Canadian visas and passports, but by the time I caught up with him, he'd already shut down his operation and disappeared," Jake answered, not willing to admit he'd let the man slip through his hands. So there it was, the bare bones of Gouderhoff's life, and most of Jake's too, truth be told.

"And you believe this man is responsible for the bomb here?" the man asked.

"I do."

"Why? Does this Gouderhoff have a political agenda?" This time the question came from the man on Medlington's left, and again no names were given.

"I believe it's purely financial," Jake answered.

"Any information about the device used in the bombing?" Medlington himself asked. Jake nodded towards the woman opposite him.

"With respect to your EATA agent, they seem to have more information than we do at the moment." He gave her his best smile, but in return she narrowed her eyes and glared at him, pursing her lips together on her long oval face. The man next to her turned.

"Well?" he demanded.

"Our information is still limited," she said. Of the four Europeans present she was the only one not English, and Jake guessed her accent to be French.

"What do you mean by limited?" the man demanded. Those pursed lips tightened even more.

"So far, EATA agents have just found a pure and intact sample of this bomb," she answered.

"And out of curiosity Agent Mann, what's Gouderhoff's degree in?" Medlington asked. Surprised by the question, Jake hesitated for a moment.

"Chemical engineering," he answered.

"Is this a designer bomb then?" Swayne asked.

"At a guess I'd say yes, but again, EATA are the experts on it," he answered, redirecting attention back to Bianca. Jake didn't think it possible for her face to get any harder, but she proved him wrong.

"Well?" the man beside her demanded again.

"Yes, it's designer. A new chemical configuration. As I've said before, we've only just found a sample of it, and our engineers are still trying to figure it out," she answered them.

"And from what we've figured out, it's undetectable," Jake added. "It could be anywhere in the world, and we don't know what to look for."

"You paint a bleak picture, Agent Mann," Medlington said. "And what of the visas if the EU were to grant them to US citizens? What's the likelihood of this character producing forgeries?"

"I'd say the chances are high," Jake answered, despite a hiss from Perry.

Chapter 15

In anger, Jake threw his holdall onto a chair, and slumped onto the sofa. His moment of rest was short-lived. A knock on the door sounded just as his ass hit the cushions. While his rest was brief, his ego and sensibilities would take longer to recover. He yanked the door open, finding Swayne on the other side.

"I'm sorry," she said. He opened the door wider, allowing her in.

"It's fine. You'd nothing to do with it. That was obvious," he said.

"I still can't believe Perry threw you to the wolves like that."

"Why wouldn't he?" Jake asked. "I admitted the visas wouldn't be safe, so why wouldn't he offer me up as the sacrificial lamb to advance his cause."

"You have a harsh view of him," she said, and as he gave her an astounded look, she held up her hands. "I'm not saying it's not accurate, but if it's any consolation you'll be stuck here with me." The astonishment turned to shock.

"What?"

"It's part of the Agreement with the EU, thrashed out in minute detail after you left," she said, and he gave her a blank stare. He didn't leave, he was dismissed after he'd outlived his usefulness, only to discover he'd become part of the bargaining.

"So Perry goes home with the prize, and becomes everyone's messiah. And that leaves you…?"

"With the joyful task of implementing the policies agreed," she answered. "I think the official term is 'liaison'."

"Sounds like the official word for screwed," he said, before realising to whom he spoke. He was about to mutter an apology, but she laughed.

"You could well be right."

"I'd offer you coffee, but I just moved in."

"Then let me take you to dinner," she offered. "I doubt you've eaten yet, and it's been a long day for you." He debated turning her down, but then figured why the hell not. He grabbed his keys to the apartment they assigned him, and slammed the door, liking the heavy sound it made.

"So what does this liaison detail entail?" he asked as he followed her out. As his only ally in this place, he needed to connect with her.

"It's more a fancy word for overseer," she answered. "The Eurocrats have agreed to the visas, but with restrictions."

"Like relocating industries?"

"So, some of the details have slipped out," she commented, as they reached the street.

"One or two," he admitted, not revealing how much he'd found out.

"But you're right, a significant number of American based companies have to set up within the twenty seven countries, primarily in the countries that will be hit the hardest by returning descendants, or who are still struggling economically since Eurogedden, the Euro financial crisis."

"We help them to help ourselves."

"Very neatly put, Agent Mann."

He held up a hand.

"Seeing as we're both stuck here, Senator, it's Jake."

She took him to an American style restaurant and outlined the rest of the terms and conditions to the visas. To Jake, it sounded as though the Eurocrats were being generous, allowing a considerable number of visas, and outlining the employment conditions for Americans, including the favourable ratio of black and Native American. All this in exchange for industries moving across the water. Of course there was a catch. There always was.

"And where do I fit in?" he asked her.

"Medlington is concerned about Gouderhoff hijacking the visas, creating his own, and selling them on the black market," she said. He grunted.

"Perry gave me the impression I was to go after the bomb," he answered. She looked him in the eye.

"I'll be honest, Perry gave them free rein to do whatever they like with you, but I've spoken with Medlington, and said you believed this guy would target the visas, and where I thought you belonged."

"Thanks," he muttered.

"I'm sorry, Jake. It's the best I could do," she answered.

"I know," he said. "It'll take time to get the visas up and running. Knowing Gouderhoff, he'll have infiltrated it before it gets off the ground, and I have no idea where start looking for him." He grew wary as a smile spread across her face.

"Well, that's where I have some good news," she said.

"Interpol and EATA know where he is?"

"I can tell you where he's likely to be."

He looked at her, but she toyed with him, and let slip a mischievous side, knocking a dent in his assessment of her.

"Stop teasing, I'm far too young," he dared to play back.

"Cheeky pup," she laughed, reassessing her initial assumption of him. "Okay, I'll spill. Much to everyone's surprise, well on the US side anyway, the Eurocrats have already implemented a visa strategy."

"What?" he said, astounded.

"At a place called Shannon."

"The airport in Ireland?"

"The very place. It's a stopover point for all flights into Ireland, and an immigration point for Europe. Jonathan told me about it after Perry left."

"Jonathan?" he queried.

"He's not too young," she replied. Good for her, Jake thought, knowing Swayne's history, or at least what he'd read in the papers.

"Did Jonathan tell you anything else?"

"Quite a lot," she answered.

Chapter 16
Shannon Airport, Ireland

Matt tried his damnedest not to stare, but found the task difficult. It wasn't everyday his ex-fiancé walked back into his life to work alongside him, only with more authority. So far, she seemed pleasant enough; no hint things between them ended on a sour note. She fixed her attention on the Director of TARCO, the Trans-Atlantic Relocation Co-Ordination Unit, established in Shannon to handle, process and produce all the visas and permits for the Americans.

The Director addressed these experts before him, outlining the specifications and requirements, something Matt himself should have been paying attention to, but couldn't. Every now and again, she threw a glance towards the French security consultant, and Matt saw the look the French woman gave her in return. He was happy not to be on the receiving end of either glance. Perhaps that explained her lack of animosity towards him. She had a greater adversary in her sights.

The Director moved onto the introductions, naming first the appointed civil servants already assigned to the team, pulled from the relevant departments. He then moved onto the consultants, introducing the French woman as Isobel Piquet, a specialist in on-site security systems, listing off her impressive résumé to everyone in the room. Next up was Daniel Fisher, the American specialist in the US social security systems, and then Leigh Harte.

Her résumé stunned Matt even more. She had been busy since she'd left him, and left the civil service. It seemed a lifetime ago to Matt. The Director then handed the floor over to Matt, the head of the development team. He found Isobel's stare hard, and Daniel's expectant, but Leigh seemed amused. Matt took a sip of water, and cleared his throat, feeling the build-up of pressure that bordered on panic. He hated speaking in front of people.

"Erm… yeah, just to echo what the Director said, welcome to TARCO, and as you've already heard, most of Europe is already linked up in terms of immigration and work permits. What the Director didn't mention is that the US social services will process applications for visas, and those selected will be chosen randomly. The European database should be able to match up their skills with available jobs, especially when the American companies move over, and get up and running. So Daniel, you'll be working with our people from Social Protection, configuring the data from the US to link with ours. The plan is to have vermits ready as each immigrant arrives."

"Vermits?" Isobel asked, to which Leigh chuckled.

"Visas and permits?" she asked, and Matt grinned.

"Shortens the conversation," he said. "And you're here to make sure no one can hack into the system, and issue bogus vermits."

"That's the plan," she answered.

"Okay, let's get everyone settled in," he said. "You guys are lucky to get your own offices. It's been hell getting the space we needed."

He gathered his papers before assigning members of his team to escort Daniel and Isobel to their respective offices while he hung back with Leigh.

"You look a little shell shocked, Matt," she said when everyone left.

"Just surprised to see you, that's all," he replied. "So what's new with you?"

"Got this cool new job," she shot back.

"I see you haven't lost your sense of humour."

"I see you still haven't found yours."

She held the door open for him as he followed her out.

"So what's the story with you and that French woman?" he asked as he showed her to her office.

"What do you mean?"

"She doesn't seem to like you."

"She doesn't. Not since I shot her."

He hesitated, not sure he'd heard her correctly, or perhaps her bizarre sense of humour ran riot again. She dropped her papers and security badge on her desk, and turned to face him, seeing the confusion and perplexity on his face.

"Eh, why?" he asked, playing for time, trying to figure out if she was serious or not.

"Because she'd been beating the shit out of me, and it pissed me off," she answered.

"Fine, don't tell me," he said, storming out of her office, and she let out a small laugh. Sometimes the truth was far stranger than fiction, and she rubbed the small scar on her forearm, a souvenir from one of those beatings. Isobel entered having overheard the exchange between them.

"There's history there?" she asked. Leigh glared at her.

"Yeah," she admitted. Working alongside Isobel didn't mean she had to befriend her. "What's all that bullshit the Director read out, French Police, and French security services?"

"What makes you think it's bullshit?"

"Because the file I broke into in Huntington said you'd been arrested for terrorist activities." Isobel closed the office door behind her, a clear reminder to Leigh to be mindful of who might be listening. Leigh didn't need the hint, she had a good view of the corridor, and of anyone approaching. A better view than Isobel had at that moment.

"And what of the bullshit about your computer skills? Am I to believe you're that good?"

"Who do you think fucked up your files at Huntington?" Leigh replied, taking pleasure from the anger rising in her French counterpart.

"So what's your brief?" Isobel demanded.

"Officially or unofficially?" Leigh answered, cold and calm, that same iciness as when she'd reloaded her gun on the practice range, and shot Isobel. The bulletproof vest saved the French woman's life.

"Why did Lantry send you here?" Isobel asked.

"He thinks the visas may already be compromised."

"That's what he told me," Isobel said. She sat, making herself seem relaxed in front of Leigh, making a show of not being afraid or wary of her, but something about Leigh's icy and hard demeanour unnerved her. To deflect the tension Leigh sat on her desk and looked around the room.

"Needs a coffee machine," she said, but sighed and relented. "The official brief is genuine. I'm responsible for the encryption of the visas and...well, the vermits, and developing the housing allocation system. Unofficially, I'm to embed a tracking subsystem to detect any hint of hacking or tampering."

"Tampering? Doesn't that imply?"

"An inside job? Someone already infiltrated into the team? Yeah, but I'm guessing that's where you come in."

Isobel gave a nod.

"The story about the team being threatened is true, and I have expertise in terror tactics," Isobel admitted. "There've been several threats towards the facility. It seems there's a lot of anti-American feeling out there."

"And for a so-called security expert have you even considered the possibility that this room is bugged?" Leigh threw at her. A smirk spread across Isobel's face as she held up a small electronic device in her hand.

"Until I get to carry out a proper sweep, this should distort any electronic signal," she answered. Leigh grunted.

"Well, that would explain why mine is going mental then," she said, turning over what Isobel assumed to be her mobile phone, engaging in the geeky equivalent of a male pissing contest.

Their brief history together was far from pleasant. Training at Huntington could only be described as brutal and harsh, with the concept of team building omitted from the curriculum. It was each man, or woman for themselves, and building relationships was not encouraged, especially not with those who used you for target practice, or a human punch bag.

The only one in her group without a criminal record, or army background, Leigh found the training gruelling, and as the perceived weakest link, was singled out from the start by the others. Out of sheer aggravation, she'd resorted to shooting Isobel with cold deliberation, with a rewarding effect. They all left her alone after that. Even Lantry ceased his own brand of terror tactics, sending the trainers to pull them out for manoeuvres at god awful hours of the night, subjecting them to long periods of confined isolation, sensory deprivation, and intense anti-interrogations techniques.

That stopped too, after she barricaded herself into the bathroom, and slept in the bathtub, while the rest were hauled off on a twenty kilometre hike. Her absence was not appreciated by the others, and Lantry retaliated by having the bathroom door removed. His reign over her ended when she broke into his quarters, hiding out there for a peaceful night's rest, while locking Lantry out. Whether he stopped out of frustration, or because of her losing it with Isobel, she didn't know, but she doubted it was out of concern for her well-being.

Now she faced her main antagonist from those intense months, challenged with working together, and Leigh hoped it wouldn't become a constant battle like their time at Huntington. Besides, Leigh had better things to concentrate on than dealing with Isobel and preventing a fraud. She wanted to catch the man behind it, and the man Lantry told her had killed her parents.

Chapter 17
The Quays, Waterford, Ireland

The warehouse looked the same as any of the others spread along the docks, with boxes of legitimate items stacked and stored in precise order. The difference between the warehouse and others along the quay was the secreted hi-tech communications centre Karl Gouderhoff built for himself beneath the warehouse's commercial façade. Constructed to withstand pressure from the sea, and sound proofed, it became the perfect hideaway, and a fortress into which Karl liked to retreat, especially after his antics of the last few days.

His current employer expressed disapproval at the bomb, but the point needed to be made. 'Dallas' needed the lesson. Bringing that woman along wasn't part of the plan, and it didn't take long to figure out why. Karl reasoned with his employer, who conceded to the need for the lesson, just not the result. In this he was justified; the bomb wasn't meant to kill, just to frighten and threaten. The death of the Californian Senator was regrettable, and it almost put a halt to the whole operation.

In silence, Karl made himself a large mug of tea. No radio or television blasted incessant noise, no sound filtered down from above. It was just how he liked to live, and the silence suited him. In his youth he'd spent time in this country, and it held a lot of memories for him, most of them good, some not so.

With his brew in hand, he returned to his operations room, one wall covered in an array of monitors and screens. Not all of them were in use, just the ones he needed for this job. The active ones showed him the current events within the EU Commission as they happened; images streamed from the various micro cameras concealed around the conference room and office of the British Commissioner, strategically placed state-of-the-art cameras and listening devices, with anti-detection and scrambler capabilities to avoid detection by the sweeper teams. So far, his little toys withstood seven security sweeps.

Karl timed it well with his cuppa, returning as figures appeared around the table on screen. Medlington stood and shook hands with Senator Swayne and from Karl's observations on the Commissioner, this was a warm, almost intimate handshake. Swayne then turned to introduce the newcomer, and Karl stared at the screen in disbelief as Jake Mann stepped into view.

He turned up the volume a notch at the control console, listening with interest as Jake gave a good account of Karl's life. There were a few inaccuracies, some missing details, but so far Jake was the only agent Karl had encountered who'd proven his worth in terms of dogged determination, and in learning everything he could about his adversary. Jake's un-agent-like unpredictability and unconventional methods threw Karl more than a few curve balls in the past, unlike previous agents hunting him, and he appreciated Jake in his life, even if it was to remind him of life's precariousness, and how vicious a sense of humour it had.

He watched on as both Perry and Medlington dismissed Jake, a toy they'd outgrown. At least Swayne had the decency to seem abashed by the treatment of the agent, but Karl turned the volume up another notch, and listened to the plans they made concerning the visas, his visas, and assigning Jake to the case. How easily these politicians played with people's lives, Karl thought, again wondering about the effect of the bomb on Perry. It hadn't appeared to have frightened him half enough, but on the upside, Karl had Jake to play with for a while.

With the meeting over, he returned to the contents of the other screens, the documents he'd been reading before taking a break. The contents of the documents fascinated him. Displayed before him were the financial accounts of Senator John Perry. Karl felt a twinge of jealousy at how well the man covered his tracks, and it took time to untangle the complicated, and often misleading, information. One thing was certain; Perry knew now to cover his ass. He'd known the Senator was a conniving, scheming bastard, but he never realised the full extent of the man's activities, nor did he realise the number of companies that sat in his pocket, and he in theirs.

Movement on other screens caught his attention, as the conference room in Shannon airport showed activity, and again he adjusted the volume. Most of the faces he recognised by now and knew each of them. Files and background checks on them were on his servers, but the three new people captured his attention the most.

From his surveillance, he knew of the American's arrival, of his role to link up the US and European systems. Introducing the security expert didn't surprise him. They'd had demonstrations at the airport, outcries at the perception of Americans taking jobs and housing, and none of these demonstrations were organised by Karl. He didn't need to. This was a backlash to the US's immigration clampdown some years back. Nor were the demonstrating participants all Irish. Other European nationalities joined in the protests. Appointing a security expert was a clever move, but the third name shocked him to his core, knocking all other thoughts from his mind.

Leigh Harte. Now there was a name from his past. Using the controls he panned the hidden camera around as far as it would move, zooming in to get a better look at her. His breath caught in his chest, seeing a younger version of her father, down to the same characteristic clenching of the jaw that had been a permanent feature of Lee senior. The last time he'd seen her in person was after the funeral, and even then he hadn't dared get too close to her. His instincts saved him that time; she'd been under surveillance, and had he tried to approach her, he'd have been shot. Back then she'd been a waif of a child, terrified of the world. Yet over the years Karl maintained tabs on her, and her whereabouts, when he could. He wasn't the only one keeping a watchful eye on her either. Because of Lee, several differing agencies maintained surveillance on her, until their fears of her following in her father's footsteps proved unfounded.

As he watched her now, he felt a twinge of guilt at how much he'd failed her in the past fifteen years, unable to help when she succumbed to drugs, and unable to find her when she disappeared during her first year in college. While that boorish oaf, Tom, seemed to have sorted her out, her disappearance set off alarm bells for Karl, and he suspected she fell back into bad habits again. Yet again, Karl was powerless to help, but he was surprised when she resurfaced, and her name appeared on the enrolment list for the Goethe Universität in Frankfurt.

That she took a clerical job in the Irish Civil Service after she graduated also surprised him, but she'd always been a shy kid, so maybe a stable desk job was the best thing for her. However, that didn't last long. She disappeared again less than two years later. Concerned, Karl tried tracking her down, finding hospital records for a medical procedure in Kilkenny, but she'd fled to Frankfurt for another couple of months.

She returned to Ireland sometime later with a bang, her company set up, and a list of clients already on board. That those clients had connections to her dad, Leigh didn't need to know. The same people who trusted Lee's encoding now put their faith in his offspring, but without dragging her into the dark and seedy world her father inhabited. Her reputation grew and word in the IT world was she didn't disappoint, her encryptions and computer skills surpassing Lee's.

That still didn't explain how or why she'd landed the job at Shannon, and Karl didn't believe in coincidences. Lee senior taught him that. In this underhanded world, there were no such things as coincidences, and the presence of young Leigh rang an ominous bell in the back of his mind.

Chapter 18

"'The Yankees are coming'. It sounds like a Civil War cry, but this time Americans are united in their struggle." Louise Donohue of BSI News stood outside a State Department sub office, doing her best not to be jostled by the gathering masses, who awaited their turn submit their applications.

"While authorities claim that selection will be based on a lottery system," she went on to the camera, "many have raised concerns over the need to register their skills, qualifications and experience. This has prompted fears that the so-called lottery will turn into an elitist selection process. Government officials have denied this, claiming it a necessity for the allocation of jobs, and housing, in Europe. Senators Perry and Gerrard have returned to the US with the body of Senator Michaels, but details of funeral arrangements have not yet been released. Senator Wilma Swayne remains in Europe to campaign for more visas, and to secure the rights of Americans lucky enough to get to Europe...."

The aforementioned Senator reached for the television remote, silencing Louise and her rhetoric. Wilma never did like the journalist.

"I didn't know what you liked for breakfast, so my cook made everything," Jonathan said, placing a tray beside her on the bed.

"If you have waffles and maple syrup, I'm yours for life," she joked. He playfully kissed her before pulling away, lifting a lid from a plate.

"It must be fate, sort of. Pancakes, but I've been assured the ingredients are the same," he said, kissing her again as he sat beside her. She pulled away, the food distracting her, but continued to regard the man as he picked at a strawberry, at odds with his public image.

On lazy days like this, he was unkempt, dressing in baggy sweats and a well-worn, well-loved Cambridge t-shirt. He stretched out on the bed, entangling his legs with hers and picked at a croissant. Gone was his frosty demeanour, and all his airs and graces. Last night he'd invited her to dinner, and over a warm, fruity bottle of red wine and a game of chess, he'd kissed her. When asked if she played chess she'd announced her successes in high school, but admitted to not playing for years. Jonathan produced a board and challenged her. Initially she suspected him of trying to distract her with the kiss, especially as she'd beaten him twice, but it turned out not to be the case. He used the game as his foreplay, using it to figure her out, to unlock the deep and dark places where she hid herself, and she allowed him in, yielding to his intense passion, and giving back as good as she got. He liked that, loved the returning ferocity. She stirred her legs, knocking him from his reverie.

"There's an art exhibition opening tonight, some American artists."

"Artists such as?" she asked. He shrugged and shook his head. She laughed at that. "I thought all you aristocratic types were cultured."

"Art was never my forte," he defended himself. "If it's appealing, then I like it."

"And if it isn't appealing?"

"I never take an interest in anything but the best."

"And last night?"

"What about it?"

"Just a passing interest?"

"Why? You have regrets?" His tone turned sombre.

"No," she answered. "You just surprised me, that's all."

"Really?"

"You go on with your frosty British, stiff upper lip," she teased him. "Who knew the passion you've hidden?" He blushed, and distracted himself with his cup of coffee. She chuckled. "You're not the hard-ass you make yourself out to be."

"Please don't tell my adoring public," he said.

"Somehow I don't think I'd be believed," she shot back.

"And you're not a mere passing interest, I assure you of that," he admitted. Years of reading people told her he spoke the truth, and she blushed. It had been a long time since anyone expressed such a desire to be in her company. "So how about that date, Senator?" he asked.

"Date?"

"This art thing. We're both invited, and I would be delighted to accompany you."

"Then I'd been honoured, Commissioner."

It turned out to be a gala affair. Euro dignitaries and royalty, heads of governments and US ambassadors, all turned out for the opening, showing a united front to the world that this new alliance would be embraced, and accepted by all. Yet the mood within the Metropolitan Art Museum remained sombre. Behind the genteel façades, many governments doubted this new scheme would work, viewing it as a threat to the hard fought economic stability Europe managed to restore itself to.

Swayne arrived late. Jake, as her security detail didn't bat an eyelid, but the company of Sir Jonathan Medlington continued fuelling rumours of how the US secured concessions on jobs and housing. The trashier tabloids sprung into frenzied life with idle speculation. Since the tragic death of his wife over a decade ago, Medlington was rarely seen alone in the company of other women, and his office leaked to the press that his association with the American Senator was purely on a political and professional basis, in an attempt to offset any damage their relationship could spark off. That tactic backfired as the press created their own 'politics and strange bedfellows' analogy.

Once inside the museum they were beyond public scrutiny, and Jake left the pair to it. Wilma gave him a grateful nod as he did. He gave her a knowing smirk in reply, secure in entrusting the Senator to Medlington. Jake investigated the man at the first opportunity, but found Medlington to be above reproach, and a man of simple values. Like Swayne, Medlington achieved everything he set out to do, instigating many of the social and economic reforms that, not only pulled Europe from the brink of bankruptcy, but also improved social standards in many of the struggling nations.

His wife died in a car accident fourteen years previous, and Jake dug up old newspaper articles relating to the accident. The story was widely covered, and Jake delved deeper for any hints that the accident was more than just an accident, but his fears were put to rest. Medlington's wife drove that fateful night, and it was what it was, a tragic accident. Medlington miraculously survived, but at the cost of a year in hospital and rehabilitation, while his body repaired and healed. Jake reckoned Swayne was in safe hands. Besides, he didn't think she'd allow any old, smooth talking politician to sweep her off her feet. As the child of a savage drunk himself, Jake knew what it took to stand up to that level of brutality, and he admired the Senator for it. However hard his life was, he could only guess at the difficulty she'd faced with children in tow. From the look on her face as Medlington stroked her hand, it was obvious to anyone that she was happy.

Behind the couple another figure came into view, and Jake's eyes narrowed in annoyance at how a perfect evening could turn sour so quickly. Bianca Monterey knew how to make an entrance, pausing for effect and glancing around the room. Her shimmering dress caught the light as she sashayed through the room, making her way to the bar, and towards him. He turned away, ignoring her. She stood beside him, and ordered a drink, before turning to him. He could feel her cold, hard eyes drilling into him, but he refused to acknowledge her presence. He was being petty, but he didn't care. His new partner was a prize bitch, and he planned to play her at her own game, figuring her to be the kind of woman who got what she wanted, with men willing to fall at her feet. He was determined to be the exception, and that was the plan, until he felt her hand on his arm. He turned to her, finding himself staring into her deep brown eyes as she smiled at him, coyly.

Chapter 19

Shannon Airport

The scent of coffee assaulted him as he entered her office.

"Still take your coffee by the slice then," Matt said, crossing the threshold.

"Near enough," Leigh answered. "Want a cup?" She waved to the machine installed in the corner. He shook his head.

"No thanks. Can't drink it when it's strong enough to resurface roads." She ignored his comment. He stepped closer to the extra monitors she'd requested and installed, different applications and codes open on each one. "Whoa," he said leaning closer to one of the screens. "I've never seen code like this."

"And you won't."

"Yours?"

"Of course." There was that icy detachment again, Matt thought, but it seemed she made a visible effort to rein it in. "It's a Neo-Dynum Configuration."

"And that?" he pointed to another screen.

"Siege Sentinel Nova Bug."

"You're making this shit up, aren't you," he accused her, and she laughed.

"The siege sentinel is designed to trace any attempts to break into our systems, before going supernova on theirs."

"Nasty," he murmured, though impressed by the code's complexity.

"That's the reason they called me in, it's what I specialise in," she answered. He glanced around the room. She'd changed the layout, moving the L-shaped desk into the corner, maximising on the floor space. Except for the coffee machine, he found no other personal items. Not unusual for her, but time it seemed, made her more distant.

"I hear congratulations are in order," she said, staring at one of the screens. "You and Tina had a baby girl."

He searched her face for any sign of anger, or bitterness, but found none. She'd kept her voice even, but losing the baby all those years ago had been the breaking point in their relationship, especially as he'd been more relieved by the loss than her.

After that, she withdrew even more, and he'd returned home to their apartment one evening to find she'd moved out, took two weeks leave from work, and never returned.

"Thanks," he answered, noticing the tiny twitch of her jaw, and knew not to go into details.

"And the reason you're here?" she asked. They were interrupted by Daniel's unwanted arrival.

"Oh, hey, coffee. Mind if I grab some?" he asked.

"Knock yourself out," she answered.

"And it will knock you out," Matt commented, ignoring her glare. With a mug in hand, Daniel sat at the small conference table, pushing folders and papers out of the way, and opening his own file.

"I got the preliminary list of companies who are in a position to transfer over," he started. "Most of these already have branches somewhere in Europe, so they're already complying with Company Laws. The rest on the list still have to establish a base, but I've got a team liaising with European officials to move and start up as soon as suitable locations can be found."

"That quickly? What about existing employees?" Matt asked.

"For the most part there are none. A lot of these companies were Californian, Colorado or Nevada based, and most of them were destroyed either by the earthquakes, or volcanoes. Others were damaged by a mix of natural disasters, flooding, mudslides, you name it. Where possible, salvaged machinery will be shipped across the Atlantic to its new home."

"What we need to watch for, are bogus companies trying to set up as legitimate ones to get their hands on vermits, and using them to start trafficking people," Leigh added. A frown crossed Matt's forehead.

Maybe he knew this was going to be a complicated project, but all these unquantifiable variables started to cause a headache. He needed that coffee after all.

"Did you upload that list to the server?" she asked Daniel, and he nodded.

"It needed reformatting, but its uploaded to the test database. So far, the application, and test data, seem to be working with the job skills allocation," he said.

"What's happening on the American side?" Matt asked.

"The lottery is not going to be as random as it seems," Daniel admitted.

"There's a surprise," Matt muttered, and Leigh threw him a hard look. Daniel's face also hardened.

"Don't mind him," she said to Daniel. "Sarcasm's his default setting." Daniel gave Matt a glare before returning to his notes.

"We've already put together a test batch of people to come over," Daniel said, and Matt was reassured to see Leigh was just as surprised. "They're construction workers, highly skilled, and already vetted with no criminal records," Daniel added.

"I think you'll find enough construction workers throughout the EU," Matt said.

"Naturally, but your new EU Directives now state that certain percentages of Americans have to be employed. And, if we're to do our part in getting houses ready for living in, and getting companies set up, then you need all the manpower you can get," Daniel said, unable to keep the smugness from his voice. He noticed Leigh's attempt to hide a smirk. Daniel sized the pair up at their initial meeting, noting the familiarity between them. Ex-girlfriend, Daniel then concluded, and ex-girlfriends seemed to delight in all things that upset their ex's.

"ETA?" she asked him.

"State Department's still working on it, but I'd say they could be ready in the next few days," Daniel answered.

"ETA?" Matt asked.

"Estimated Time to Arrival," she answered him, in a tone that said he should've already known that. A bad breakup, Daniel determined.

"So we've about a week to pull all this together," Leigh said, and Daniel nodded.

"I figured we'd take this as an opportunity to test run the whole system. Flight details and passenger manifests, will be sent just before the plane takes off, and with a seven or eight hour flight, that should give us enough time to have the vermits, and onward travel arrangements, made," he said. Leigh agreed.

"Sounds like a solid plan," she said. Matt remained quiet, annoyed at how they'd progressed to this, and without much input from him. But they were the consultants, he reminded himself, and doing what they were employed to do.

"Any chance we can get this info sooner than just before take off?" he asked.

"As soon as it's finalised and I get it, then you'll get it," Daniel replied.

Chapter 20

Brussels

Medlington threw the newspaper onto her desk.

"Have you seen the headlines?" he growled. Wilma shook her head and reached for the publication, one of the more intellectual journals. She inhaled sharply. A picture of Perry, and the title 'Euro Tricked', blasted across the front page. She read the article, horror and anger growing with each word of the journalist's account. She was incensed. She'd known Perry was a scheming bastard, that he hadn't acquired his wealth and position by hard work. To be confronted by the man's deceit and treachery, in this way, threw her.

"Bastard!" was all she could think of saying.

"I couldn't agree more," Jonathan said. "This is going to put you in a very difficult position."

"How?"

"By association. You were also on that negotiation committee, it'll only be a matter of time before someone thinks of turning to you. Perry very conveniently left you behind," he answered.

"Just what the hell are you saying?" she demanded. "Do you think I'm an accomplice in all of this? That's bullshit, and you know it. But if that's the line you want to take then fine, you can get the hell out of my office, and out of my life." To her surprise, he grinned at her.

"With a fighting spirit like that, it's small wonder you haven't taken over the world."

"What would I do with it?" she shot back.

"For what it's worth, this is my office, which you have the courtesy of using, and Senator, I have no intentions of leaving, either my office, or you. I've grown fond of your company, and I wouldn't dream of forsaking it, nor do I intend to abandon you to the mercy of the press."

"So your intentions are honourable, sir?" she asked in a somewhat haughty manner.

"Yes madam, most honourable." He tried to be solemn, and almost succeeded, but a soft laugh broke through, and he kissed her. "Do you always go on the attack like that," he murmured as he pulled away.

"Only when I plan on conquering the world," she answered, with a laugh of her own, but her mind churned with their present dilemma. "This will also put you in a very awkward position. You're the one who agreed to the visas, and you're consorting with the Senator most conveniently left behind, as you put it. The press is already hinting at our relationship. Any effort we make now will be misinterpreted."

"I'm aware of that," he replied. "My press secretary is working on a damage limitation strategy which will, hopefully, distance us from this mess. Damn that Perry. This was supposed to help alleviate America's problems, not add to them, or ours for that matter. The Anti-American groups will have a field day with this, and individual countries already unhappy about this will use it to reverse the decision."

"We'll figure it out," she assured him, but with no idea how to begin achieving that goal.

Jake groaned and rolled over, feeling disorientated. For a moment, he couldn't remember where he was. He reached out, finding the bed empty and cold, and very little recollection of the previous night, but as he rolled back over, his back hurt. He reached behind him to touch the site of the pain, and his fingers traced along torn skin. What the fuck, he thought, confused and bewildered.

He got up, taking a moment for his head to steady itself, before making his way to the bathroom to check out the damage, finding his injuries to be more than just torn skin. Bruises bloomed on his body, and the tears looked to have been made by sharp nails. He had no memory of receiving the injuries. He tried to think back to the last thing he remembered, finding it to be Bianca's smile.

She'd engaged him in conversation and to his surprise found her to be quite witty, with a wicked sense of humour, at odds with her work persona. The throbbing in his head increased as he stood, and he reached for the painkillers, sensing he wouldn't get through the day without them. A knock on the door pulled him out of the bathroom, and he rummaged around for a t-shirt and boxers before answering, glancing at his wrist for the time, but not finding his watch. He didn't remember taking it off.

The knock came again, more insistent. He opened it without checking, and Swayne looked at him crossly.

"Sorry, did I wake you?" she asked, sounding anything but apologetic.

"What time is it?" he asked.

"Midday," she answered, stepping inside without an invitation.

"Shit!" He answered, stunned. He never overslept, not even with a hangover.

"You're here on assignment, Agent Mann," she said, and he knew he was in trouble for her to address him so formally, but for the life of him he couldn't think what happened. "While your private life, and free time, are your own business, I would ask that in future, you act with a little more decorum in public than you did last night," she said. He stared at her, stunned before realising he stood in front of her, half naked, leaning on the door.

"What?" he asked, puzzled.

"Don't you remember?" she quizzed him, and he shook his head, regretting doing so.

"Not a god-damned thing," he admitted. "All I remember is arriving with you and the Brit, standing at the bar when Agent Monterey arrived. She got me a drink, and that's it, that's all I remember."

Swayne stared at him for what felt like an age, something his grandmother used to do, and he felt as small now, as he had then. Swayne sensed he told her the truth.

"Agent Monterey carried you out last night. You could barely stand," she informed him. He frowned, disturbed. He'd never lost control like that before, not even when he planned on getting drunk.

"Sorry," was all he could think of saying.

"That's not the reason I came," she said, handing the paper to him. He took it and read the headline.

"Fuck!"

"That's a fair assessment of the situation," she commented.

"The bastard was on the take?" It was more a statement than a question.

"You expected boy scouts in the Senate?" she said.

"And you?" he dared to ask, looking her straight in the eye. It hurt to stare, but he wouldn't back down until he knew, until she either confirmed, or shattered, his belief in her. Her returning stare was hard, angry.

"I'm neither a boy scout, nor am I receiving payments for any activities, illegal or otherwise," she answered. That was all he needed to hear.

"This explains a few things," he said looking away, a little abashed to have questioned her integrity, but he needed to know. He turned his attention back to the paper. "Perry gave me the impression he didn't want Michaels' death, or the bomb, to be investigated."

"By impression are you saying he deliberately told you not to?"

"Pretty much," he admitted. She took a deep breath and sat down, mulling this over. "Perhaps you should get dressed, Jake," she suggested without looking at him, and he complied without question, disappearing into his bedroom.

Chapter 21

Shannon

The short drive in the AC Cobra scared the crap out of Matt, and Leigh hid a satisfied smirk as she J-turned the car into a parking spot. She didn't know why she'd taken the sporty car to Shannon, but the look on Matt's face was worth it. He got out at the hotel by the airport.

Isobel exercised her authority and commandeered the hotel as the new residence for the TARCO teams. She claimed it was for everyone's personal safety after a recent assault on one of the team members as they returned home. This new measure hadn't gone down well with everyone, but rent free accommodation, meals on demand, and leisure facilities, managed to soothe most grumbles. Matt was not one of those so placated, not with a disgruntled wife and new baby he couldn't go home to.

This new measure suited Leigh's covert purposes. Someone had attempted to copy her code, tried accessing it from inside the facility, but so far no part of her encryption code was copied. If it had, an embedded subroutine would've kicked in, corrupting the file's contents. Yet, the unanswered question remained; who tried, and from where? Very few people had the security clearance to enter the server room, and the entry logs didn't correspond to the time of the attempts. It puzzled her, but at least they were now confined to the airport compound.

"You coming in?" Matt asked her as he took out his holdall. She shook her head.

"Going home," she answered.

"How the hell did you manage that?" he demanded. She shrugged.

"Guess my security clearance is higher than yours," she answered, waiting for him to shut the door. He slammed it closed, and she winced as the car shook.

"Lovers tiff?" Daniel asked as he passed by, having just stepped off the shuttle bus, and witnessing the slam.

"Shut the fuck up," Matt snapped, and stormed off.

She pulled out of the parking space, and tore up the road, towards the exit. Not wanting to draw any more attention to herself than the car already did, Leigh kept below the speed limit, but that still didn't stop the cops from sitting on her tail along the motorway. She ignored them, and they soon moved along, probably after checking the registration details, and finding nothing. Sometimes she was grateful for Tom, and his less-than-soft ways with her.

However rough Tom's methods were, they paled in comparison to her treatment at Huntington, and she used long learned disassociation techniques to push those traumatic memories from her mind. Instead, she concentrated on the two obstacles she now faced; catching the person breaking into the servers and catching the man Lantry told her about, the man he said killed her parents, Karl Gouderhoff.

On that, she had a reason to return home. The last journal she'd decrypted, and read, before Lantry hauled her off to Scotland, mentioned a young Gouderhoff, and she hoped the third journal would reveal more about him. As was Lantry's usual method, he delivered this profound news about her parents in a blunt manner, no preamble, or handholding, to ease her through the shock. He'd placed the scene photographs before her, not giving her a moment to steel herself, and picture after picture she'd felt her resolve weaken, but she was determined not to breakdown and cry in front of this man.

The sky ahead of her darkened, and Leigh drove into a storm for the final part of her journey. She opted to stay on the main roads, though the country roads would have gotten her home quicker, but she didn't want to take the chance, not in the Cobra. Only the storm greeted her as she eased up her driveway, opening the garage doors with a remote fob before driving straight in, squeezing past the Mini and the Triumph. Why had she taken the Cobra? Probably to piss Matt off, she admitted to herself, knowing in advance who'd be at Shannon. Well, almost everyone. Isobel Piquet had been a surprise to her, as much as her presence was to Isobel. God, Lantry liked to keep his secrets, but did he know she and

Matt shared a history? It was hard to tell with that man. Meeting Matt again had been tough. Not that she'd admit that to anyone, and yes, the car was a mixture of pissing him off, and to impress, to show off how well she was doing, financially at least. Emotionally, she still didn't want to deal with what happened, and she shut out that part of her life.

As she exited the garage, and made a dash in the pouring rain to the back door, she remembered she returned to an empty house. Jessie was dead, shot as he'd tried to bite at the men who'd attacked her in her home. Too tired and drained to attempt any work, she crawled into bed, only pausing to take off her boots.

She rolled over the next morning, still expecting to hear a yap, but she willed herself to get up and go for a run. She'd always been keen on keeping fit, but the training at Huntington drilled this daily ritual into her. The rain eased, but not abated, and it seemed this side of the world was destined to suffer in such a fashion, with rain and more rain.

Spray from passing cars made the run almost intolerable, but she ignored the discomfort, and allowed all thoughts and emotions to ebb away with each pounding step. When she returned home an hour later she felt more relaxed, clear headed and less weighted than the night before. After a shower she set to her task, scanning the third journal in, checking the key inside the cover. Her father used the tenor clef this time, and she smirked, remembering the difficulty trying to read cello music in that clef, for her final year music exam. With music in mind, she opened the media player and loaded up the latest album from Thirty Seconds to Mars, released while she'd been at Huntington.

While the decryption executed, and music played in the background, she logged onto the servers at Shannon, the embedded encryption access module allowing her into the systems, satisfied to note no one else attempted to access them during the night. She pulled up the log files and cross referenced the dates and times of everyone who hit the program files. For the most part, access to the systems resulted from upgrades and developments to the coding, tweaks to the applications, minor adjustments to data arrays to accommodate the incoming files from around Europe.

Her threat assessment and risk analysis saw the incoming files as a potential for a security breach, but with the likeliest breach coming from the US side. While that was Daniel's area, something niggled at the back of her mind. Maybe the mild flirting from him unsettled her, but she reminded herself these things happened in an office environment. Lantry's information on the American showed no reason for concern, though Daniel was too interested in her coding for her liking.

She delved deeper into the log files, trying to trace the interloper back to their origin, but found herself at a dead end. The music fell on deaf ears as this latest development consumed her. Even when the decryption beeped to say it finished, she ignored it. How could someone hit the program without leaving a trace? That just wasn't possible. The only possible answer lay in the server room itself, and she now itched to get back to Shannon to see if her hunch proved right.

She left her office on realising the extent of her hunger. Heavy rain returned, and she watched it as the microwave cooked a frozen meal. The beep that sounded, breaking her from her daydreaming wasn't from the microwave, and she checked her phone, finding a message with bizarre contents, and knew Lantry wanted to contact her.

She waited for the food to finish cooking and returned to her office with it, before logging onto Lantry's secure site. She had to admit, she felt somewhat reassured to find she hadn't been recruited into a rogue spy outfit, but into the British Ministry of Defence's European Intelligence Branch. Still, given the calibre of her comrades, she questioned just how high up the strategic chain Huntington was.

She silenced Leto's crooning as Lantry's face appeared on the screen, a face she hated by now, and understood the depth of her fathers feelings for this man. As an afterthought she activated her security protocol, seeing the status bar twitch, as Lantry tried to get around her systems.

"Well?" he demanded, his face taking up most of the screen. She sat back and paused, still refusing to jump whenever he demanded it.

"Well what?" she asked back, knowing that would have earned her a nasty blow if she'd been standing before him at Huntington, though not from him. He never laid a finger on her. He just had one of his minions do it instead. On screen, he made a visible effort at holding his temper.

"What's happening at Shannon?" he said.

"Oh, that," she answered, knowing she was winding him up, and taking great pleasure from it.

"Yes, that," he snapped back.

"The visa application is almost ready, but someone is trying to break into the system. So far they haven't succeeded, and I haven't managed to find out who it is, yet," she reported, knowing she couldn't continue her surliness without repercussions.

"Gouderhoff?" he asked, but she shrugged.

"I don't know, but maybe he already has someone on the inside," she answered.

"So the attempted breach is internal?"

"It looks that way, or it's being made to look that way."

He found her terse answers annoying. Where had she learned that? Did she know her father used to do it also? Impossible, he thought.

The status bar crept closer to the midway point, and she knew she needed to end this conversation soon.

"Is that all you wanted?" she asked, raising an eyebrow, but keeping the smirk from her face.

"For now," he conceded.

"Tootle pips then," she said, and severed the connection. She picked at the food, but lost most of her appetite after talking to Lantry, until she remembered the decrypted journal and the reason for decoding it. Gouderhoff. The man responsible for her parents' murders.

She downloaded it to her e-pad, along with the new music, and packed up to leave, leaving the showy cars behind and taking her regular one instead. Hitting the motorway hard, she reached Shannon in record time. She went straight to the terminal, weaving her way through passengers, not that there were many, but the airport still had domestic flights in operation. She headed for the development facility, but halted as she spotted a figure making his way towards her. At the sight of her he stopped, looking to be as startled to see her as she did him. She reached around for her weapon but remembered she couldn't bring it into the airport without setting off alarms. Isobel appeared beside her.

"There was a security breach at the facility. My beeper just went off. Is that him?" she asked, and Leigh nodded. Isobel unclipped her reserve gun from under her jacket, and handed it to Leigh. "Think you can hit him?" Isobel asked.

"I'll damn well fucking try," Leigh growled. Faced now with two adversaries, Karl Gouderhoff turned and ran, disappearing into the crowd.

Chapter 22
Paris

Jake sat up, disorientated, taking a moment to realise he was back in Bianca's Paris apartment. How the hell did he end up here again? The last time it happened he'd promised himself there wouldn't be another time, but it happened, again. He checked his watch and groaned, finding it was almost midday. Another day almost wasted. He rolled out of bed, his body feeling like mush, and he started to panic. There was no reason for him to feel this way, but the memory loss worried him the most. He couldn't recall anything after going out for dinner the previous night.

His memory lapses were part of the problem, and each time his body suffered. He struggled to the shower, the hot water stinging the fresh cuts to his skin, and he cursed himself for feeling eighty years old. Still, he took his time, closing his eyes to the stream of water hitting his face and shoulders, and the hypnotic rhythm of the shower almost put him back to sleep, but a thought jerked him awake.

He stepped out and dried off, returning to the room to begin the now familiar hunt for his clothes. Finding them, he dressed, and set about the task in mind. He started in the main room of her apartment, leaving no clues that he rifled through her things, but found nothing there, with the same results in the kitchen. He moved to her study, unlocking the file drawers of her bureau with a deft touch, but only finding household bills, some EATA documents, and credit card statements. A quick glance through those revealed her expensive tastes, but he found nothing out of the ordinary.

He moved back to the bedroom, the last room to search, and went through her dresser, noting with detached amusement the expensive lingerie. A glint from the corner caught his eye as he went to move onto the next drawer, and he found a foil pack, half concealed in something black and frilly. About to dismiss the pill pack as her contraceptives, he realised they weren't like any he'd seen before, and he popped a pill out from its pod. He turned it over, recognising the few letters inscribed on it, and the pieces began to slot into place, the drunken stupors, the memory losses. He heard the apartment door open, and he put the foil pack back, closing the dresser and sat back down on the bed just as Bianca re-entered the bedroom, and he made a show of fumbling with his tie.

"We may have a breakthrough," she announced.

"Oh?" Jake said.

"My colleagues at EATA believe they've worked out the configuration of GS1."

He stared at her, unsure how to take this new development.

"How?"

"Another bomb alert last night. They got a sample before the bomb disposal team contained it."

"Gouderhoff?"

"No."

Her answer surprised him.

"Then who?" he demanded.

"One of the anti-American groups."

"And they had GS1?" he asked, getting pissed off at having to prise information from her, but she nodded.

"I've been at EATA most of the night while they tried to reverse engineer it."

"Why the hell didn't you wake me?" he demanded.

"Don't you think I tried?" she fired back, "but you were impossible to wake." Yeah, I'll bet, Jake thought darkly to himself, now knowing the bomb could've gone off beneath him and he'd never have felt a thing. "I came back to get you," she added, and Jake looked at her in surprise. She was finally including him in this investigation? Well, wonders would never cease.

He followed her, allowing her to drive to EATA's Paris base of operations, on the outskirts of the city. It looked like a disused warehouse, but inside told a very different story. The internal structure was heavily fortified, with state of the art security and technical systems, making it the foremost anti-terrorist force in the world. He followed Bianca to the heart of the complex, its gleaming lab a far cry from Winebeck's humble little office that was overrun with printouts. Bianca approached the lab's only occupant, a man hunched over a laptop, furiously punching codes.

"Find anything definite?" she asked him in French, and Jake caught the man's muttered reply.

"Still trying to figure out the last strand of the bomb sequence," he answered. "We've got part of it, but I'm just trying to see if the computer can come up with some variation that will complete the structure. This puzzle is worse than my wife's jigsaws." Jake heard the exasperation in the man's voice. Bianca turned to Jake, and shrugged.

"Still nothing," she told him in English.

"Nothing at all?" Jake asked, pretending he hadn't understood a word the other man said.

"No, the bomb is still a mystery," she lied to him.

"That's disappointing," he said. She turned back to the scientist, and Jake listened intently, while maintaining a bored expression. The man pointed to the screen, and between their heads Jake could just make out the outline of a chemical configuration. He jotted down as much he could before one of them turned to him. He slipped his slim notebook up the sleeve of his jacket when Bianca turned back to him, leading him away from the computer.

"That's it, we came all this way for nothing?" he said to her and she glared at him, hating every minute she had to spend with him.

"So it would seem," she answered. "I'm sure they'll figure it out soon."

Chapter 23

Karl watched one of the monitors as the icon moved erratically. Paris thought using an electronic voice modulator to alter his voice and distort the image on screen kept his identity safe, but Karl still knew how he really was. Karl conducted his business in this manner, protecting himself more than his employers, adhering to the principle of the less they knew, the less they could reveal. His enterprises depended on discretion and secrecy, but he made a game of eluding the law.

"Dallas is no longer a concern," Karl answered.

"How can you say that? He's made counter allegations that could ruin this operation," Paris put to him, and Karl thought he caught an edge to the voice despite the distortion.

"How can he ruin it? He has no proof, and no names," Karl assured him.

"Payments can be traced."

"That's assuming payment was made."

"It wasn't?"

"No. Dallas reneged on the original agreement, he forfeits his payment. The greedy man tried to use this opportunity to expand his power base, and that is where I attacked."

"You're responsible for the press?" Karl heard the anger that time.

"I am," he answered.

"You should've discussed it with me first. Your action could result in a backlash here. Dallas' allegations are going to give rise to an investigation." The modulator couldn't disguise the harsh tone.

"They have no proof, and our identities are unknown to each other," Karl lied with ease.

"That's not the point," Paris shot back. "And it's going to have serious repercussions on this venture."

"I disagree," Karl answered. "Dallas has unwittingly helped the scheme."

"How?"

"He's made the European visas more attractive. The authorities will no doubt tighten up security, making them seem harder to get, and human nature being what it is, people will want what they can't have. They'll be prepared to pay whatever price is asked once the visas make their way onto the black market."

"Simple economics," Paris mused.

"The simplest, supply and demand. With the accusations against Dallas, he's already stirred a demand for them."

"It appears you have a talent for business, as well as destruction and mayhem, but in future you should discuss your actions with me first," Paris said, and Karl gritted his teeth in annoyance. No matter who the employer was, they all reacted the same when they got to this point.

"You agreed I had a free hand to run this in any way I chose," Karl answered, allowing his characteristic hardness to creep back into his voice. "I don't interfere with your end of this, and I expect the same from you, or would you prefer the same route as Dallas?"

"Are you threatening me?"

"No, I'm merely outlining your options," Karl answered. "After all, you have more to lose than I."

He disconnected the link and sat back, putting the bureaucrat out of his mind, and turned his attention to the development in Shannon; Leigh Harte, and that other woman, the security expert.

It was obvious she was more than a programming expert, and she'd recognised him, both of the women recognised him, before charging after him. He could think of only one person behind it, Lantry. Somehow he'd gotten his hands on her, dragged her into this world, a world she didn't belong. She'd stared at Karl with that same cold, hard stare her father had. It terrified the life out of a very young Karl then. It scared the hell out of him now.

He retreated to the safety of his own quarters another level down, taking up the entire subterranean space. Down here he felt safe enough to let his guard down, and he threw himself onto the oversized sofa, allowing the past to flood him with memories of his time with the Hartes. He thought about Lantry, and how he'd created the perfect little assassin in Leigh, using her anger and hate to kill him. Many of Lantry's agents tried over the years, but no one could have gotten close to him as easily as Leigh would have, but he saw the hatred in her eyes, her determination, and he didn't doubt her conviction or capacity to kill him. He'd seen that same look in Lee too many times, knew it well enough to understand the deadly force that lay behind it.

He went to his safe, punching in the eight-digit code before the locks tumbled and the door opened. From inside he retrieved a metal box, the steel holding his past, which he rarely opened. He carried it back to the sofa and entered the code to open the box, shuffling through old photographs, pulling out one of him and Lee. The photograph showed smiles all round, but that hadn't always been the case, not at the beginning anyway.

Beside the stack of photos, his hand came to rest on a handwritten journal, Lee's last, and to this day Karl still hadn't figured out the secret that lay hidden within the pages. Did Leigh get the others? Did she break her father's code? Was that how she'd ended up in this world? That wasn't Karl's intention when he'd left the other two with Lee's solicitor.

He held the last journal in his hands, the one Lee entrusted him with for safekeeping until Leigh was ready. But with her sights set on him, now what was he to do with it?

Chapter 24

Journalists camped outside the EU building, and despite the police arresting and evicting them, they still returned, waiting for the British Commissioner, or the American Senator, to appear, waiting with serious questions and allegations to throw at the pair. Of the American committee, Swayne appeared to be the only one not receiving any form of payment, but the press just assumed she was cleverer at covering her tracks. Medlington was an entirely different story, and he hadn't been seen for two days, fuelling speculation.

Wilma slipped out of the EU offices without fuss, Medlington's driver taking her deep into the Belgian countryside. She allowed herself to relax as the car took her away from the city, but her mind refused to let their current situation go. Coming to a stop outside Medlington's country home, she was greeted by the security guard posted at the door. He allowed her in, and she met Jonathan's private secretary as she entered.

"How is he today?" she asked, and the man shook his head.

"I haven't seen him this despondent in years. He's in the study. Would you like some tea?" he asked, and she smiled. How very British, she thought. The world was falling apart, but there was still time for tea.

"I'd love some," she answered, ascending the stairs. She found him sitting, staring into the cold empty fireplace and ran her fingers through his hair, startling him.

"You're early," he said.

"No, you've just been daydreaming," she said.

"Not daydreaming," he answered handing her a file. "This whole thing is spiralling out of control." She heard the weariness, the defeat in his voice.

"How much worse can it get?" she asked.

"I've now been implicated in this mess, and I'm guilty until proven otherwise. Even then, there will always be doubts, the investigation will become an addendum to anything I do."

"We'll both be exonerated, you'll see."

"My dear, your optimism is commendable, but sadly misplaced. You and I will forever be spoken of together in the same breath as Perry. Scandal is one thing people never forget."

"Both of us are innocent, and I for one am going to do everything I damn well can to prove it," she replied, growing angry at his apathy. "How can you just sit there and accept this. You have an unblemished career and character, yet you're prepared to allow yourself to be tarnished, and put in the same category as Perry. You're god-damned crazy."

He glared at her.

"I'm putting up little resistance in an effort to save my career and character," he said sharply. Her look of confusion didn't surprise him. "It's a form of reverse psychology. If I appear too eager to help the investigation, or give out too much information, then I draw attention to myself. Whoever is investigating this whole bloody affair will suspect my motives for being so cooperative, and will believe I have something to hide." Wilma looked even more baffled.

"You're all insane," she concluded, shaking her head.

"Trust me, it's not the first time Commissioners have been investigated, and it's always the ones most eager to prove their innocence who turned out to be the guiltiest ones. I'm not a psychologist, I'm at a loss to explain it, but it's the way it happens. As for the investigators, I suppose it's human nature to distrust what's simply handed to you."

"Always look a gift horse in the mouth, sort of thing," she surmised.

"That's exactly the sort of thing," he replied, softening. "But you Americans, you're an impetuous race."

"That's because we're still so young. We believe in the good guys wearing white hats, and the bad guys get out of town."

Jonathan shook his head.

"I bet you still believe in the tooth fairy," he said as he stood, and wrapped his arms around her. The look of mock horror she gave him made him laugh.

"You mean there ain't no tooth fairy? Next thing you'll cruelly shatter my belief in Santa Claus."

"I'll say nothing of the sort. You can set up your own Select Committee to investigate that one," he answered, and kissed her.

Chapter 25

Isobel followed Leigh into the server room, and watched as the Irish woman squeezed behind the back of the servers, scrutinizing every cable plugged in.

"That was definitely Gouderhoff, wasn't it?" Isobel asked.

"Yes," Leigh answered.

"Why are you after him?"

Leigh's head appeared over the bank of machines.

"Why are you?" she countered.

"Lantry's orders."

"Same here. So why would Lantry send us both after the same person?"

"I have a personal reason," Isobel added. Leigh's head popped back up, frowning this time. There were those coincidences again, and she didn't like it. She disappeared again, doing her best to avoid becoming entangled in the cables. She reappeared with wires in her hand, and a slender black box.

"What are those?" Isobel asked.

"How he tried breaking into the visa application. He hard wired access to the servers, and used this remote access modem to connect to them. Was the security breach in here tonight?"

Isobel shook her head.

"No, the safe room, where the visa and permits are stored. He didn't get anything; I'd already upgraded the security in there."

"I guess your time in terrorist boot camp came in useful after all," Leigh replied sarcastically. "I want this room locked down as well." Isobel's eyes narrowed in annoyance at the insult, and now being given orders by Leigh.

"I'll restrict the access to just you and me," Isobel answered, and Leigh nodded, though she was more interested in scanning the room, looking for anything that seemed out of place. Something caught her attention, a thin cable that shouldn't have been there, and she pointed it out to Isobel.

"Is that what I think it is?" Leigh asked, and the French woman climbed up the metal frame, that housed the bank of servers.

"It's a detonator cable," Isobel confirmed, tracing the cable to the tiny charge hidden in the frame. "He's going to blow this room?"

Leigh thought about it for a moment.

"Probably after he downloaded the application, and got his hands on the blank cards. He'd have genuine, untraceable visas." She looked around the room again before turning to Isobel. "Find the rest of the charges, and place this room in lockdown," she ordered, her tone not brooking any arguments, and left Isobel to it.

In spite of physically being the runt of their training group, Leigh's ability to read a situation, and make hard calculating decisions, pushed her ahead in the leadership stakes, and then as now, when the opportunity arose, she took command without hesitation, expecting her directions to be carried out without question.

She went to the hotel, collecting her key card at reception, and went to her room, unimpressed to find herself sandwiched between Matt and Daniel's rooms, but strangely reassured to know Isobel was across the corridor. That Gouderhoff got away annoyed her, but she couldn't have taken the shot without endangering innocent passengers in the terminal. Whatever Lantry turned her into, she refused to let that be a callous or trigger-happy killer.

Exhausted, she fell onto the bed, but her mind churned, so she pulled her e-pad out, her thumbprint unlocking the device for use. She opened the third journal and began to read, surprised to discover how much Karl Gouderhoff had been a part of her young life. That startled her. She didn't remember him. However, she detected a tone of affection in her father's writing, almost the son he never had, in spite of the bad start. Karl, it seemed, was a deeply troubled child, and her father soon knocked that penchant for destructive behaviour out of him. By the end of the journal, details of Karl's induction, by Lantry, were brutal and graphic.

Leigh herself began to feature quite a lot, with notes on her school achievements, and it caused her to smile at the pride in which he wrote. She put the e-pad down, and rubbed her tired eyes, still unable to sleep. That Karl worked with her father was no startling revelation, Lantry had told her that much, but how her father treated him only deepened the sense of betrayal, turning on the people who provided him with a home. She regretted not scanning the fourth journal, but she hadn't anticipated reading the third so quickly. With Gouderhoff showing up at Shannon, could she risk another journey home? Would he make another attempt, knowing they were onto him? Yet she felt answers lay in the last journal.

Chapter 26

Senator Swayne sat in stony silence, but every now and again, her eyes flickered down to the pill on the table, before returning her gaze to Jake. He'd returned to Brussels as soon as he could, and she recognised the pill straight away. He maintained eye contact with her, feeling those deep brown eyes burning into him.

"You're sure about this?" she asked, and he nodded.

"What reason would I have to make it up?" he countered.

"I'll be honest, I find it hard to believe a man of your experience, and calibre, would be so easily overpowered."

"But I hope it explains my behaviour. I should have wised up to it sooner," he said. She leaned in, and picked up the offending pill.

"Don't be too hard on yourself. I'll admit, you had me worried for a while, and this date rape drug explains a lot," she told him, then shook her head. "I've seen too many girls' lives destroyed by this drug, and they've all gone through what you're going through, the guilt, the humiliation. I admire your bravery for coming and telling me." His smile was humble. He did feel humiliated, and the strange need to talk to someone. The Senator was the only one who came to mind.

"Does she suspect?" she asked, and he shook his head.

"I left the pills where they were. If they disappeared, she'd know I was on to her."

"A wise move, but why? What would she have to gain by drugging you, or raping you?"

"I don't think I was raped," he answered. His pride shuddered at the thought of it, and she frowned at him. "Mixed with alcohol, that drug effectively paralyses its … victim." He grimaced at the word, not wanting to think of himself in those terms. "Let's just say, I wouldn't have been able to rise to the occasion."

"Still, she took the opportunity to inflict what damage she could, if your injuries are anything to go by," Swayne answered. His injuries gave credence to his claims. "But the question remains, why?"

"Aside from disgracing me, and getting me sent home, she has nothing to gain, unless..." he paused, another piece of the puzzle falling into place, but he wasn't sure where it was going to land. "That's if she's on the level."

He stood and paced, thinking aloud.

"To date, all we've done is chase an elusive explosive. At every turn, I've been stopped from investigating the visas."

"You think she's working for Gouderhoff?"

"It's a possibility," he answered. "Someone is keeping me away from the visas, and using Bianca to do it. Who else could it be?"

"As plausible as it sounds, it's still a big leap," she cautioned. He scratched his head.

"Yeah, I know. All I have to go on is creative guesswork."

"I promised I'd help in any way I could, but with this visa scandal..."

"You're not being investigated," he assured her. At her surprised look, he continued. "You were the first person they ruled out. The only thing stirring trouble for you is the media, and you're in the firing line because you're over here."

"And how do you know this?" she asked.

"Let's just say I know the wrong sort of people," he answered. "The reason there's so much hype over here, is because of a major corruption scandal a few years ago, part of the financial Eurogedden crisis that involved most, if not all, the big players in the Commission." Swayne's eyes widened in disbelief. "Jonathan wasn't involved."

"What do you need from me?" she asked.

"I need more info on Bianca. Her credit card statements had some pretty high priced items on it, too high for an investigator's salary, unless my Euro equivalent is paid better than I am."

"I'll talk to Jonathan. He seems to have a connection with EATA. He may be able to help there. And the bomb?"

"Designer, just like we thought. I emailed Dave Winebeck what little I could write down, before they turned around."

"And they have no idea you speak the language?"

"None."

"Any other languages you've neglected to mention?"

"A few," he answered, and saw her features harden.

"I have to admit, Agent Mann," she began, using his title, and he knew he was in trouble with her, again. "The more I discover about you, I find the less I know. Any particular reason why pertinent details, like your language skills, are omitted from your file? I would appreciate knowing exactly who I'm working with."

He stood still, knowing he couldn't talk his way out of his past this time, and if he wanted her help, he had to trust her. In confiding about Bianca, he'd opened the door to her, and the Senator now jammed her foot right in.

"Seven languages," he conceded. "Including French and English, I also speak Russian, Polish, German, Turkish and Slovak."

"All political hotspots," she answered. "But it's a start. So who exactly are you, Jake Mann?"

Jake knew a time like this would come. He feared it, but he felt calm now. This woman inspired faith and hope in others, but at the back of his mind a disturbing question remained, would she continue to have faith in him when she learned the truth? He sat back down.

"You realise, I have to kill you, as soon as I tell you."

"You can't, you're sworn to protect me, remember?"

"Damn, you've got me on that one. So what do you want to know?"

"Let's start with your name, your real name."

He took a deep breath before answering.

"It's Jaran Baenleaski, I'm of Polish descent. My grandfather was a Polish engineer, in the Russian army during the Cold War, but he defected to Western Europe when he saw the atrocities happening around him. My grandmother was from Quebec..."

"Hence the French," she interrupted him, and he nodded.

"She was a Red Cross nurse, based in France, when my grandfather and others defected."

"Love at first sight?" she asked, and he smirked.

"She swears she hated the sight of him. After being debriefed, he volunteered to go back into occupied Germany, working for the Americans. He was well educated, spoke German and Russian, he was a gift handed to them. He met my grandmother again, sometime later, after one of his former commanders spotted him, and shot at him. It's a classic nightingale case. She nursed him back to health. After that they moved to America."

"Not back to Quebec?" she asked, and he shook his head.

"My grandfather proved to be too good of an asset, and the intelligence agency kept him. They gave him full American citizenship, and he could've had a whole new identity if he'd wanted, but he kept his name, said it reminded him of where he came from. He and my grandmother married, had two boys, my father, and then my uncle. My uncle died when he was seventeen. The official report claims it was a boating accident on the Chesapeake."

"But?" Swayne asked. Jake shrugged.

"But what? All I have to go on is the suspicions of an old woman."

"But she thinks your father was involved." Jake's stare was hard, and his jaw clenched. Over the years she'd seen many stares, some desolate, some defiant, most not wanting to face the truth of what happened to them, but never a stare so hard.

"Apparently my father was... unruly. Back then it was a polite way of saying he was an uncontrollable sociopath. Because my grandfather was away a lot of the time, often for months, my father grew out of control. At first, they thought it was just attention seeking, that he rebelled against everything my grandfather stood for, but then he got my mother pregnant with me. He did the righteous thing, and married her, even though they were both far too young. It turned out he couldn't hack the responsibility thing, started getting loaded on alcohol, and whatever drugs he could get his hands on. It got worse after I was born. He blamed my mother for everything that had ever gone wrong in his life, including getting pregnant. When I got big enough, and old enough, he started taking it out on me."

"How did you stop him?" she asked.

"What makes you think I stopped him?" he asked.

"Call it a hunch," she answered, and he sighed.

"I turned him in," Jake answered.

"You did the right thing," she assured him, but Jake held up a hand.

"I don't need reassurances for what I did, I've already done the therapy crap, but as it turned out, my mother and I weren't the only defenceless creatures in his path. A total of thirty five waitresses, call girls and hookers lined up to give evidence against him for severe assaults, and the cops reckoned he was responsible for the disappearance of several girls, but couldn't pin it on him. After that my mom changed her name. Grandpa used his connections to do an airtight job, told me to do the same."

"So where did Jake Mann come from?" she asked, and he smirked.

"I went to live with my grandparents after the trial. My mom couldn't cope, so she checked herself into a place to straighten her nerves out, but she died about six months later, from a Valium overdose. At the time I couldn't decide on a name, but I read one of grandpa's old Russian books, some obscure spy thriller, where the bad guy was an American called …"

"Jake Mann," she answered, and he nodded.

"That's what I wanted to be, the All American boy, with no past, no history."

"What about the undercover work? I'm guessing you followed in your grandfather's footsteps."

"Something like that. Because of my father, they put me through some pretty thorough tests, but thankfully it didn't show up any sociopathic tendencies like his. I excelled at languages, and figuring stuff out, and given my grandfather's credentials..."

"They recruited you," she concluded, and he nodded. "How old were you?" she asked.

"Which part?" he countered, and she understood then. This happened to him over years, the beatings, the devastating losses.

"Any part you like?"

"I was recruited at fifteen."

"You only show up officially when you joined the Bureau about two years ago," she said, and he nodded.

"Before the Bureau, I was posted here, well Europe, but I felt I was losing my edge, so I requested a transfer home before I got myself killed."

"And Gouderhoff? Where does he fit into all of this?" she asked, and his jaw strained as he clenched it.

"Karl and I go back a long way, but I doubt he remembers me from back then."

"Why not?"

"I looked much different then. I was nineteen when I first met him. I was assigned to get close to him, to gain his confidences and get information, then kill him. My cover was as a recruit in the German Army, under my original name."

"So what happened?" she asked, entranced by his story. He shrugged, but his face looked haunted.

"I walked into a trap. A bomb went off, and I was badly injured. I needed reconstructive surgery on my face, so I don't look anything like I used to."

"I'd never have guessed," she said peering closer. "There's no scars, no tell-tale lines."

"It's had plenty of time to heal." His answer sounded sour.

"Wait, were you the cadet who was supposed to be killed?" she asked, seeing his features harden again, but her insight shouldn't have surprised him, and he nodded. "But you reported he died in that blast."

"To maintain my cover, but it finally put Jaran to rest."

"Was Gouderhoff behind it? The bomb?"

"Yes."

"So you're after him for revenge." It sounded more like a statement than a question, but he didn't answer.

Chapter 27

The knock on her door woke her, and her e-pad also beeped at her, and a tired Leigh answered the door, finding Isobel there.

"Someone triggered the sensors again," she said, pushing her way into Leigh's room.

"Twice in one day, he must be getting desperate," Leigh answered, reaching for her e-pad to silence the beeping,and check what set it off. "Someone tried accessing the code as well."

"Busy night. What are you waiting for?" Isobel asked. Leigh rubbed her eyes before reaching for her jacket, and Beretta.

"What the hell time is it?" she asked.

"Just after 3am," Isobel answered. Leigh stifled a sigh and followed Isobel out, checking she had a full cartridge loaded in her weapon. She closed the door softly, not wanting to disturb, or alert anyone else on the floor, and they descended the two flights of stairs.

Leigh let Isobel drive, and used the short drive to the terminal to calm her mind, and the myriad of questions that arose from the last journal. At the airport, they kept their weapons concealed, Isobel's security pass allowing them entry without setting off the metal detectors.

They split up, approaching the facility's entrance doors from opposite sides, and once out of sight of any witnesses, armed themselves. Leigh took the long way around, rounding the final corner, and finding Isobel unconscious on the ground. Leigh advanced up the corridor to her, scanning for any hint of movement, but turned too late to check behind her. She felt a sharp pain at the back of her head, and darkness came crashing down.

A soft glow shone overhead, but the light hurt her eyes, worsening her headache. She rolled over, putting her feet on the floor, and tried to figure out where she was. She didn't recognise the room, a bedroom. Her gun lay on the bedside locker, and a quick check confirmed it was still loaded. She stood, and surveyed her surroundings, but the photographs, arranged in a column on the wall, caught her attention. She peered at them, surprised to find black and white prints of her parents, caught unawares in an embrace, a few of her father and another man, who looked like a very young Gouderhoff, and the last one of her, taken a very long time ago, a picture she hadn't posed for.

With her gun at the ready, she took a defensive posture, something Lantry's instructors drilled into her, and left the room, finding a short hallway. She came to the end, and it opened into a generously sized living space. Gun at the ready, all senses on high alert, she stepped from the hallway, keeping her back to the wall, thinking of all the thriller films she'd ever seen where the bad guy waited out of sight to take a shot, but no one lay in wait for her. She stepped further into the space, anxiety and confusion beginning to win the emotional battle within her, until she found him in the kitchen, his back turned to her.

"Coffee?" he asked, surprising her, as he looked over his shoulder. Here was her nemesis, the man who'd murdered her parents, acting as though she'd just popped in for a cuppa and a social chat. He turned, carrying two mugs with him as he came closer to her, extending one of the mugs towards her. She eyed it suspiciously.

"It's not drugged or poisoned, look," he said, and he took a swig from the one he'd offered her, but grimaced. "How do you drink this without sugar?" he asked, extending the mug to her again. She refused to take it, so he placed it on the coffee table between them instead, and sat down on one of the small sofas. She was at a loss to explain his behaviour, but it didn't seem the actions of someone intent on killing her.

"Leigh, sit down. If I meant you any harm, you'd already be dead," he said. She watched for any sign of tension, any betrayal in his body language, but she found none. He was as calm and relaxed as he appeared to be, and she lowered her weapon. If possible, he seemed to relax even more.

"What do you want?" she demanded, and he smirked. So like Lee, he thought, direct and to the point.

"Just to talk," he answered. "To explain. Please, sit." He indicated to the sofa opposite him. She hesitated, deliberating what to do. Should she put a well-deserved bullet in him or...

She had questions, lots of them. Would getting answers soothe her conscience when she carried out the task? She took the proffered seat, resting one foot on the opposite knee, resting the gun on her thigh, clicking the safety back on, and Karl chuckled to himself. Lee used that very same technique and posture during interrogations, to give his prey a sense of comfort and safety, but he doubted she knew that.

"Why?" she demanded.

"Why what?" he countered, taking a sip of sweetened coffee from his own mug.

"They took you in, they gave you a home. What has to go on in your twisted mind for you to murder them like that?" She saw his jaw tighten, but he sighed.

"It wasn't me," he answered, and saw her grip tighten on her weapon. "I didn't do it." He'd leaned forward as he spoke, as though to emphasise the point, and almost convincing her of his sincerity.

"Prove it," she challenged him, and he sat back again.

"Don't you think I would, if I could?" he countered. "Whoever is responsible did an excellent job of directing all the blame towards me. Your father knew who it was, but I haven't been able to figure it out." His accent and English were perfect and neutral. If she hadn't already known his origins, she'd be hard pressed to place him.

He rose and went to his safe in the corner of the room, extracting an object before returning to his seat, and throwing it onto the table. That, he noted with some satisfaction, was enough to shake her icy demeanour. She sat forward, and reached for the journal.

"Where did you get this?" she demanded in a dangerously low tone.

"Your father, where else?" he countered.

"Why you?"

"Because he knew I'd keep them safe."

"Them?"

He nodded in reply.

"Lee always kept a journal. I think he wrote them to appease his conscience, but he uncovered something or someone, maybe within the Ministry, I don't know. He wouldn't tell me, but he grew more secretive, and decided to encrypt his notes. The first two he put into a safety box, and gave to his lawyer. The rest he sent to me as soon as he'd wrote them."

"Sent them to you?" she interrupted him, and he nodded.

"He sent me away, back to Germany. He used his contacts to get me into the army, thinking I'd be safe there, but he was wrong. We both were."

"So where are these journals now?" she demanded, and he laughed at her, a humorous laugh.

"You obviously got them, and decrypted them, or you wouldn't have become embroiled in this world," he returned the challenge. "After their deaths, I followed your father's lead, and delivered two of the journals to that lawyer in another box."

"And what else was in this alleged box?"

"Your father's weapon, photographs, and the keys to the Mercedes. As part of the cover up, Lantry arranged to have the car destroyed, but I rescued it. I'd put too many damned hours helping Lee rebuild it, so I was not going to allow it to be crushed."

He watched her. While her face remained impassive and hard, small little things gave away the myriad of thoughts and emotions he could only imagine she was going through. He sat forward again, and looked her straight in the eyes.

"I didn't kill them Leigh. Why would I? How could I? You were the only real family I'd ever known. Whatever else I am, I'm not their murderer." He must have convinced her, he thought as she put the gun down beside her, and flicked through the journal. She examined the inside covers, and he guessed she didn't find what she sought when he saw her mouth tighten. "Think you can decipher it?" he asked. She shrugged, and looked at him, a hard and calculating look he'd so often seen in Lee.

"I don't know," she answered. "Unlike the others, there's no key, and it looks like different cypher methods were used." She opened on a page. "The cypher used on this page is not the same as the one used on the next one." He nodded. After keeping it safe for fifteen years, having thumbed through it many times, he'd already come to the same conclusion.

"Take the journal, and figure it out," he told her, standing up. She looked up at him.

"You're just going to let me walk out of here, with the one piece of evidence that could clear you?" she asked, and he nodded.

"Who else would I trust to give it to, and who else could work it out," he answered, and she stood.

"And what makes you think I haven't already been tracked?"

"You've no mobile phone, or any other devices on you, and there are security measures here, preventative measures."

"And you're not getting your hands on those visas."

He laughed.

"The visas aren't important to me, only to the people who hired me, but you can continue to try stopping me." It sounded like a challenge. He checked his watch. "There's a train leaving in about forty minutes to Carlow, and we're only a short walk away."

"Not back to Shannon?"

"And risk being tracked back to here? Besides, I'd have thought you'd want to lock that journal away."

"Where would I put it?" she asked, but he understood why. She probed for any chinks in his story, in how valid his claim of Lee confiding in him was.

"There's a safe, hidden behind the fireplace, in his office, your office." That won her over. He disappeared down the short hallway, returning moments later with a sweater. She stared at it.

"It's what it looks like, a sweater. No hidden devices, no bugs, no trackers, but if you're getting on public transport I'd suggest you wear something that will hide the gun from sight," he said.

"Why are you doing this?" she asked.

"It's what your father would've done," he said. "It's my way of preserving his memory, his decency." She took the sweater from him, feeling the roughness of the Aran wool in her hand before putting it on. She tucked the gun into the waistband of her jeans at the small of her back. He ushered her to the small elevator, and she hesitated getting in.

"Still hate small spaces?" he asked, and she glared at him, more shocked by the question than surprised. "Do you remember what happened, how it happened?" She shook her head, frowning as he smirked. "As a child, you liked to hide, especially from me, but you got yourself locked into a small cupboard, and couldn't get out. I heard you crying, and had to break the door open to get you out," he explained.

"I don't remember that. I don't remember you," she admitted, before taking a breath and stepping into the confined space. A myriad of things went through her mind as she digested what had just happened.

He in turn watched her, trying to make out the facial expressions that were Lee's, and the ones that were uniquely hers. She narrowed her eyes as Lee did, clenched her jaw in a similar manner, but with a quirky twist to her mouth that was hers alone, along with the arching of her eyebrow. In this confined space a younger version of his mentor, his best friend, his substitute father, stood beside him, and he wanted to hug her, embrace her, something he'd been unable to do all those years ago.

As the elevator door reopened she found herself in a warehouse, and Karl led her to one of the smaller cargo doors. As it opened she was grateful for the sweater against the late evening chill that blew in. As they exited she looked around, recognising the hotel across the road.

143

"We're in Waterford," she said, and he nodded, taking her by the arm to guide her on, and she knew the train station was on the other side of the Suir river. They crossed the bridge, buffeted by the breeze, until they reached the relative haven of the station. With no wallet or cash on her, he purchased her ticket from one of the automatic machines, handing it, and twenty euros, to her.

"For another cup of coffee on the train, and a taxi to get home," he explained when she hesitated taking it. He walked her to the gate, unable to go further without a ticket himself, but she turned to him before going through the barrier.

"Thank you," she said. He shrugged.

"It's what Lee would have done," he stated, pulling her close and kissing her. She pulled away, a little startled by his action.

"Is that how you and my father would say goodbye?" she asked, and he laughed.

"We didn't have that kind of relationship, no," he answered, still laughing. From his back pocket, he pulled out a slip of paper and handed it to her.

"What is it?"

"The codes to get in, if you feel like talking."

"You're putting a lot of trust in someone you barely know, and who's been sent to kill you," she said, but he shook his head.

"You're your father's daughter, and I trusted him with my life." He kissed her again, before walking away.

Chapter 28

Jake didn't like the answers he got from the team based in Shannon. Admittedly, his temper hadn't improved since Bianca's abrupt announcement of their departure to this god-forsaken place, where the weather did nothing but rain heavily since they landed. Bianca gave him very little notice, pounding on his door in the early hours of the morning, expecting him to pack there and then. She gave out little information about where they were going, or why.

Their unannounced arrival not only caused a hostile reception, but it seemed they'd landed while the personnel were in the middle of a crisis. Their security consultant had been found unconscious, and was sent to Limerick hospital with a concussion, while their so-called programming whizz remained unaccounted for. The security cameras showed the two women entering the airport at an ungodly hour, but nothing else, nothing that would explain one unconscious woman and one still missing. The only two people with access to the servers and the visas, and Jake didn't like coincidences like that.

The guy in charge was downright hostile towards him, and Jake checked the file on Matt, noting the recent change in his parental status. With civil service wages, and a new baby, Jake considered him an easy target for Karl to tempt financially into service. So far though, the guy seemed on the level. The only one forthcoming with answers was the American, and he latched onto Jake like a long-lost friend, adding to the deterioration of Jake's mood. He'd never been a team player, and in truth never quite fit in, nor understood the buddy mentality.

Leaving Bianca to interrogate the others, he searched Harte's office, appreciating her choice in coffee, as well as the level of security on her systems. Her file told of her experience as a programming expert, with no suspicious gaps in her record, nor did she struggle to make an income from her freelance work. Her credentials were impressive, especially the level of security clearance she'd obtained, working her way up, not too smoothly that it looked staged, but no unexplained jumps either. A perfect file.

Receiving a soaking as he dashed from the parked taxi, he let himself into Harte's hotel room, and surveyed the space. The bed hadn't been slept in, but the covers were rumpled, and under a ruffle in the duvet, an electronic device caught his attention. A mobile phone sat on the locker, explaining why the woman wasn't answering any calls. He picked up the e-pad, but found it locked. It required a thumbprint to gain access, and while he appreciated her attention to security, he wondered what she had to hide. Then again, her file screamed geek, and she was likely to have such a security app because she could.

Getting past the thumbprint wouldn't be a problem for him, and finding no wash bag, or any other personal items in the bathroom, he turned his attention to her holdall, but his suspicions grew as he found a magazine clip, a .45 if the size of the bullets were anything to go by. He continued searching until he found her make-up bag, and using her powder and brush, he dusted the bottom corner, satisfied at the ridge detail the powder highlighted, hoping it would be enough to access the e-pad. Covering his thumb with a latex glove he kept inside his jacket pocket, and pressed it onto the e-pad and it sprang to life.

He scrolled through the directories, but either she was clever enough to give innocent and innocuous sounding file names or… He went to the recent history section, opening the last file she'd accessed, surprised to find it a diary of sorts. An accomplished speed-reader, he scanned through the entire document within an hour. He sat back on the bed, not realising he'd been hunched over, and tensing, at each page he'd read. He took a deep breath at the magnitude of what he held, Gouderhoff's origins. How was it possible she had this? She'd have been far too young to know him, unless she worked for him, but even then, Karl would never allow anyone to have this kind of information about him. It made finding this woman a priority now.

Unable to get access to her car keys, Leigh opted for the shuttle bus to return to the airport, the inclement weather worsening her temper after finding her room locked, and reception under orders not to give out a replacement key. The receptionist muttered something about a security lockdown. If this was Isobel's idea of a joke she was going to get hell from Leigh. At least her security pass still worked, but rather than trying to explain the Beretta she still carried, she went the way Isobel brought them the previous night, avoiding the metal detectors, and made her way to the facility. She was barely inside the door when Matt caught up with her.

"Where the hell have you been?" he demanded.

"Out for a jog," she replied, not in the mood for an interrogation. "Where's Piquet?"

"Limerick hospital," he answered, and she stopped short.

"What? Is she okay?"

"Concussion, but she'll be fine. They reckon she'll be released later today."

"Then who locked down the hotel?" she demanded. Matt looked to movement at the end of the corridor, and pointed.

"They did. He's American, she's French. Flashed badges and stormed their way through here a couple of hours ago."

"What for?"

"Something about investigating the visas. Apparently they're already on the US black market, some scandal about them?"

"One of the Senators negotiating for the visas seems to be involved," she told him, but watching the approaching pair.

"Leigh Harte?" the tall man asked, his deep voice echoing down the corridor.

"Who wants to know?" she countered, and saw his jaw clenching, a man used to getting more straight answers. The retaliation didn't come from him, but from his partner who turned Leigh around, slamming her against the wall. She snatched the e-reader from Leigh, and handed it to

Jake. She then discovered the gun, which surprised almost everyone. Bianca handed the gun to Jake, and decided a more thorough search was in order as she repatted Leigh down, getting too close and personal for comfort as she painfully squeezed Leigh's breasts. Leigh reacted with a reverse elbow to the woman's face, spinning around to face her. She found herself looking down the wrong end of the barrel of her gun as Jake took aim on her. Prudence won out, and she held her hands up in surrender, but the stunned look on Matt's face was priceless, and in spite of her predicament, she fought to keep a smirk from her own face.

"Immigration has an interview room, lock her in there for the moment," Jake said, as Bianca wiped her bloody nose. "And trust me," he said to Leigh. "I wouldn't recommend hitting her again."

Bianca glared at him, but hauled Leigh away. Jake turned his attention to the e-reader, and turned it on, finding no security measures installed, but found another diary. Ignoring Matt he went to Leigh's office, the only place to get a decent coffee, and started reading.

He found Leigh lying on the table in the centre of the room, flat on her back, knees bent, and feet upon the table. She looked to be asleep, and didn't stir, or open her eyes, as the door opened. Slamming his hands on the table either side of her head did the trick, and she found his face dangerously close to hers. Something about her stare told him intimidation and threats wouldn't work on her.

"Tell me about the journals," he said.

"What journals?" she countered, calmer than she felt.

"The ones on your reader," he said, and she shrugged.

"Bought them online."

He slammed his hands down again.

"Don't fuck with me," he growled, and she sat up to face him.

"Wouldn't dream of it. Besides, from the way your partner groped me, I got the impression she'd be my best bet for that." His eyes narrowed in annoyance, and he leaned in closer, but she didn't lean back as most people would, just stared resolutely back.

"The journals, who wrote them?" he demanded. "When were they written?" he added when she refused to answer him. "Who are you working for?" About to give a smartass reply to the last question, the door opened, forcibly enough to slam against the wall. Tom Barnett stood in the entrance, his warrant card in his hand, the gold and blue of the Garda Siochána badge glinting in the light.

"Leave," he told Jake, who straightened up to meet Tom's challenge.

"I have authority from the EU, and you're interfering with an official investigation," Jake answered, but Tom barked a laugh at him.

"Yeah? Well now sonny boy, my badge trumps yours, and the EU leave enforcement to the local authorities, and I outrank you, so to use one of your euphemisms, 'beat it'." Age and authority won out as the American left, and Tom slammed the door behind Jake, before turning his temper on Leigh.

"Where the hell have you been?"

"Out," she replied, before reeling back from the force of the backhanded slap to her face.

"Where were you, Leigh? Believe me, I won't ask a third time," he said. Now she understood what her father had written in the first journal about this man.

"Someone tried breaking in again last night. Isobel and I came to investigate, and we decided to come from two different sides, but by the time I got around, she was already unconscious on the ground."

"And then what?"

"I took a blow to the head, and woke up in the middle of nowhere," she lied.

"Where in the middle of nowhere?" he pushed.

"Somewhere in Westmeath. I saw signs for Kinnegad and Mullingar," she answered.

"You were just dumped there?" It didn't sound like he believed her, but she just shrugged, keeping silent.

"Why?" he asked. "Why not interrogate you for the encryptions?"

"Maybe those two showing up upset plans," she offered, but it was a question she'd already asked herself. Why didn't Karl probe a little about the codes?

"That's why Lantry and I were trying to get a hold of you and Isobel, to warn you they were coming," he said.

"Yeah? Well, your timing's impeccable," she answered smartly, anticipating another blow, but it didn't come.

"He's an American agent who's also after Gouderhoff, and she's with EATA," he explained. "We only got wind of their arrival when they were on the way. So now your cover's blown."

"I can still do what I was sent here to do, stop Gouderhoff from getting the visas," she answered.

Jake stood on the other side of the one-way darkened glass in the adjacent observation room, listening and watching, and concerned at the roughness with which this man treated her. No wonder Jake couldn't intimidate her, not when she had that man to face. He was clearly her handler, but the name Lantry surprised him. It had been a very long time since he'd heard that name, and if they were connected to him, that would make them both British, or EU Agents, and from the sounds of it, after the same quarry.

However, the electronic journals troubled him, and with Tom's meeting with Leigh over, he returned to the reader and scrolled back to the last few entries. If what he read was true, then he had a problem. But how could it be true? He needed to get Harte to talk.

Chapter 29

Jake brought her back to the hotel, manhandling her into her room, slamming the door as he pushed her onto the bed.

"The journals," he growled at her, his patience wearing thin. Lying prone she watched him warily, trying to anticipate his next move. "You're Ministry of Defence, aren't you?" he questioned.

"I don't know what you're talking about," she said. "I was only hired to do the encryptions."

"How long have you been MoD?" he continued to push, coming closer to the bed, looming over her. "I know who Lantry is," he said, but she still seemed unfazed by him. "And if you're connected to him, then you're MoD."

"Seems like you have it all figured out," she answered.

"I want to know about the journals," he said again.

"Why? They've nothing to do with you."

"They contain information about someone I'm chasing."

"They're over fifteen years old, how can they be relevant?" she asked. He straightened up.

"In the immortal words of Lao Tzu and Rage Against the Machine…, know your enemy," he replied.

"Funny, I had you pegged as a Michael Bublé fan."

He gave her a sour look.

"Just tell me about them," he said, pulling a straight-backed chair into place in front of her, and sitting down. She sat up, matching his pose and posture.

"They're ancient history. Your enemy has moved on."

"How do you know that?"

"Are you the same person you were fifteen years ago?" She'd made a fair point, but he sensed there was more to it.

"I can do this all day," he threatened.

"Go for it," she challenged, settling in for a long waiting game, but a beeping distracted them both, and Jake got to the e-pad before Leigh could. He grabbed her roughly at the wrist, forcing her thumb onto the screen to unlock it, before pushing her back onto the bed, hard.

Once he'd accessed the screen he found a video call coming through, and he answered it, even more surprised to find a much older man than he remembered appearing on the screen. The years hadn't been kind to Lantry.

"Ah, dzień dobry, Jaran." Leigh heard Lantry's unmistakable clipped tone. The name threw her, the name of someone who was supposed to be dead.

"It's been a long time, Chris," Jake answered in English.

"And you look much better than you did the last time I saw you," Lantry replied. "You're with Leigh?" Jake nodded. "Trying to interrogate her?"

"Trying being the operative word," he said.

"Good luck on that one," Lantry answered, and to Leigh it almost sounded like a laugh, but with the old man she could never be sure.

"She's one of yours?" Jake asked, but Leigh didn't hear the reply.

"Are you still after him?" Lantry asked.

"Every chance I get."

"Then she'll be of use to you." Leigh felt anger and indignation rising at being such an expendable commodity, but she did her best to hold onto her temper.

"But there's a problem," Jake answered.

"With Leigh?"

"No, with what happened in Germany," Jake answered, and received a kick from Leigh. He glared at her, about to retaliate, but she shook her head, looking furious.

"What about it?" Lantry repeated, before Jake looked back to the screen.

"I'd rather talk to you in private about it," Jake answered.

"Fine. Anything you need in the mean time?" Lantry said.

"Yeah. There is one thing. I can't seem to get a file on the other agent with me, Bianca Monterey. You know anything about her?"

"I'll send on anything I find," he said. Without speaking to Leigh, Lantry disconnected the call, and Jake rounded on her.

"Now you're going to tell me everything about the god-damned journals, including why you're hiding them from Lantry."

"Lantry tried interrogating me for three days about them, and I didn't tell him anything. What makes you think I'm going to tell you?" He grabbed hold of her by the arms, and yanked her closer.

"Tell me," he said with a low, threatening growl.

"Tell you what? That according to the journals, you're supposed to be dead?" He thrust her away from him. Falling back onto the bed, she saw the furious look on his face.

"Who wrote them?" he demanded.

"My father. He worked for Lantry."

"But it said the bomb was meant for Karl." His voice trembled as he spoke, and she nodded. "That's not true, it can't be."

"Why not?"

"It just can't. And Lantry doesn't know about them?"

"He suspects my dad wrote them, but my father didn't trust him with his notebooks, so why should I?"

"But what your father wrote…" He didn't get a chance to finish as Bianca let herself in, looking at the pair with suspicion.

"The other one is back from the hospital. Why don't you interview her, and I'll take over here," she said.

"No, I'm not done," Jake answered.

"And how much success have you had? You'll be more effective on the other one," Bianca countered, putting herself between Jake and Leigh, and leaving him no more room for argument.

Leigh watched the interaction, picking up a bad vibe between the two. Jake relented, much to Leigh's surprise, thinking he'd want to find out more about the journals. Seeing the sneer on Bianca's face, Leigh thought she'd figured out Jake's game plan. After a session with this woman, he reckoned Leigh would be more than willing to talk to him.

Bianca confirmed that notion as Jake closed the door behind him, and she sent Leigh reeling across the bed from a blow. However rough Leigh estimated Jake would be, it couldn't compare to his partner, who surpassed all expectations of viciousness.

When Jake re-entered a short time later, expecting the Irish woman to be more forthcoming, he found the pair out on the small balcony in the pouring rain, Leigh tied to the seat he'd vacated, but flat on her back, the chair kicked over. The rain hitting her face mixed with blood from cuts; a slash above one eye, a bloody nose and a split lip. Bianca's gun was pointed at her head, but Leigh still maintained that icy calmness. Jake caught hold of Bianca's arm, twisting just as the shot rang out, the bullet embedding into the wall.

"What the hell do you think you're doing?" he asked his surprised partner. So consumed with her rage, she hadn't heard him return.

"She's refusing to talk," Bianca answered.

"Yeah, well, shooting her in the head will reduce her chances of talking even more," he said.

He twisted the weapon out of her hand. "Thankfully, the other one was a little less stubborn, and confirmed they're MoD," he went on, as much for Leigh to hear as Bianca. "We're on the same side." Again, the comment was directed at both. Bianca made a noise, the words indistinguishable. She pulled her arm free of his grip.

"If we're all on the same side, then what has she got to hide?" Bianca hissed at him.

"Maybe she has nothing to hide. Ever considered that possibility?" he put to her. The look on her face told Jake that the thought never crossed her mind. Was she trying to take out the major obstruction to Gouderhoff getting his hands on the visas? Did the man hate this girl that much? What could have happened to turn him so much against the family that appeared to treat him fondly, as one of their own?

Using his pocketknife Jake bent over, cutting the plastic zip ties Bianca used to tie Leigh to the chair, fastened so tight they cut into her wrists and throat, making it difficult to get the blade under them without inflicting more damage.

Leigh took it stoically. Only the involuntary intake of breath betrayed the pain it caused. Once released, she sucked in air, but that too caused pain, and Jake checked under her wet and bloodied shirt, finding bruises blossoming on her midriff, where it was distinguishable from the other artwork he found. So he wasn't the only one Bianca used as a punch bag. He helped Leigh up, and out of the rain.

"She needs medical attention, and you need to cool down," he said to Bianca, who said nothing but gave the pair a venomous look. He helped Leigh into the car, and as he started the engine, looked across at her.

"I'll bet I'm looking pretty good as an interrogator now," he said, and she laughed, still holding her side. "You ready to talk?"

"Maybe," she answered.

"And where the hell did you learn to take a beating like that?"

"Bondage club, in Germany."

"Yeah. Funny," he answered, pulling away from the curb.

Chapter 30

Despite the early hour, Leigh found Karl in the kitchen preparing coffee, wearing nothing more than a pair of tight boxers.

"Do you always greet your guests so fashionably?" she asked.

"In all the time I've lived here, you're my first visitor," he answered.

"Dressed like that, I'm not surprised, you'd frighten the locals," she said, smirking. For a guy heading into his forties, he kept himself in good shape, with no extra pounds to spare. His physique belied his age, and the tousled hair, and state of undress, meant she'd gotten him out of bed. He ignored her last comment, and turned on the coffee machine.

"I see an old friend of mine arrived in Shannon," he said, approaching her, about to greet her with a kiss, but she stopped him, placing her hand on his bare chest. He noticed the marks on her face, brushing curls out of the way.

"You need to sit down," she said, in a tone that told him there'd be no arguing with her, and again, so like Lee. He did so, and she sat opposite him. "Tell me about the bomb," she said, and he looked at her curiously.

"Which one?" he asked, and she shook her head, realising there could be hundreds to choose from.

"The one in Germany. The one you escaped from, that dad wrote about," she answered. Karl shrugged.

"What's to tell? Knowing Lee, he'd have written down everything I told him, at the time."

"Any idea who planted it?"

He shook his head.

"Lee thought whoever he was after, was trying to intimidate him."

"By blowing you to pieces? That's a bit extreme, for intimidation."

"Again, part of the reason your dad sent me away. He saw it as a warning, a message to back off."

"Again, a little extreme."

"Possibly that's why your dad didn't involve me, he knew he was dealing with someone very dangerous. Why are you asking about this?"

"The guy he wrote about, who died..." she went on, ignoring his question.

"Jaran? What about him?"

"Did you see the body?" she asked, and he sat forward.

"They carried him out in a body bag."

"Did you verify the body? Did you see him?" she pushed.

"No," he admitted. "I didn't think I needed to, and ... I couldn't bring myself to do it. The kid followed me into that storehouse, and when I realised what I'd walked into, I turned and ran, shouting at him to get out, but it was too late."

"What if he didn't die?"

"Impossible," he said, his voice barely more than a whisper. He heard the coffee machine click, as the brew cycle finished, and he stood up, distracting himself with getting mugs, pouring the coffee. Leigh followed him, cautiously, unsure of the conclusion he'd reach.

"Not impossible, but he was severely injured, to the point where you wouldn't recognise him today," she said, stopping behind him. His whole body tensed, his shoulders hunched as his hands pressed down on the worktop. He turned to face her.

"Jake?" he asked, and she nodded. He ran his hands through his messed hair as he took a deep breath. "Wow," he said, calmer than she expected him to be. "It explains so much, why he chases me with a passion. He thinks I set that bomb, doesn't he?"

She nodded.

"He did, until he got his hands on a copy of dad's journal," she answered, and he took another deep breath.

"I rarely carry guilt for what I do, or allow a job to affect my conscience, but his death was my fault. He followed me in, and I couldn't save him. He was only a kid."

She made a face.

"He wasn't quite so innocent," she told him. "He was undercover, sent in to get close to you and, if he had the opportunity, to take you out."

"How did you find that out?"

"You knew?"

He shrugged.

"About getting close? Yes, I figured he'd lead me back to whoever set it up, but…"

"But what?"

"You're sure about the elimination part?"

"Yeah, why?"

"Because he had plenty of opportunities to carry that out at the time. You're sure?" he pressed.

"That's what the file Lantry sent me said, along with that bullshit about Bianca."

"What makes you think her file is bullshit?"

"It's a total fabrication, and she tried putting a bullet in my head. That tends to set off alarm bells."

"What?" his voice dropped dangerously low.

"She's one of yours, isn't she?"

"Possibly. She did that?" It was more a statement than a question as he pointed to her injuries. She sighed, and nodded, as she sat up on the worktop, taking a sip from the coffee he'd prepared. He moved closer to her, putting himself between her legs, making a try for another kiss, but she moved her head to the side, deflecting him again.

"Tell me about Isobel Piquet," she said.

"Who?"

"She's the other agent Lantry assigned to Shannon, and she seems to have her own personal grudge against you." He stared at her, but seemed deep in thought.

"Her father," he answered. "He was part of the Nouveau Movement Socialiste or New Socialist Movement, a Basque off-shoot, but with a more aggressive agenda. He was their main strategist and buyer, and my first solo run, my first assignment without your father."

"Who gave you the assignment?"

"Lantry, who else? He was Assistant Chief of Operations by that time, said I was good enough to do this one on my own. Why?" he asked, seeing a frown deepening across her forehead.

"Too many coincidences," she muttered.

"Your dad always said there were no such things."

"I'm beginning to think he was right," she muttered. "Tell me about him?"

"What do you want to know?"

"What was he like?"

"You're a lot like him actually, mannerisms, quirks but there were times when he could be very hard, cold and calculating, with no conscience about using an asset in whatever means necessary. I don't want to paint a bad picture of him, he wasn't a bad man. You and your mother were the most important people in the world to him, but I don't want to give you a rose-tinted view of him either," he said, and she understood.

"It's fine. That came across in his journals, that deliberate, callous calculation."

"He was brilliant at it, and he was a good teacher. Not necessarily the most patient man in the world," he added, and she smiled. It sounded like what she remembered. "How did Lantry drag you into this?"

"More like I tripped, and fell," she admitted. "I got the journals," she began, going on to explain about the forgotten boxes, finding the key to decrypting them, and curiosity being too great to let such a puzzle go.

She opened up about the training at Huntington, the brutality of it, and not just from the trainers. She admitted about snapping and retaliating on Isobel, of how on the target practice range she'd turned, reloaded, and shot her at close range, then walked up to the fallen woman, placed the gun to her head, and threatened to pull the trigger if she didn't back off. What scared both women, was the cold calmness in which Leigh delivered the threat, sure of her ability, and capability, of carrying it out.

Leigh had no idea why she felt the need to purge her soul, to unburden it in such a fashion, and to a man she not only barely knew, but was also under orders to assassinate. But he'd been to Huntington, and he knew her, he'd understand, even if he was purported to be the enemy. Perhaps Bianca threatening her in a similar way made her realise the full extent of her actions, but Bianca lacked control, and in that tiny detail lay the heart of what scared Leigh about herself the most, the calm and callous approach, and just, it seemed, like her father.

Karl woke hours later, reaching across the bed, but found it empty and cold. Leigh was long gone, and he sighed. She had inherited more than just her father's temperament, but Karl had no intentions of revealing how calculating Lee was when it came to seducing and exploiting most of his targets and assets, and not just the women. Men also succumbed to his charms, when the occasion required. Yet somehow the man could distance himself from his actions. Maybe that was why he kept the journals, a means to purge his soul, and Karl smiled, thinking of Lee's choice of words, if he knew what he'd gotten up to with his daughter. More than likely Lee wouldn't have said much, perhaps leaving a bullet on Karl's bedside locker, as a subtle message.

"She's not a little girl anymore, Lee," he told the ghost of a memory. And however capable Leigh was in the IT and business world, she was also a force to be reckoned with in the bedroom, aggressive, with no reservations or coyness about what she wanted, liked and didn't like. A 'take no prisoners' attitude, and again, like Lee Senior. Did she know about his peculiar, and often deviant, tastes? Hardly, he reasoned. She would have been too young to know about such things.

The tattoos and piercings surprised him the most, all hidden beneath a layer of well-dressed respectability. She called it the result of much angst, but the level of detail in the tattoos belied the idea they were spur-of-the-moment decisions. The intricate dragon, snaking up her left side from just above her hip to under her breast, one wing spreading around to her shoulder blade, was not a snap decision, taking hours, and a number of visits to complete. As for all the piercings? That was her pristine, corporate public image ruined, if what lay beneath her pinstripe suits, and tailored clothing, ever got out. Karl laughed at what he imagined Lee's reaction to the tattoos to be. He would have freaked at the piercings, but Karl recognised it, or at least thought he recognised it for what it was. With her, it would be more than just rebellion against the world, it was self-expression, but it also revealed a strong, determined core, a person who knew their own mind. That she'd kept them hidden, said she'd done it to prove something to herself, and to no one else. Yet, her obvious disassociation worried him.

Lee possessed that same disassociation, but not to the same extent as it seemed with her. To Karl, it seemed as though she'd shut down that entire part of her life, archived it off, and sent it to long-term storage, never to be retrieved, or thought of again. From bitter experience he knew such disassociation had a backlash, having suffered the psychological trauma, until he learned to deal with what he did. What he'd told Leigh about feeling guilt was true, but it took him years to get to that point. Perhaps having Jaran's death to hold onto, to beat himself up over helped, the scourge he punished himself with, purging him of his other sins.

Now, even that was shattered. Jake was Jaran, but he couldn't conjure Jaran's face. The image of that kid blurred, and only Jake's hardened features came to mind. Perhaps it was time to rebuild a bridge, he thought and dressed, a task in mind that would also remove a potential problem for him. One he hoped would also protect Leigh.

Chapter 31

Tom waited for her return, and she refrained from her usual smartass responses to his questioning, though still giving him unhelpful answers. While they weren't outright lies, they were still far from the truth. The main crux of his inquiries centred on her latest disappearance, which she answered as tersely as possible, not surprised he didn't believe a word she said. That stemmed both from his history with her, and his natural inclination as a detective.

That she found Lo-Jack tracking devices on most of her cars also told her how much they didn't trust her to play by the rules. She was grateful for having the Gullwing as a backup, an untraceable means of transport, grateful to Karl for saving the car from destruction. That sentiment was hard to maintain though, as she drove to Waterford, her arms tired from the lack of power assisted steering, and her shoulders stiff from exerting control.

She hid her discomfort from Tom as the topic turned to Jake and Bianca. How much did she know about either of them? Aside from the files Lantry sent, she had very little to add. Tom grunted at her responses, pausing every now and again for dramatic effect, in the hope she'd blurt something out, but he was sorely disappointed. Two generations of Hartes, he thought, as he watched her, only the second generation seemed harder than the first. In truth, it made her a good agent, or would do, if her natural talent for quiet anarchy could be harnessed, and controlled.

Like Lee, she had an ability to quickly assess a situation, and formulate a plan to deal with it, though not always in a manner others would think to use. To say she operated outside the box would barely do her justice, but if her programming was anything to go by, then she was gifted with the ability to come up with uniquely creative solutions to problems. Lantry relayed how she'd dealt with the Piquet girl, an almost paternal pride in his tone, but in truth, both men found the resemblance to Lee unsettling, and uncomfortable.

Jake joined them, but not out of choice. Tom's attempt to make the order sound like a request failed, and only a word from Lantry ensured Jake's cooperation. As quick as Leigh was at solving problems, Tom could see the cogs spinning away, as she tried to work out how the American was involved with Lantry. Not even Tom knew, nor did he want to know. Sometimes safety lay in not knowing. The tension between the three was palpable, Jake clearly not happy with this new arrangement, nor having to answer to this boorish man. He still wanted answers from Leigh that were, so far, still not forthcoming.

Tom delivered the updates they'd both been waiting on, mostly about Bianca, and the concern over her lack of history before joining EATA. They moved onto Leigh's developments on the encryptions, but aside from removing all the hard wired connections, and the remote access modem, there was nothing more to report. She hadn't made any progress on locating the source. Tom ended the meeting in his usual abrupt manner. After he'd left, Leigh handed an e-pad to Jake.

"What is it?" he eyed it cautiously.

"The start of the whole story," she answered. "I loaded up the first two journals. It should put what you've already read into context." He took it, noting the need for a thumbprint to unlock it.

"And how do I access it?"

"Oh, there's no need to yank my arm off either, your own print will do the job," she answered humorously, getting ready to leave, noting with a sense of satisfaction his puzzled look at how she'd gotten his thumbprint.

"You're going?"

"Believe it or not, I have real work to do here. In case you've forgotten, I'm overseeing the visa and permit applications, and we've got a plane load of people due in a matter of hours."

"Anything I can do to help?" he offered. She paused and thought about it.

"You could scan the list, see if anything triggers your infamous antenna. Otherwise, just stay the hell out of my way."

"My infamous ... what?"

"Okay, so I'm paraphrasing, but Lantry's file on you says you have an instinct for things that are not quite right."

"Oh it did, did it?"

"You want to help or not?"

"Yeah, why not. It'll give me an excuse to avoid her as well."

"You always have such a close and intimate connection to your partners?"

"I usually work alone."

"Really? I'd never have guessed."

He thought he detected a hint of sarcasm, but she'd delivered her answer so deadpan it was hard to tell.

Back at her office she set him to work, giving him access to the lists, and it wasn't long before he spotted a problem, just as Matt entered to tell them the plane had taken off from Newark.

"Newark? Not Dulles?" Jake asked, and Matt shook his head.

"Snowed in," Matt answered. "Something about a severe arctic front that hit Canada and North America."

"Fuck," Jake exclaimed. He'd left in the middle of a heat wave. Sudden and severe snowstorms would've been the last thing he'd have anticipated.

"Yeah, lucky for us we only get a deluge of rain," Matt answered.

"So far," Leigh added. "Or have you forgotten about the two-month long bout of snow a couple of years back?"

"Oh yeah, the whole country shut down for weeks," Matt answered.

"The whole country?" Jake asked.

"We don't cope well with the pretty white stuff," she answered, and that time he heard the sarcasm. "What's the problem?" Her quick redirection back on track made him smirk.

"It's the numbers," Jake answered, pointing to the screen.

"They all checked out," Matt said.

"I'm sure they did," Jake answered, and unlike with Leigh, the sarcasm was hard to mistake. "Who did the crosscheck?"

"Danny first, then I checked them on an independent system," Matt answered, sounding defensive. He tried looking to Leigh for backup and support, but found her stare harder than the American's. Only when she looked away did Matt find he could breathe again.

"What *is* the problem?" she asked again of Jake.

"On my first ever assignment, I spent days trawling through pages and pages of printouts…" he began.

"Any chance we can have the reader's digest version, not the 'American blockbuster full background before we get to the point' version?" she interrupted, and he glared at her. "Time's a-wasting," she added.

"These numbers are bogus. They're part of a batch that were corrupted about twenty years ago, and marked on the system, never to be used again," Jake explained.

"You remember that?" Matt asked.

"Like I tried explaining, it was my first ever assignment, and I have an almost eidetic memory," Jake answered.

"Eidetic?" Matt asked.

"It's a fancy name for perfect recall, or photographic memory," Leigh explained.

"Why didn't he just say that in the first place?" Matt muttered.

"The point is," Jake went on, raising his voice, "these numbers shouldn't exist."

"Okay, we'll flag them, so when they step up to get their vermits, we'll have Immigration pull them in. Do you and super-bitch want to do the interviewing?" she asked Jake.

"You don't want to do it?" he asked, surprised as she shook her head.

"Interrogation's not my thing," she remarked.

"You're pretty good at withstanding it though," he commented. Matt listened to the interaction, with nothing of value to add to the conversation. Leigh always had a quiet almost shy side, but that seemed to have changed to secretive, and Matt found her a complete stranger to him. They both turned to stare at him, catching him studying them, trying to figure them out, but in turn, he became the rabbit caught in the headlights, and unable to control himself, gave a little start.

"I'll flag them on the system," he said, but Leigh shook her head.

"I'll do it here," she said and turned back to Jake. "I'll set it up so they don't flag until they get to the Immigration desk for processing."

"What? You don't trust me now?" Matt demanded angrily, and Jake had to admit he admired how calmly she turned to Matt, and delivered her answer with aplomb.

"No. I don't trust anyone here," she said, "so don't take it personally. What you can do, is alert Immigration on what to expect." She turned back to the computer and pulled up another database, typing before turning to Jake. "Update the relevant records," she ordered, and he gave her a mock salute, before sitting down to work his way through the file. Ignored again, but having been given an order, Matt left without another word.

"You're being a bitch to him," Jake commented, after he'd left.

"Yeah, well, sometimes payback really is a bitch," she answered.

"Working with an ex, huh?" She gave him a cold glare before returning to her own screens. "I'm guessing you're not the sentimental type," he added.

"Sentimentality is a waste of time and energy," she answered.

"But there's something more," he probed.

She signed, and turned to him.

"Gouderhoff's got people in here, but I haven't figured out who they are yet," she admitted.

"What makes you say that?"

"The night of the break-in, when I got around the corner and found Isobel on the ground, I just about caught sight of her attacker disappearing, before I went down."

"Karl could have been one of those attackers," Jake suggested, but she shook her head.

"Just before I lost consciousness I heard another man's voice, away from whoever attacked me, and no way could it be Isobel's guy. He couldn't have gotten around that fast, without being breathless. Even if one of them was Gouderhoff, that leaves at least two men, and one of them has to be already working here to get access to the servers."

Jake chuckled to himself.

"What?" she demanded.

"You *do* realise that's the longest, and most informative answer you've given since I've met you?" he asked. "Voluntarily," he added.

"We're supposed to be on the same side, remember?" she shot back.

"So's your handler, but you don't seem as forthcoming with him."

"Yeah? Well, wait until you read the first two journals."

"Based on his current level of charm, I'm guessing he makes for interesting reading."

She grunted in reply as she got up to leave.

"Now where are you going?" he asked.

"The vermits should be printing, and I want to check the batches. Want to join me, make sure I'm not secretly working for Gouderhoff, and attempting to subvert the visas somehow?" she put to him.

"Seeing as you put it that way, perhaps I should."

Chapter 32

Jonathan's blunt reply surprised Wilma. After promising to find out whatever he could about Bianca Monterey, he returned to say he could do nothing. All avenues of information were closed to him. He then left, as abruptly as his announcement, leaving Wilma perplexed. His only explanation was the ongoing investigation, that the investigators were taking far too much interest in his affairs, restricting where he could access such information. This left Wilma baffled, and while she understood the pressures he faced, she found his sudden change in attitude disturbing. Finding him unavailable for the rest of the evening, she returned to her apartment alone. Having received very sparse updates from Jake, she decided to phone him, to break the bad news. He answered on the first ring, and she heard as he excused himself. He made his way to Leigh's office, confident his conversation wouldn't be overheard there.

"Senator," he said.

"Bad news Jake, I couldn't find anything on Bianca," she said, and he thought he detected an angry tone in her voice.

"She seems to have covered her tracks well," he commented. "But she's definitely not playing by the rules, and we're not the only ones trying to find Gouderhoff through the visas."

"What?" Clearly, this was news to her.

"The Brits have a team here as well, with Karl top of their hit list," he informed her. "One of them is a computer tech working on the encryptions to prevent him from hacking into the system. So far, it's withstood several hits."

"Are they any closer to catching this man?"

"Not yet, but ..."

"A link?"

"Yeah, I think so. Bianca physically assaulted the programmer, almost shot her in the head."

"What? Why would she do that?"

"The only conclusion I can come to, is Leigh wouldn't give up the encryption codes to the visa program."

"Leigh?"

"The kid working on the encryptions."

"And she's MoD?"

"Yeah, along with a French woman, who's taking care of the physical security measures."

"Any connection between the two French women?"

"None, that I can see," he admitted.

"France is a big country, but their intelligence community isn't," she reasoned. "Can we trust these new contacts?"

"I think so…"

"But?" she asked, and he smirked at her motherly tone.

"Coincidences," he answered, and paused, but she waited him out. "This kid, Leigh, is connected to the bomb in Germany."

"The one where you were injured?"

"Yeah."

"But Jake, if she's only a kid …" She left the rest unsaid.

"She wasn't there, obviously, but she has documents that puts my perception of what happened into doubt. She's connected to the man who sent me in after Gouderhoff, and as a child, she had a connection to Karl."

"Coincidences like that don't just happen, Jake."

"I know, but she's after Karl as well."

"The enemy of my enemy is my friend?" She chuckled.

"Yeah, something like that. And Bianca was adamant about interrogating her alone."

"Are you sure you're not reading too much into her motives? That perhaps she's just trying to stay ahead of you, and in control?"

"Sure, anything's possible, but you should see this kid's injuries. Bianca's definitely not in control. More like trying to eliminate a threat."

"Which brings us back to where her true allegiances lie, with us or Gouderhoff."

"They're not with us, that's for sure. And it gets better."

"Go on."

"Leigh asked if I'd look at the list of Americans en-route, and there's a problem."

"Which is?"

"A batch of very old, and corrupted, social security numbers was used."

There was a pause on Swayne's end.

"I'm not sure I follow," she said.

"They were a batch of numbers that were stolen over fifteen years ago, and used at the time for smuggling people into the States. A high-end operation. You got the whole package, a new life, good credit rating, and solid record for employment and education, and you paid for it."

"How did you know about it?"

"My first real assignment was tracing back the numbers. Shit like that tends to stick in your mind."

"But again, the coincidence Jake, that you should be the right guy in the right place, at the right time, with the right information."

"It's fluky alright, but as you already pointed out, the intelligence world is too small."

"Is the problem on the US side then?" she asked.

"So far that's all we've found, which is troubling."

"How so?"

"How do you find a needle in a haystack? Where do you start looking? Is someone in the State Department wilfully entering these numbers, or is someone here manipulating them?"

"Is it possible the State Department is recycling old numbers?"

"They were locked down, or supposed to be."

"So, it looks like someone held onto them for that many years? That's a hell of a long-term business plan," she said. Jake laughed again.

"I'm not saying Karl had a crystal ball to foresee this, but he's a meticulous planner, almost obsessively so. Something like this, he'd have filed neatly away."

"You think he had the original batch of numbers?"

"That's what I was investigating when I went undercover in Germany."

"It's coming full circle."

"It always does, if you wait, and live long enough."

"Very philosophical for one so young."

"Cynical, more like," he replied.

"What's your next move?"

"I'm going to stick close to this kid. I have a feeling she's the key to the old and historical stuff, and it might shed some light on our current situation. She's also proving to be pretty resourceful, so I'll use her to try dig up something on Bianca."

"So you trust her?"

"About as much as I trust anyone in this game. She's a tough one to figure out though," he confessed.

"In what way?"

"She has this almost impenetrable wall, comes across as quite cold and harsh at times, but yet, there's no sense that she's hiding anything."

"Perhaps she's an experienced agent," Wilma offered.

"No, that's the thing, she's not. This is her first assignment. She's fresh off training, with only a boorish ass to rely on for support."

"Well, be careful," she said, and he heard that motherly tone again.

"I will, and I'll let you know as soon as I find out anything."

"I'd appreciate that, Jake," she answered and disconnected the call, feeling happier to hear of progress on the visa end of things, but concerned over the number of issues it raised.

She detected a hint of something in his voice, a softening of his tone as he spoke of this new woman, but if she was MoD, why didn't Jonathan know about her, and if he knew, why hadn't he said anything to her? It was Jonathan who initially told her about the visa programme, well in advance of the public announcement. Surely he'd have known if British agents were also on site. Questions only begat more questions, without any forthcoming answers.

Swayne's phone rang, surprised to see Jake's number.

"What is it?" she asked.

"When's the last time your apartment was swept for bugs?"

"I didn't think there was any need," she answered, taken aback by the question. "Why?" she asked.

"Did you tell anyone about my past? Jonathan, perhaps?"

"No, no one. Why?" she asked again.

"There's a leak somewhere," he answered.

"What do you mean?"

He heard the concern in her voice.

"I just got an envelope delivered to me," he said.

"And?"

"It's in German, and inside there's a disk addressed to Jaran. Get a sweeper team in your apartment, now."

He disconnected abruptly, disconcerting her even more. Was her apartment bugged? The very thought of it made her shudder.

Jake looked at the note on the disk, handwritten in a script that he recognised as belonging to Karl. It was unsigned, but Jake knew where it came from. The note read 'peace offering.'

If it hadn't leaked from Swayne, that only left one possibility, Jake thought. Two possibilities actually, but they were connected. Had he completely misread Leigh? Lantry, he never trusted anyway, but what about Leigh? Connecting an external disk drive to the e-pad, he inserted the CD and accessed the contents of the disk.

Chapter 33

A total of seven people were returned to the States, courtesy of Jake's observant eye, and memory. Both he and Bianca carried out the interviews, with other members of the Shannon team, Matt sitting in with Bianca. In the observation room, sandwiched between the two interview rooms, Danny watched on as Leigh's jaw twitched at Bianca's hostile interviewing technique. In the other room, Jake's interviewing method was dangerously subtle, his calmness and lowered vocal tone ensnaring his prey.

Leigh recognised most of his tricks, completely at odds with Bianca's intimidation tactics. At least he refrained from threatening to blow someone's head off. Jake got more people to return to the US voluntarily than Bianca did, and got a better lead on where they'd bought their new identities. Armed with the names of the returnees, Leigh returned to her office to update the systems. With the system becoming more streamlined, it would be capable of highlighting such cases, before they even got off the ground.

With the rest of the vermits successfully distributed, and those travelling put onto European flights, or public transport for relocation within Ireland, Leigh heard a cheer echoing down the corridor as the last file was processed. Secluded in her office, she continued to work on closing off any remaining loopholes.

Still, she allowed herself a smirk at the success of the test run. From now on people would be arriving at a faster rate, and on a more regular schedule, but before then Leigh secured a begrudging agreement from Isobel to allow everyone at the facility to go home for a few days, confident the system was robust enough to withstand any new cyber-attack. And Leigh had an ulterior motive to return home. She had the final journal to figure out.

She'd let the problem run riot in her brain, thinking about the encryptions every now and again, making notes on her e-pad. Jake found her in her office, and without invitation, he entered, helping himself to freshly brewed coffee.

"What are you up to?" he asked, in a deceptively jovial and conversational manner.

"Just hacking into the CIA database, in an evil attempt to take over the world," she replied.

"Their database isn't the way to go," he answered. "If you want to control the world, you break into the financial hub."

She turned in her chair to look at him, not sure if he was being serious or not. He made it harder again by shrugging nonchalantly.

"I do have access to that database, but I need a secure system to access it on," he added, looking intently at her.

"I'm getting the impression you're not asking me if you can use my systems, more like telling me," she said. He hid a smirk behind his mug as he took a sip, but the look he gave her unnerved her a little.

"Not here," he said. "I understand you're planning on going home for a few days."

"And?"

"You have a guest room," he said, again making a statement, not a request.

"I guess I do now," she shot back, not allowing him to intimidate her. He placed his half empty cup back beside the coffee machine.

"Good. You can pick me up at the hotel in about thirty minutes." He didn't wait for confirmation, just took it for granted his demand would be met, and Leigh sat back in her chair, not quite sure what just happened. She'd never been good at figuring guys out, but this guy was hard work.

She met Isobel on her way out, and they exchanged updates on their respective areas. The software systems where locked down, with the facility also to be locked, and under constant surveillance. Isobel was leaving on the next flight to Paris, planning to spend the next few days with friends. Leigh simply nodded, and gave a pleasantry in reply, without getting into an extended conversation.

Jake's directive was foremost in her mind, and she found him waiting in the lobby. Without prompting, he picked up his bag, and followed her out. She noticed he travelled light, taking only a small backpack with him, but he held onto the e-pad, sitting in the passenger seat without a word.

If she thought his behaviour odd, she didn't comment, but as soon as they hit the motorway he began questioning her on the contents of the first two journals, quizzing her on details. She did her best to answer, but she pointed out that many aspects of the journal were just as much a mystery to her, as to him. She didn't know her father well enough to give any deeper insights into what he was thinking at the time.

"So Barnett was always that charming," he commented, and she grunted. "Lantry is pretty much how I remember him," he added. She shot him a glance, but refrained from asking. Given his current behaviour, she wondered if this was yet another tactic of his, baiting her with a tantalising morsel. Instead, she focused on the road ahead, and said nothing.

"What's your impression of Danny?" he asked, in another change of direction.

"He makes me uncomfortable," she admitted, "but maybe that's because he's been hitting on me."

"Got yourself a little admirer, huh?" he teased, and she glared at him. "And Matt?"

"Ancient history," she told him, and he wilfully ignored the hard tone that implied he drop the topic.

"How ancient?"

"Why do you need to know?"

"Oh, I don't know, two people thrown back together in a highly charged situation, tends to set off alarm bells."

"You think we're conspiring on the visas?"

"Are you?"

"Most assuredly not." While her tone couldn't be described as fiery, it was the most passionate reaction he'd gotten out of her, so far. Passionate enough for it to be true, and still a tender and sore point he reckoned, convincing him of Matt's connection to her miscarriage and hospital admission in her early twenties, which he'd read about on her file from Huntington. Typical of Lantry's information; comprehensive, but devoid of any sensitivity.

With no more questions, silence reigned in the car from Portlaoise to Carlow, and Jake watched her fluidly change gears as she drove, but he noticed her begin to relax as they neared their destination.

"You hungry?" she asked, breaking the silence.

"I could eat," he answered.

"It'll have to be take-out, all I have is pasta," she said.

"Pasta's fine with me," he answered, and she gave him a quick glance before stopping at a red light, and then turned in the direction of home. The security sensor light came on as she drove around to the rear of the house.

"You own this?" he asked, surprised at the size of the place.

"Yeah," she answered, turning off the ignition and getting out. Unlocking the patio door she entered and disarmed the alarm while Jake followed her.

She gave him directions to the guest room, and while he climbed the stairs, she went to her office, still there when he returned, finding her deep in thought, and holding a leather bound book.

"Is that one of the journals?" he asked, startling her, and he got a sense of just how solitary a creature she was, and that he'd just invaded her innermost sanctum. He surveyed the room, impressed with her setup.

"It's the last one, the fifth," she answered.

"You said there were only four."

"Four that I could decipher. This one has no key, and the cyphers change at intervals." She got up, moving to the whiteboard mounted on one wall, drawing a line down the centre of the board. On the left, she wrote the page numbers where the cyphers changed. On the right, she listed out the existing journals, and the keys to decoding them, drawing the musical symbols. Taking a step back, she studied her work, knowing the key to unlocking the fifth lay on that board.

Not wanting to break her concentration, Jake took her vacated seat at the workstation, and finding her systems unlocked, set about his own task. Leigh turned around at the sound of keys clicking, but caught sight of the Agency's insignia at the top of the screen, and decided not to ask. Returning to the board, she circled the words 'music' and 'key'.

"I didn't realise you were a leftie," Jake commented.

"I'm not," she answered. "Not naturally, anyway. My dad made me practice writing with both hands when I was little. I find it helps when I need to think outside the box."

"Ever stop and wonder if he was training you for a life of intrigue?"

"What?"

"All this, the codes, the handwriting, mechanics… I'll bet he even taught you basic self-defence techniques, and your driving skills…"

She shook her head.

"There's no way he wanted me in the middle of this."

"But here you are, and if I hadn't seen your file, I'd have thought you'd been at this for years."

"I'm a fast learner."

"Or you had a good teacher," he answered. The computer beeped, its search finished, and Jake turned his attention back to the screen, frowning at what he read. She returned to her board, confident the key was an actual musical key, not a clef this time. Only when she scanned in the journal, and tried the keys, would she know if her theory proved correct. A thinner journal than the rest, it wouldn't take long to scan in the five sections, but she'd have to wait until Jake finished.

The scent of food pulled Jake's attention away, and well-timed, finishing his investigation, but disturbed by what he'd found, including a less than respectable description of Lee Harte, a man who was both admired, and feared, in equal measures, if the Agency information was anything to go by. Jake had no doubts that had he lived, young Leigh would be more dangerous than she already was. He followed the scent to the kitchen and she handed him a bowl of pasta and sauce. Simple fare, but at that late hour, was enough to quell the hunger pangs. Accepting a bottle of cold beer, he followed her to the den, an alcove off the kitchen.

"The left-handedness," she started. "My dad was a leftie, but back when he was a child it was seen as abnormal, and they tried to beat it out of him." She saw the horrified look on his face, and she shrugged. "It's what happened in those days, ignorance of something different, but he learned to do everything right-handed, and defying them all, still learnt to write and use his left hand."

"So the apple didn't fall far from the tree then," he commented, "that defiance."

"I guess not, but he taught me to write, with both hands, when I started school. You really think he was preparing me for this... career path?" The very idea bugged her, though her dad claimed in the letter that he didn't want her involved in this kind of life.

"He was being a father," Jake answered. "Knowing how potentially short the lifespan is in this career, he probably wanted to make sure you could take care of yourself. From reading his journals, I don't think he wanted you sucked into this. So what happened after they died?"

"In what way?"

"Did Lantry try to recruit you then?"

She shook her head.

"I didn't know about him until I read the notebooks," she answered. "Barnett, on the other hand, became an instrumental force in my life, stepping in at the time to straighten me out."

"Why, what did you do?"

"Everything," she admitted. "Underage drinking, underage sex, drugs, you name it."

"Ah, the classic knee-jerk reaction. What stopped it?"

"A couple of nights in a cell, and Tom getting a bit tough."

"The good old scare tactic," he concluded, and she laughed.

"Yeah, it worked, for a while. What about you?"

"You've read my file."

"I've read *a* file, but I'm thinking it should start with 'once upon a time'." Her stare was intense, exaggerated by the wounds still healing on her face. It lent her a dangerous look, and he thought back to what he'd read about her father. "According to the journals you, or some guy called Jaran, allegedly died in a bomb meant for Gouderhoff," she said, and saw his returning stare harden. "You've been chasing him all these years because you think *he* was trying to kill *you*."

He put his half-finished meal on the coffee table.

"Very astute of you."

"Confucius once said, 'before you embark on the path of revenge, first dig two graves'."

"You're quoting Confucius at me?"

She sat back, watching, but waited him out.

"How true are the journals?" he asked, and she shrugged.

"The author's not around to verify them, but so far, everything he wrote about Huntington, Lantry, Barnett, his assignments, they've all proven to be true, so why would I doubt the rest of it? Is it so important to you to have them proven wrong?" The question threw him, and he hesitated. "You *need* them to be wrong, so you can feel justified in continuing your personal vendetta, so that you haven't wasted all these years chasing him."

"You're not just a pretty face," he answered, but she stayed quiet. "Okay, fine, I've been after him since I got out of the hospital, after nearly two years of painful reconstructive surgery and rehab. I didn't recognise the guy in the mirror anymore. Hate and revenge were all I had to hold onto at the time, just to get through it."

"And the journals now threaten that belief, threaten the foundation," she said. He took a long drink of his beer.

"What they tell me is that I've been wrong, that I've been chasing the wrong guy and, as you've so eloquently put it, I've been wasting my life all these years."

"You didn't waste them, someone else did."

"What do you mean?"

"Someone set this up, someone set all this in motion."

"Who? Why?"

"You're better at this Jake, you figure it out." It almost sounded like a taunt.

"Your father?" he asked, but she shook her head.

"No, but I think he found out, and that's what set the whole thing in motion."

"But that was over a decade ago."

"There's another old saying that goes 'it's possible for two people to keep a secret, but only if one of them is dead'."

"What do you do, read a book of quotes on a regular basis?"

"Every morning, before breakfast," she replied, and he laughed, releasing his own tension. Except for Swayne, it had been a long time since he'd felt this relaxed with anyone. A strange sensation for him, but one thing continued to niggle at the back of his mind.

"Do you still think Gouderhoff's responsible for their deaths?" he asked, and saw her jaw clench.

"That's what I was told," she answered.

"That's not what I asked," he countered. Her eyes narrowed.

"I honestly don't know anymore," she admitted. "You've read the journals, the same as I have. My father treated him like a son, took him in and gave him a home, and from my reading of them, dad sent him to Germany to protect him, what reason would Gouderhoff have to turn on them. And besides, my impression of dad is he'd have had no hesitation in taking Karl out, if he ever considered him a threat." Jake nodded, consistent with what he'd read about the man.

"And certainly if he ever posed a threat to you, from my reading of them," he said. "Hence my earlier question, about him teaching you all that stuff. He seemed very protective of you, but he wasn't going to bubble-wrap you, and hide you from the world. He sounded like a decent guy."

"Yeah, from what I can remember of him. He was strict, but... when he taught me stuff, like cars or codes, he had this quiet passion. So what about yours?" she asked. He took another drink and sat back.

"Mine wasn't such a contender for Father-of-the-Year," he answered, making it clear the topic was uncomfortable for him, and she let it drop.

"I've got work to do, so if you're finished your super-spy stuff?"

He nodded, and she let him to his thoughts. Before going to bed he checked in on her, finding her engrossed in scanning the final journal. Early the next morning he found her in her own room, half undressed under the covers. A light sleeper by nature, new surroundings added to his inability to fall into a deep sleep, and he'd heard her ascending the stairs in the early hours of the morning.

She woke shortly after he did, movement in her own home waking her, despite working late into the night. A bare pantry was all the excuse they needed to head into town for breakfast, but every now and again Leigh's mind would wander, as the ongoing problem of the key to the final journal consumed her. During the night her program scanned the document, but none of her possible keys came up as solutions, and the puzzle continued to eat at her.

They sat in the corner of a quiet coffee shop.

"Can I expect a visit from a clandestine American Agency in the next few days?" she asked, pulling herself back into the present.

"Not this time," he answered.

"Who were you looking for that couldn't be researched in Shannon?"

"Your old man for one," he admitted.

181

"And the other?" That he'd checked Lee out didn't surprise her.

"Bianca," he answered.

"Gouderhoff's?"

"If she is, then she's fallen out of favour."

"I don't understand," she confessed.

"He's the one who told me where, and what to look for. He called it a peace offering. Any idea why he'd do something like that?" He watched her closely, but the question threw her.

"Maybe she's become a liability, and he has to get rid of her. What better way, than by sacrificing her? So who is she?"

"Ex British Military."

"British?"

"Yeah, not French."

"That explains why Isobel never heard of her, and couldn't find anything on her. I take it Bianca's not her real name either."

He shook his head.

"It's Melanie Banks."

"I'm guessing there's a reason for the change of name."

"A dishonourable discharge. What they kicked her out over, was the least of her offences."

"Not her devastating charm?" she asked. The conversation died as their coffee arrived.

"You never told me what happened in that room," he said.

"She tied me to a chair, and beat the shit out of me, what more do you need to know?"

"What you talked about, what questions she asked you."

"She was more of a physical, than verbal kind of girl, not big on asking questions, but when she did, they were about the encryptions."

"And she was prepared to put a bullet in your head for that? I don't buy it."

"If I'm out of the picture, and no one else can crack the codes, then they have to start over again, with a new programmer, new encryption codes and someone a little less resistant to her... brand of persuasion."

The answer seemed plausible, but something still niggled at him, at the coincidence between Bianca's brutal assault on Leigh, and Karl's ensuing sacrifice of Bianca, almost a retaliation for the attack. Jake kept it to himself for the moment.

Chapter 34

Jake did more digging, but the Bianca/Melanie scenario left him with more questions than answers. Leigh gave him access to her systems, and again, deemed it prudent to remain ignorant. During the previous night she'd delved into Jake's past, finding very little about Jake Mann, aside from the cover stories put in place.

Jaran Baenleaski however yielded a lot more information, and made for an interesting read but also, it seemed, set off security alarms somewhere. A more in-depth search gave links to two other men, Marek and Pitor, both with the same surname. The links to Marek gave articles and details of his trial. The case against him made for compelling reading, and it was what kept Leigh up for most of the night.

Marek's list of alleged crimes was extensive, and the newspapers printed picture after picture of his victims who'd survived, including a picture of a very young Jaran, and a distraught mother. If it occurred in the present day, his picture would never have appeared in the public domain, but back then there'd either been no legislation, or very loose adherence to it, where protecting a young boy was concerned. Perhaps the press justified it to themselves. The public needed to be aware of a potential new threat on the horizon. After all, he was the son of a convicted serial rapist, and suspected serial murderer. Apples like those tended not to fall far from the tree.

Now she understood when Jake said he no longer recognised his face in the mirror. The surgery altered his features, squaring his jaw and chin. If anyone put the before and after pictures of him side by side, they'd never suspect they were of the same man.

That brought her back to the bomb that changed the course of all their lives, but specifically the lives of two men, setting them on a collision course, time and time again. But who was behind the bomb? Jake had been convinced it was Karl, but Karl was convinced it was whoever was behind the murder of her parents. Were either of them telling the truth? If Jake was sent after Karl, had he also been sent to take out her parents as well? After all, Jake was genetically predisposed to homicidal behaviours. And Karl? Did he have it in him to ruthlessly dispose of anyone in his way? She already knew the answer to that, of course he did. However, the journals threw a spanner in her speculations. Were they fabricated? A very clever ruse to deflect suspicion from the real killers. But why go to such lengths, an intricate encryption which no one could figure out. And if you were the guilty party, holding the documents that proved your guilt, why keep them? Not only keep them, but ensure their safety?

Her sleep-deprived brain struggled with all the probable, and improbable questions that sprang to mind. This was why she preferred working with computers, and very much alone. Computer problems had logical solutions, unlike dealing with humans, where it seemed only the most illogical solution appeared to work. On that note, she retired to bed, too tired to undress properly, and just about managing to pull the duvet over her.

Having delved as much as he could, Jake finally took a break. His shoulders ached from where he'd hunched over the keyboard for considerable time without realising. He found Leigh asleep on the sofa in the den, and after her late night he couldn't blame her. That left him unsupervised, and his instinct to snoop kicked in. The closed doors in the house were too much of a temptation, but he justified it to himself, that he wanted to understand Leigh, and the Hartes, better.

He began with the room beyond the office and stairs. The double doors, made of solid wood and unlocked, opened silently inward. A grand piano dominated the room, but uninterrupted dust on the floor told him she never came in here. The dust cover on the piano was also grey, as were cloths covering other shapes, which he figured to be other instruments.

"My mother was a music teacher," Leigh said, startling him as she appeared beside him without warning.

"I thought you were asleep," he said, trying to defend himself.

"I was," she admitted, "but you stomp around the place like a herd of baby elephants." He knew that wasn't true, he'd been as quiet as he could. "She used to teach in here," Leigh went on. He stepped over the threshold, and went to the piano, lifting the cover and the lid, hitting a few of the keys. Surprisingly, it didn't sound out of tune, given its lack of use.

"You play?" he asked.

"Used to. That, and the cello."

"Not anymore?"

"Not since my college exams, and those I did in Germany. I don't come in here much." His footprints in the dust emphasised how much she'd neglected the room, and the instruments.

"Too many memories?" he asked, and she nodded. "But you did a music degree, as well as your computer stuff," he added.

"The music was mostly theoretical, I only played what I had to, and only when I had to."

"Pity," he commented, as he pulled the dust cover off the seat, and sat. He played *chopsticks*, badly, but an easy and old favourite of all children learning the piano. He turned and grinned at her. "That's about the extent of my playing," he confessed, and she chuckled.

"My mum hated when kids came in and played that."

"I guess it would grate on your nerves, if you heard it constantly."

Leigh laughed.

"She caught me playing it once, made me do awkward scales and finger exercises."

"Oh, tough punishment."

"Yeah, but good practice for playing Beethoven." As though defying the ghosts in the room, she stepped inside for the first time in almost a decade, and he noticed a slight catch in her breath. He'd noticed a faint tremor in her hands as she typed, both in Shannon and now here, but it became more pronounced as her fingers touched the keys of the piano, playing a major chord. He took hold of her hand.

"You're shaking," he said.

"Nervous disposition," she admitted.

"Even when you're programming?"

"Especially when I'm programming," she answered. Her hand was cold, perhaps explaining part of the tremor.

"Bet that made playing concerts interesting."

"I never played in public… I couldn't. Nerves always got the better of me," she admitted.

"You don't strike me as the nervous type."

"I hide it well," she said, pulling her hand away, and departing. She stopped at the threshold. "You fancy dining out tonight?" she asked.

"That sounds tempting."

"Then I've got a phone call to make, and you need to get dressed."

"How well dressed?"

"Something a little classier than jeans and a hoodie," she answered, and left.

Jake appeared from his room a short time later, hiding his surprise at seeing her in a short, well-fitted dress, but her expression dared him to say something, anything, smart-assed. He held his tongue, feeling it to be a wiser tactic. A furtive search of her belongings didn't suggest a strong feminine side, but he liked it, and followed her out without comment. She drove into town, parking in one of the hotel's reserved spots.

He'd discovered her investment in this place, and wasn't surprised to find they had a reserved table, in an almost secluded section, the manager personally escorting them to the table. Her phone call to make the reservation, and for once invoke her owner privileges, surprised him, and now she arrived with a tall and handsome stranger, which only added to the intrigue. Word spread like wildfire throughout the hotel, stunning those she normally worked alongside. Leigh Harte, it seemed, was officially on a date. Jake sat opposite her, a suspicious smirk on his face. She tried ignoring it, concentrating on the menu instead, but gave up.

"What?" she demanded. He gave her an innocent look, and shook his head, but she persisted.

"I'm your first date here, the first time you've taken advantage of your position?" he asked, intrigued.

"Don't let it go to your head," she shot back.

Her choice of food was modest, he noted but, from what he already knew of her, he wouldn't describe her as a hearty eater. He deferred to her choice of wine, but by the time they reached the dessert, she was starting to feel the alcohol taking effect, and only then realised he'd been slyly topping up her glass. Unwittingly, she'd drunk more than she'd intended, pushing her over the limit to drive home.

Jake sat beside her in the back of the taxi, close enough to detect the subtle fragrance of her shampoo, and the faint scent of perfume. He was coming to realise just how understated she was, on the surface at least, of the façade she presented to the world. Anyone taking her at face value, did so at their peril. Her financial records showed her to be worth a comfortable fortune, but she lived modestly. Yet, beneath that modest, almost plain exterior lay... Well, he wasn't sure.

She had a keen and penetrating mind, with a hint of obsession, when it came to solving problems. But it was the body art, and other modifications, that revealed the most about her. At her core, he guessed, she could be quite passionate, but she kept that contained Pinstripe suites, and crisp white shirts, hid that side of her from the world. Yet, she kept a tight rein on that aspect of herself, almost as if she was afraid to allow that part out, to express itself, perhaps afraid of what would be unleashed.

Jake took the lead as they arrived back at her house, the wine helping to drop his own reservations, and he pulled her close, kissing her.

That cool exterior responded stiffly, at first, but she soon replied to his passion, with equal vigour.

Leigh was nowhere to be found the following morning. Her own room showed almost no trace of her, the only exception was her dress dropped on the floor. Running shoes were missing, but he had no idea what other items were gone.

He returned to his room and packed his things, planning to return to Shannon, and felt relieved as he heard her arrive back. She seemed surprised to find him in the kitchen as she entered. Dressed in running gear, her face still a little flushed, he guessed she'd gone for her run into town, and collected her car. In the cold light of day, her shield was back up, that cool demeanour back in place. Ah, nothing like that awkward morning-after moment, he thought, as she muttered about needing a shower. A short time later she returned, suited up, her façade firmly back in place. Her phone beeped, and she frowned as she checked the message.

"What is it?" he asked.

"Looks like someone's in Shannon before us," she answered.

"Perhaps Isobel's arrived. She's flying back today, isn't she?"

"She's still at De Gaulle airport, her plane's due to take off shortly. She wouldn't have set the alarm off, and wouldn't be trying to break into my systems," she answered, with a hard edge to her voice.

"How long will it take to get there?"

"Under optimal conditions, it would take two hours."

"I'll rephrase the question. How fast can you get us there?" he asked, and was answered with a dangerous looking smile.

Chapter 35

Neither of them spoke. Leigh concentrated on driving, at speeds well in excess of the limits, and Jake remained silent, not wanting to break that intense focus. The only thing to disturb the silence was a call from Isobel, to say she'd landed in Shannon, and that a perimeter alarm sent her a text message just as her plane was taxiing on the runway. Handing Jake her phone to answer, he updated Isobel with the limited information to hand, and warned her to stay put until they arrived. As far as Jake was concerned, he was still the senior agent, and if Lantry gave him authority over Leigh, then that extended to the French woman as well.

Isobel didn't answer their call when they got there, and no sign of her where Jake ordered her to wait. Connecting to the security system, Leigh accessed the video link, and played back the previous hour in fast motion, visibly startled as she saw Isobel falling to the ground in one of the corridors.

"What is it?" Jake asked, moving to look over her shoulder, and Leigh replayed the scene. "Guess that explains why she's not here. Any idea who, or how many we're up against?" he asked. She shook her head.

"All I can make out are shadows."

Armed, they entered the facility, Jake taking the lead. With years more experience, Leigh put her trust in him, watching as he combined stealth with speed. He barely made a sound as he checked doors and rooms along the way. He disliked working with others, disliked having to trust and rely on them, but Leigh followed him, and his instructions, without question. His checking ensured no one would surprise them from behind, but he left the job of monitoring their rear to Leigh as they advanced into the complex.

From their brief surveillance of the place, they had an idea where to go. Isobel's body also acted as a signpost, lying in a pool of blood. Jake checked her gun to discover she didn't even get off a shot. He shook his head in dismay. Of the two women, she had the most experience, and should've had more sense, and caution. Her over confidence in her abilities cost her her life.

Leigh froze at seeing her body, and only Jake's gentle squeeze on her shoulder broke her from her paralysis. She knew she needed to refocus, and while she took a shot at Isobel back at Huntington, the blood made it different. Witnessing the violent act unnerved her, and it was nowhere near as poetic, or glamorous, as the movies portrayed.

She steeled and willed herself to move forward, that cold detachment slipping back into place, joining Jake as he checked around the next corner, and down the corridor. Shadows in the light betrayed the others, and Jake signalled a stop, which Leigh obeyed. Matt appeared, followed closely by Bianca. Matt looked shocked at seeing them standing there, guns at the ready, but Bianca reacted quicker, wrapping her arm around Matt's neck, using his body to shield herself, and jamming the barrel of her gun into his ribs. With one gun digging into him, and two more aimed at him, Matt looked terrified, and Leigh couldn't blame him.

"Let him go," Jake said.

"You expect me to just surrender? Have you any idea who you're up against, of who I work for?" she demanded.

"Oh, I know all about you, Melanie," he answered. At the mention of her real name her arm tightened around Matt's neck, and he squeaked. "I know all about your dishonourable discharge from Special Forces, and then you got a second chance with Lantry, but you blew that too when you betrayed him." That was news to Leigh. "So what's it going to be?" he asked, still maintaining that low even tone.

Leigh wondered how he was going to bring this to an end. Based on her experience with this woman, there would only be one outcome.

"You wouldn't dare kill me," she returned to Jake.

"What makes you think that?"

"I know too much. You need me."

"Again, what makes you think that?" That threw her, but a flicker of her eyes betrayed her. Jake turned Leigh around to face behind them,

191

timing it well as another accomplice entered the scene. Leigh took aim on Danny as his opening shot went wide. Bianca counted on Jake reacting, taking a shot at him. His retaliation was swift, a through-and-through hit Matt in the shoulder, continuing on to impact into Bianca. She stumbled back, releasing Matt, unable to hold him as he crumpled to the ground. Danny disappeared down the corridor, and instead of chasing after him, Leigh turned back to the action behind her. Undeterred by her wound, Bianca took aim again, this time at Leigh, but already poised for action, Leigh shot first, hitting the other woman in the chest, causing her to fall back against the wall. She hit it with a thud, the force of the bullet driving her back, before she slumped to the ground. Jake moved first, checking the body for any signs of life, a little disappointed to find her dead. He turned back to Leigh.

"You ok?" he asked. She continued to stare at Bianca's body, her first confirmed kill.

"Yeah," she answered, turning away. She looked at Matt still sitting and sobbing, cradling his injured shoulder. "Who else?" she asked him in a dangerously low tone.

"Just Danny," he admitted.

"That explains the numbers," Jake commented.

"You knew?" she asked, but he shook his head.

"I suspected, but I couldn't prove it," he answered.

"I'll deal with him."

"Be careful," he said, turning his attention to Matt. He hunkered down in front of him, reaching out to assess the extent of the injury, but his grip caused Matt more pain.

"So who else is there?" Jake asked him.

"No one," Matt screamed, before gasping for breath.

"It's not a serious injury, so I could keep this up all day. You, though, might pass out from the pain, and I'm not sure I've either the time or the patience to wait for you to come back around." Matt didn't need any further convincing.

"If there was anyone else, I don't know about them," he said.

"Who recruited you?"

"Some guy. I only met him once, and then that bitch arrived. I thought you were working with her, but then she threatened me, warned me not to say anything to you."

"Yeah, she's not known for her subtlety," Jake commented. "The guy, was he German?"

"Honestly, I couldn't tell." Sensing he'd gotten all he could, Jake stood and helped Matt up.

"Know where to find Danny?"

"I think he went to delete the files," Matt answered. That meant Leigh's office, and Jake pulled the injured man along with him.

From Danny's condition, Jake suspected Leigh of trying to extract information from him, but upon closer examination, Jake concluded Danny's injuries were the result of a fight between them, and one in which she'd come out the victor.

"Get anything of use from him?" Jake asked.

"No, but I stopped him deleting the files," she answered.

"Good."

"So now what?"

"We call in the cavalry," he answered, pushing Matt towards his accomplice.

"Lantry?" she asked, and he nodded, making the call.

"We need to make a copy of whatever he was doing," he said, and in a moment of serendipity, the computer beeped at completing the copy to a flash drive.

"Done," she answered, placing it with the rest of the evidence she'd collected. Silence and tension reigned while they waited for reinforcements to arrive. Isobel had already alerted Lantry before her ill-fated attempt to tackle the situation herself. Barnett arrived with the reinforcements, taking command, and scrutinising every aspect in his

193

usual slow and meticulous manner. He took in every detail, especially about the two bodies.

Barnett's team took Matt and Danny into custody, leaving Jake and Leigh to make their reports, which they did, separated and isolated in the interview rooms. With adrenaline wearing off, Leigh found her hand shook as she tried to write details of the events as they happened, but she stalled, and shivered, as images of shooting Bianca flashed before her eyes. She forced herself to write each act, and action, that she saw. Only when she described the entire chain of events, did she feel she'd exorcized some of the demons, and guilt.

Being better equipped, and experienced to deal with what'd happened, Jake finished first, and was the first to be debriefed by Barnett who then, armed with the facts and his initial assessment of the scene, had intimate knowledge of Leigh's part in it. Lee would've been proud of her, but watching her from the other side of the table, she seemed defeated. Barnett scanned through her report, ignoring the unusually shaky scrawl, at odds with her normally neat and tiny script.

"Tell me what happened," he said, in a softer tone than she'd heard in years.

"You read the report, everything's in there." She may have looked drained and defeated, but the hard edge belied how she looked. Definitely cast from the same mould as her old man, Tom thought. Her account was consistent with the American's, at least up until the point where they parted. And, he noted, their starting points were equally vague. Lantry gave her to the American as a resource, and Tom wondered how liberally the man had taken that. Tom didn't like it.

"How is it both of you got here at the same time?" he asked, trying to keep bitter jealousy at bay.

"Because he was with me," she answered.

"How was he with you?" he pushed.

"He needed access to American security databases, and he couldn't do it from here," she said.

"And Bianca? You delivered the kill shot. Why?"

"She didn't give much of a choice. She was hit, but refused to surrender. She was going to continue being a threat until she was suppressed, and in this instance that meant total suppression. Did you know her?" The question was unexpected.

"What?"

"Bianca, or Melanie, did you know her?" she asked, more adamant.

"How would I know her?"

"Because she was one of ours. Lantry recruited her about the same time as..."

"As?"

"They were killed." She watched him closely, enough to know this was news to him.

"How do you know this?" he asked.

"Does it matter?"

"It does if it's not true."

"And if it is?"

"If it is..." he hesitated. "If it is, and it was Lantry's op at the time, then keep your nose out of it. That's some friendly advice, heed it this time."

"This time?"

"Yeah, this time. You got yourself into this mess because you didn't listen to me the last time. And get a bag packed."

"Why?"

"You're finished here. Lantry wants you back at Huntington for a full debrief, and seeing as you've just proven your worth, you'll probably be part of the next phase, so you'll need to be there for that meeting. And if I were you, I wouldn't be asking too many questions." He closed the file and left.

Chapter 36

The shooting left Leigh with an uncharacteristic need for physical human contact, not that Jake minded when she knocked on his door. He tried to get her to talk, but she disregarded his efforts, overpowering him, not that he put up an effort to fend her off. Her emotions were in turmoil, and they fuelled her passion, making her more aggressive. He understood the emotions driving her, and even with his experience in the field, situations like they'd just encountered, often caused him to react in a similar way.

He tried to pull her back into bed, but she twisted her arm free with little effort.

"I have to pack," she murmured, the most she'd said all night.

"That won't take long, and the flight isn't until this afternoon," he answered. She continued dressing, but gave him a smile, one of the cute shy ones, with a quirky twist that made her look much younger in the early morning light. He watched her leave, knowing her need for solitude had returned. She wasn't that complicated to work out, once he understood her little quirks, and what lay beneath them.

He lay back, closing his eyes for a moment with every intention of having a quick nap. He woke hours later with his phone ringing, and Leigh pounding on the door.

He took a seat in the departure lounge, scanning people dotted about, more out of habit than anything else. He glanced back at Leigh as she waited in line for coffee.

"Guten tag, Jaran." The unmistakable voice came from behind him, as Karl walked around and took the seat opposite Jake, giving him a friendly tap on the arm with the large envelope he held.

"Was willst du? *(What do you want?)*" Jake demanded. "Irgendwie habe ich glaube nicht, dass du hier bist, sich zu ergeben *(somehow I don't think you're here to surrender)*."

"Nein, das kann nicht *(no, not quite)*," Karl answered, opening the jacket of an expensive suit. They looked like two business men having a chat.

Karl glanced across at Leigh, and caught her watching them with an inscrutable expression on her face. She then turned back to order from the barista. Another expression scarily like her father's, Karl thought.

"Did you get my peace offering?" Karl said.

"I did," Jake answered.

"In custody?"

"Dead."

"Probably the only way she was ever going to go quietly," Karl conceded.

"Why?" Jake asked, and the question surprised Karl.

"There's a proverb about gift horses."

"You're not known for your generosity," Jake shot back, and Karl laughed. It seemed surreal to Jake, like two old friends just sharing a laugh, like they used to do, a long time ago. Karl watched as Leigh approached them.

"Perhaps we have a mutual friend to thank for that," he answered. Leigh returned with three steaming cups, handing Jake his first, before giving one to Karl, and sitting down with her own brew.

"What are you doing here?" she asked him, and her conversational tone stunned Jake. Karl held up the large envelope before lobbing it across to Jake.

"Everything you need on the visas," he told them.

"What do you mean by everything?" she asked, glancing at the package.

"I mean everything, who hired me, who was involved, everything."

"Why?" she asked, before Jake could.

"The visas don't interest me, it's just business, same shit just a different commodity. Maybe I'm tired of running, of having to hide from something I didn't do," he answered to Leigh, but glanced at Jake. He

197

checked the departure board. "Well, that's my cue," he said standing. He looked to have more to say, but instead he just gave Jake a nod, before leaving. Jake turned on her.

"How? He's the guy who killed your folks, and you just handed him coffee, like he's your best friend?" The anger in his voice was unmistakable.

"I don't think he did it," she answered.

"How can you be so sure?" he demanded. "Have you slept with him?" She sat back, keeping a tight rein on her temper. "Are you working with him?" he pressed.

"I'm not working with him," she answered.

"But you've slept with him?" Jake inferred from the unanswered question.

"No," she answered. He looked relieved. "But then again, I haven't slept with you either," she said, adding more fuel to the blaze. "As I recall, there wasn't much sleep involved."

"So you lied to me? You had sex with him?"

"That wasn't the question you asked," she answered in that cold manner that began to infuriate him. "He sent the third and fourth journals to my solicitor for safe keeping. He personally gave me the fifth journal to decrypt. If it does contain information about who's behind all this, then why would he give it to me, if it was him all along?"

"Did he hand over the journal before or after you had sex with him?" Jake pressed. She clenched her jaw to stop herself giving him a bitchy remark.

"Before," she answered.

"So you did have sex with him," he stated. "What was it, to say thanks?" She leaned forward, bristling with anger.

"What the fuck is your problem? You've had sex with Bianca, and no doubt with loads of other women who've crossed your path, but when I start behaving like a man, your pride takes a beating? Who I do, or don't have sex with is none of your concern."

"Oh yes it is," he shot back.

"You have no exclusive rights, or privileges, here. Or is it because it was Karl? Would you react the same way if it had been Matt?"

Her remark and question stung. The look on his face was all the answer she needed, and she felt a smug sense of satisfaction at hitting on target. This was the very reason she opted to stay free of emotional entanglements. It just got too messy. She picked up her bag, and went to the departure gate. With their flight number flashing on the boarding screen, he knew he'd have to follow her.

He grabbed the envelope Karl left, deliberating what to do with it, before stuffing it into his backpack until he had a chance to assess the contents. He wondered about Leigh. What was she playing at, or had Karl somehow managed to turn her? He boarded the plane and buckled himself into the seat beside her.

"And FYI," he said aggressively. "That psychotic bitch had to drug me to get me into bed."

She bit back another snippy and scathing retort.

"So was he better?"

She turned to look at him, astounded by the petty question.

"No," she answered. "But neither were you."

Suitably humbled, he sat back, ignoring her for the rest of the flight.

Heading to the awaiting car, he caught up with her.

"Anyone would think you were acting like a jealous lover, or a wounded boyfriend," she said, breaking the silence as they reached the doors. "Lantry is going to pick up on it, so if that's what you want, then by all means, continue to sulk, but you'll give him another weakness that he'll have no hesitation in exploiting."

"What do you mean 'another weakness'?" he demanded.

"You believe Karl set that bomb, and Lantry continues to exploit your hatred of him," she answered. She got into the back seat of the car, sliding across to make room for him. He got in beside her, mulling over what she'd said. She was correct, he had no right to feel jealous, but damn it, did it have to be Karl?

She was also correct about Lantry. That man was an excellent manipulator, but was she correct about Lantry exploiting his hatred of Karl? Had he fuelled that hatred? He sat back, watching the countryside pass by, but his mind was elsewhere as he thought back to that horrendous time, remembering the agony of the surgeries, the excruciating pain as his face and body healed.

"I never questioned him," he muttered, keeping his voice low enough so the driver couldn't overhear.

"Question who?" she asked, with no trace of animosity.

"Chris, when he said Karl was responsible for the bomb."

She chuckled.

"Is that how he phrased it?"

"Pretty much word for word."

"Then he didn't lie to you. He simply allowed you to interpret it in the way you did. If what we've discovered is right, then it was meant for Karl, it was set up for him, he was the reason the bomb was there, and he was the reason you were there, ergo, it was his fault, and his responsibility."

"That's fucked up logic."

"It's the logic that keeps me in the lifestyle to which I've become accustomed."

"Seriously?"

"Seriously."

"I shouldn't have reacted like that," he admitted.

"No, you shouldn't have," she agreed. "Did it ever cross your mind that perhaps I'm using him?"

"Were you?" She shrugged in reply.

"I found out Bianca was his, and I found out more about my dad."

"You told him about me," he said, but she shook her head.

"I inferred, he worked it out. I just agreed with his conclusion."

"You're almost as tricky with words as Chris."

She laughed at that.

"He said he tried to warn you, yelled at you to get out."

"I don't remember that, but I don't remember anything about the whole incident."

"So it's possible he could be telling the truth?" Another question that stung him.

"It's possible, I guess."

"Lantry has put me on this path of vengeance, but I'm not going to blindly follow. It's not in my nature, and it's also bad for business to not question assumptions, or given information."

"So I'm blindly following orders?"

"You're the only one who can answer that." There it was again, that cool logic, but he had to admit, it was true. He'd chased after Gouderhoff without question, without sifting through the evidence first. So much for the intelligence part of the job description.

"I didn't think I had to question it," he said, as the car came to a stop in front of the main entrance to Huntington House.

Chapter 37

The debriefing at Huntington turned into an arduous affair, taking longer than the one with Barnett. They were barely in the door when they were escorted to the interview rooms, and separated again. A senior agent, doing what could only be described as an interrogation, tried probing deeper into the little things, such as the fight with Bianca. Leigh's analytical mind already jumped ahead, working out the agent's hidden agenda. Had she shot Bianca to prevent her from revealing something, or had she pulled the trigger before she could compromise Leigh?

The years of experience with Barnett were now worth all the aggravation and sufferance, and Leigh refused to be pushed, or bullied into admitting anything. The matter of the first journal surfaced, and yet again Leigh denied its existence, hoping Jake would also keep quiet about them. If he didn't, then it would come down to his word against hers, but he also had copies on the e-pad. Had he brought that with him, she wondered. Would her actions with Karl cause him to turn her in? She didn't think he would, but doubts crept in.

By the time she finished, a considerable time later, she found herself torn between exhaustion and hunger. Exhaustion won out, but sleep eluded her. She lay in bed, replaying the interview in her mind, analysing the questions and her answers, satisfied with her performance. Yet, she still felt troubled.

Giving up on sleep, she redressed, and headed to the Mess Hall for a snack. As a functioning operational facility, as well as a training centre, the place was well equipped to cater for everyone, but even that seemed destined to go unfulfilled as she found herself unable to eat, in spite of the hunger. She picked at her food instead, playing with it, and toyed with the idea of finding Jake, but decided to leave him be. She wouldn't exactly make for ideal company at the moment, and she doubted he'd want to talk to her. She needn't have worried, as moments later Jake appeared, looking tired and grumpy. He acknowledged her with a nod and a smirk, and joined her once he'd gotten a coffee.

"I'd forgotten how slippery that guy was," he said, sitting opposite her.

"Lantry?" she asked, and he nodded.

"He's very interested in your journals."

"And?"

"And what?" he teased, but she was too tired to play games, and waited him out. "He's still none the wiser," he told her.

"Thank you."

"Not until we figure this out, right?"

"What's this 'we' business?" she asked. He leaned in closer, keeping his voice low.

"It affects me too, you know," he said.

"I know. And Karl?"

"Still annoyed, but..."

"But what?" she asked. He shrugged, and sat back.

"It's not like you were giving him access to the visas, but I have been thinking. What if it wasn't him, after all? What if he *is* a victim, a convenient scapegoat?" he asked.

"But by whom?"

"That sweetheart, is why you need to crack that last notebook."

"You think I haven't been trying?"

"Yeah, sorry, I know you have. But please tell me it'll be worth the interrogation I just went through. I haven't encountered anything that bad in a long time."

"You too, huh?" she asked, and he recognised her weariness.

"When'd you finish?"

"Not that long ago. I think she got tired asking the same questions in different ways, but getting the same answer," she said, and Jake laughed.

"No wonder Chris wished me luck in trying to interrogate you. How the hell did you ever get that good at it?"

"Barnett," she said. He looked at her expectantly. "There's not much to tell."

"I'm all ears."

"There were times, when I was younger, when he had to pull me out of nightclubs. Most of the time, I'd either be drunk, or stoned, or both, and he'd grill me about where I'd been, who I'd been with, and where I got the drugs. At one stage we were becoming a double act, it occurred so regularly, but with Tom, you had to listen to the questions. He had a knack of tripping you up, and catching you out. Once I figured his game out, it no longer worked on me. I learned to fix the answers in my head, and just keep repeating them on cue, and block everything else out."

"Well, didn't you have all the lucky breaks," he answered.

"Yeah, aren't I just blessed," she replied. He chuckled, but pushed his half-finished coffee away.

"I have to ask, this thing with Karl…"

"It's nothing."

"But how?"

She sighed, deliberating how much to tell him.

"The night Isobel ended up in hospital with concussion, and I went missing…" she started, and he nodded. "Well, I sort of lied to Tom."

"Only sort of?"

"Yeah, I was a bit economical with the truth, and I didn't know who the hell you were, so why would you think I'd tell you anything. I was knocked out, just like I said."

"But I'm guessing not dumped in the middle of nowhere."

"No, I woke up at his place, and he behaved so bizarrely for someone I'd thought wanted to kill me. He acted so casually, made me a coffee, talked to me, then handed me the journal. Those aren't the actions of someone hell bent on killing me. So, I sat, and I listened, and I gave him the benefit of the doubt."

"And then you slept with him?"

Her eyes narrowed in annoyance at his inability to drop it.

"No, not that time." He looked at her, confused and puzzled. "I went back after my encounter with Bianca."

"But you went home that time," he stated, confirming her suspicions that her movements had been monitored.

"And all my cars had trackers on them, so you're wondering how I managed it, or that he's in the Carlow area," she put to him, and he nodded. "I have a car Tom knows nothing about."

"Karl not only allowed you to leave, but he allowed you to know where to find him?"

She nodded, astounding him. These were not the actions of the enemy he thought he knew.

"He must have sent you intel about Bianca, after he saw what she did to me," she went on, and he nodded.

"Altruism and caring are not words I associate with him."

"Me neither, but the affection for him which my father wrote about, maybe it's tempered my attitude towards him. And yes, I slept with him that time, but it got him talking, and he was quite open about things, details. From what I gather, my father also used sex to extract information from an asset, or reluctant informant. It's not something I have a moral hang-up about, it's just sex. I don't do emotional or romantic attachments. It's just pleasure, without the guilt, or the hassle." For the most part she reflected his own attitude, and he'd used that act for the same purposes. It was as she said, just sex. So why was he getting hung up about it now, he wondered.

"And meeting him at the airport?" he asked. She shrugged.

"I have no idea how he knew we'd be there."

"You didn't contact him, let him know?" he probed, thinking of all the time she'd had to herself, between the time she left him, and the time she knocked on his door. She shook her head.

"I'm not that stupid to try contacting him. I had no means to do so, without it being traced, nor had I any reason to. I do suspect he's got bugs in Shannon, the arrangements could've been easily overheard." Her reasoning made sense, and Jake believed her. He had no reason not to. He stood and pushed the seat back into place.

"I'm too tired to worry about it now," he said.

"Same here, but I couldn't sleep, that's why I came down."

"Come on, then," he said, ushering her out with him. "Let's see if we can do something about that."

He woke, surprised to find her still in bed with him, and still asleep, barely stirring as he pulled his arm out from under her. No doubt Lantry knew of their sleeping arrangements, but Jake didn't care. If it was out in the open, then it couldn't be exploited, as Leigh suggested, and he'd already experienced insinuations during his so-called debrief. Again, Leigh was correct; Lantry was more than capable of using everything, and anyone, for his own purposes. He pulled clothes from his bag, finding the envelope Karl gave him. He sat back down on the bed, careful not to wake her, and opened the envelope, pulling out a considerable number of documents. It was every intelligence-gatherer's dream, and he had to admit, he admired Karl's attention to detail and cross-referencing, but if the information was to be believed, it caused him grave concern, and Jake felt chilled. Leigh stirred, and opened her eyes, giving him the barest of smiles before stretching. She looked innocent, and so much younger when she was relaxed, like now, and in spite of only a four-year difference in their ages, he felt ancient in comparison to that seeming innocence. She stopped her stretch at seeing his expression.

"What is it?" she asked, her voice still throaty from sleep.

"I need to contact Swayne," he said, dressing as quickly as he could.

Chapter 38

"Where did you get this?" Lantry asked.

"I have my sources," Jake answered.

"Leigh?"

"She's nothing to do with it."

"And this Senator of yours?"

"That's the worrying part. She's here, in the UK, a place called Sussex."

"And she has no idea?"

"None. I made it sound like I was just checking in, giving her an update on what happened, but I didn't tell her about this. From the sounds of it, she's shacked up in some country estate, miles away from pretty much anywhere. I didn't want to spook her."

"But you're thinking extraction?" Lantry asked.

"Only if it can be done safely," Jake said, sitting the other side of the large mahogany desk from the Director.

"I'll send a hunting pack to assess the situation, and establish infiltration points."

"I appreciate that Chris, but I want to be there, just so she'll have a friendly face."

"So much for returning home to a quiet desk job," Lantry said, chuckling. "That was never going to satisfy a man of your talents and abilities. You were very efficient with eliminations, for a man of your age. It's too bad you never caught him."

Jake bit back a retort at the jibe, a dig at his continuing failure to catch, or kill, Karl. Leigh's reading of this man was on target, and he wondered how he'd overlooked these traits before, but she'd had the benefit of her father's insights before meeting him.

"Take Leigh with you," Lantry added, looking to be deep in thought, and stroking his goatee. "It'll be good experience for her, and in your report, you indicated she's capable of following orders."

"You sound surprised, Chris," Jake commented.

"Yes, a little," Lantry admitted. "She's not what I'd consider a team player, and I'm not usually wrong about those I recruit."

"Slipping up in your old age," Jake joked, but Lantry did not appear amused by the comment. Instead he scanned through the pages Jake gave him, photocopies of select pages from Karl's document.

"The intel is reliable?" he asked again.

"Unquestionable," Jake answered.

"From a cousin?" Lantry asked. God, Jake thought, this guy loved his spy talk, and while it was an integral part of their world, at times like this, it got on his nerves.

"No, European," Jake answered, seeing a frown cross Lantry's forehead, and Jake held back a smirk, now understanding the juvenile delight Leigh got from antagonising the man. Lantry assumed the source to be American. That it was European, and Lantry didn't have one of his own people on it, disturbed and annoyed the Director. Jake recalled Lantry's obsession with details, and at the time, a much younger, less experienced, and more easily impressed boy admired that trait. Now, it just seemed another form of cross-examination.

"I'll notify you when the team's ready to leave," Lantry said, effectively dismissing Jake, who nodded, but a plan of his own already formed in his mind.

He found Leigh again in the Mess Hall, finishing breakfast.

"Well?" she asked.

"He's pimped you out again."

"Really? And if I refuse to come out and play?"

"Yeah, he said you weren't a team player."

"Considering that's coming from Lantry, and the minor detail that neither was my father, I'll take that as a compliment."

He leaned in closer.

"And you were right, there's a perverse pleasure to be had in holding back information, and in him knowing you're holding something back."

"Another lesson from dad. So what does he need me to do for you?"

"We're going for the Senator."

"But you said she sounded in good spirits, and the English guy she's with has no idea we're onto him."

"I know, but if our source alerted him, or even terminated his services, it might be enough to put him on edge. Maybe that's what pre-empted this sudden break away, and return to his home."

"You think he's hiding out, and plans to use her as a bargaining chip? You really care about her, don't you, and it goes beyond any sense of duty." His eyes hardened for a moment, but softened again as he blinked. By now he knew he shouldn't be surprised by her, her often deep insights into people were at odds with her human-interaction-free lifestyle. He smirked.

"She reminds me of my grandmother, that unique mix of blunt force, uncompromising compassion and minimum tolerance for bullshit," he answered. Leigh smiled.

"I like the sound of her already."

"Lantry's putting a hunting pack together," he told her, using the code for a surveillance team.

"But?" she asked, sensing more.

"I'm thinking we just knock on the front door," he said.

"Just arrive unannounced? He's bound to have his own security. There's no way we'll get past the gate."

"Not unannounced, but if I talk to her again, if I spin it right."

"Just happened to be in the neighbourhood?"

"Something like that."

"Ahead of, or in tandem, with the pack?"

"There's no way Lantry would sanction a solo run on this, not with the evidence we have. I'll get Chris to grant me lead on this. A US Senator's life could be at stake."

"When do we go?"

"As soon as the pack's ready."

A two-man team awaited them on the ground as their military chopper landed in the Sussex countryside, along with the car Jake requested while on the way, and he let Leigh drive. Swayne expected them. Jake's brief call to her organised that, but Swayne seemed more interested in the agent accompanying him, and she greeted Jake with a hug. Leigh however received a cool reception, followed by gentle but probing questions, which she found invasive. No wonder Jake liked her, and she saw the nod of approval from the Senator.

"I think you just passed the Swayne test," he whispered to Leigh.

"I heard that," Swayne said, ahead of them as she led them into one of the reception rooms in the grand house. At least Jake had the decency to look abashed at the reproach. "So Jake," Swayne went on, sitting in one of the oversized chairs. "What's so important that you came all the way down here?" Leigh liked the directness of the woman.

"I'd be remiss in my duties if I hadn't," he answered.

"Cut the bullshit," she told him, and Leigh bit back a laugh, while Jake tried to look offended.

"It's this situation with Bianca," he said, all business-like again.

"But you said she was dead," Swayne answered, her eyes flicking to Leigh for a moment. Jake obviously told her of Leigh's involvement.

"Yes, she is, but what we're concerned about is how easily she infiltrated EATA."

"And you suspect Jonathan was involved?" Swayne asked. Both Jake and Leigh heard the defensiveness in her tone, despite an effort to remain impartial, and Leigh now understood the depth of Jake's concern. The woman was emotionally involved with the Commissioner.

"Not involved," Jake lied with ease to her. "We're concerned for his safety, as well as yours." At least the last part was true, and Leigh began to see, that in his own way, Jake could be just as manipulating and devious as Lantry, as her father. Would she become like that, she wondered. The depth of self-loathing her father had, no longer puzzled her.

"You think he's in danger?" Swayne asked, and Jake nodded. The best cover stories always had strong elements of truth to them. It's what made them convincing.

"Whoever put her in place might look for retaliation for her death, and as the Commissioner who assigned her to the investigation, both suspicion and retaliation could fall on him," he said. Swayne sat back in her chair, mulling it over, watching them both intently. Leigh maintained a relaxed posture in her seat, but it required effort. Their freedom and access within this house depended on Swayne believing, and trusting them. That she trusted Jake was an excellent start. Swayne bought it.

"So what do you suggest?" she asked.

"I can have a team brought in to secure the place," he said.

"I hardly think that's necessary," a male voice from behind them said, startling Leigh. Jonathan entered the room and Jake stood, Leigh following his lead. "Agent Mann," Jonathan said, ignoring Leigh.

"With all due respect sir, I think it is," Jake answered.

"I have my own security," Jonathan answered back.

"And I've no doubt they're very good," Jake said calmly. "All I'm suggesting is an extra measure to ensure the Senator's safety."

"You weren't so concerned when you jetted off to Shannon," the Commissioner shot back. Swayne moved to intervene.

"Jake did put together a security team for me in Brussels," she said, taking hold of Jonathan's hand. Her gesture worked as he turned his glare from Jake to her, and softened.

"Yes, you're right, of course," he said, a lot gentler now. He turned back to the agent. "Wilma tells me you're to be our guests for a few days." Jake nodded.

"Only if it's not causing you any inconvenience," he answered.

"Extra security is always an inconvenience, but needs must," Jonathan said. As he moved to leave he noticed Leigh, as though for the first time. "And who are you?" he demanded, his tone gruff again.

"She's also MoD, from Huntington," Jake answered for her. "This is Agent Leigh Harte." Leigh had to admit, she liked the sound of the title, but not the Commissioner's reaction, as he gave her a startled, and horrified look. Not a reaction she'd ever experienced before, but Medlington departed without another word.

"I think the whole Bianca affair rattled him," Swayne said by way of an apology. "It's nothing personal Leigh, he's probably just shocked to have the person who killed her in his home." Leigh nodded in understanding, her own thoughts contrary to Swayne's theory. A quick glance at Jake confirmed he wasn't buying that explanation either. He'd seen the man's expression.

With the chance to remove herself from Swayne's watchful eyes, and remain out of the Commissioner's way, Leigh opted for assessing the perimeter with a member of Medlington's security team, mentally noting where the MoD team could penetrate when necessary. Jake checked the house, Swayne joining him.

"What's really going on, Jake?" she asked him.

"What makes you think there's anything going on?" he countered.

"Because Jonathan's right, you've just put a stop to the visa problem, but this German guy is still out there. I'm sure there's a lot to follow up that should be taking up your time," she said, watching him check the windows of her room.

"What if I asked you to just trust me?"

"So there is something else, something more," she concluded, and he sighed.

"Do you, or don't you, trust me, Senator?" he asked.

"Of course I do," she answered.

"Good, then please drop it for the moment," he told her, before she could add anything more. He moved to the next room, and again she followed him.

"Have you gotten any further with your past, and what you found out?" she asked, keeping the conversation going as he worked.

"There's been some progress," he answered.

"And?"

"There's been some progress," he repeated. Her mouth tightened in mild frustration at not getting decent answers from him.

"And Leigh?"

"What about her?"

"You're in love with her."

He stopped and stared at her.

"What? No!" he denied.

"You're not that good a liar, Jake," she told him, and he heard that tone again, the one reminiscent of his grandmother.

"I... No!" he told her, brushing past to continue with his task.

She continued to follow him but she kept her distance, admiring the thoroughness and efficiency of his actions, and now and then, he'd stop and look at her before turning back and shaking his head.

Chapter 39

Wilma put her arms around him, startling him.

"I thought this trip was supposed to be a break from work?" she said, glancing at the file he'd been reading. He closed it, pushing pages back inside the cover.

"You're right, it is," he answered, swivelling around in his office chair to face her.

"And about time you realised it, mister," she teased him, and he laughed, sounding better than before. The investigation with the Commission had taken its toll on him, and this break, at his suggestion, was supposed to put some distance from the public furore. Perhaps the arrival of the agents brought the whole horrid affair crashing back around him. "I thought you left all your work behind," she added, indicating the file on the desk.

"It's not work," he told her.

"You look worried, what is it then?" she pushed. He shouldn't have been surprised by the direct question by now, but sometimes her frankness still caught him off guard.

"It's, ah, it's ancient history," he answered.

"How ancient?" she probed.

"Before Rachel..." he said, and she understood this had to do with his late wife.

"Is it having me here, in your home?"

"Oh, dear god no," he answered, astounded she would think that.

"So what is it then?"

"Perhaps it's having MoD agents in the house," he admitted. And one in particular, she thought, not buying her own explanation for his behaviour towards Leigh. She'd been expecting someone much younger from Jake's description, and his constant referral to her as a kid, but in truth she wasn't that much younger than Jake.

"How about a walk in the gardens, get some fresh air," he suggested.

"Oh, it's fresh alright, with a deluge of rain."

"Oh," he said, sounding defeated again.

"It's her anniversary soon, isn't it?" she asked. Perhaps that explained his mood.

"Tomorrow," he admitted, confirming her guess. She kissed his forehead.

"I'll leave you in peace then," she said.

"Don't," he answered, taking hold of her hand as she started to move away. "You could come, if you like, tomorrow." He sounded sad and lost, and she smiled.

"Only if you're sure," she said, and he nodded.

"I'm sure." He stood. "If the weather's that inclement how about a hot chocolate, by the fire?" he suggested, putting his arms around her.

"Marshmallows?" she asked.

"And ruin a perfectly good beverage?" he teased, and she tried to pull away, but he wouldn't let her.

"Okay okay, you can ruin it in any way you please," he said.

"And whipped cream," she added.

"Now you're pushing it," he said, but laughed, letting her go. "I'll pop down to the kitchen and ask Ruth to make some, and I'll bring them up to the library."

"I'll wait for you there," she said, watching him leave. With him out of sight, and unlikely to reappear, she turned to the closed file. Peeking through it, she found a picture of an attractive man, but the name surprised her, the same as young Agent Harte. A quick flick through the pages confirmed her as his daughter. Deeper into the file Wilma found surveillance photos of the man with Rachel. She'd seen a picture of Jonathan's wife and recognised her in these compromising photos. Little wonder Jonathan reacted in the way he did on hearing the Irish woman's name, especially if her father had an affair with his wife. From young

Leigh's reaction she was unaware of her father's connection here, but Wilma found that unnerving. It was as Jake said, there were too many coincidences, too many seemingly random elements turning out to be not so random as first thought, and all of them starting to converge. Wilma closed the file back over and left, knowing Jonathan would come looking if he didn't find her in the library. In reality, it was a glorified den, complete with oversized chairs, and a large fireplace. She'd just settled in when Jonathan arrived with steaming mugs of hot chocolate, hers complete with a generous helping of whipped cream piled on top, and covered in mini marshmallows.

The next day Medlington's driver brought them to the old cemetery, a short distance from the nearest town. This had been Rachel's home as a child, and where they'd settled after they married. Even after all this time, he never thought to move elsewhere. This was where he'd made his home, with her. Swayne stood a respectful distance behind him, watching as he placed a simple wreath of flowers at the headstone. At least the weather improved a little, the rain stopping during the night, but the drop in temperature resulted in a heavy frost, turning the countryside into a picturesque winter wonderland. Picture perfect, but treacherous for walking and driving.

Jake and Leigh travelled in the car behind them and Jake now stood behind her, watchful, scanning their surroundings, and to Swayne he seemed tense, a tightly wound coil about to spring. His partner was nowhere to be found, and she didn't want to make it obvious by glancing around. While she had no doubts about Jake's abilities, something about his movements made her nervous, and what he wasn't telling her served to heighten her own senses. She noticed when he spoke into the mic, discreetly hidden in the cuff of his coat, its corresponding earpiece in his left ear, like the ones she'd seen the Secret Service use. She presumed he was in contact with Leigh somewhere on the outer fringes of the cemetery. These security measures didn't make her feel safe. She felt trapped, and without all the facts, she felt helpless; a sensation she rarely experienced, or liked.

Jake gave Leigh the signal she'd been waiting for, but as the baby of this operation, she held back, following behind but at enough of a distance to be of some use without getting in the way. On hearing the intended schedule for this excursion, Jake and the team commander devised this plan for the 'snatch and grab'. Out in the open, they had a greater chance of success, rather than attempting to infiltrate the house.

The tactical plan was to approach from three sides. While the Commissioner faced the headstone, the assault team would come from behind and sides, while another team lay in wait. Leigh knew Jake's game plan, as he assigned her to the team less likely to make contact, but on hand for support. Otherwise their approach would be in full view of the Commissioner, eliminating the element of surprise. Jonathan however noticed movement from the corner of his eye, and reacted quicker than Jake anticipated, grabbing hold of Swayne, the very scenario Jake wanted to avoid. The weapon the Commissioner alleged to have remained hidden in his overcoat pocket. Yet Jake couldn't take the chance with Swayne's life on the line, and he signalled a halt to the approaching assault team.

"What the hell is going on?" Swayne demanded despite her predicament, but was clearly scared.

"I'm so sorry, my dear," Jonathan whispered in her ear. "It should never have gone this way."

"What shouldn't have?" she demanded of him. He didn't get the opportunity to answer as he felt the barrel of a gun press into the back of his neck. Bringing up the rear had its advantages, as Leigh stood behind him, her smaller stature going unnoticed by Medlington.

"Let her go," she growled. The prospect of death didn't appeal to him, not when he knew he could bargain for immunity from prosecution, once he was allowed to make a phone call. He let Swayne go, and Jake grabbed her, pulling out of danger, his weapon fixed on Medlington.

With her gun still to his head, Leigh reached for the concealed weapon, both relieved and dismayed to find only a spectacles case in his pocket.

"You're just like your father," Jonathan said to her. "He was a devious bastard too."

"Why, thank you," she answered, knowing it wasn't meant as a compliment, but the comment puzzled her. Nowhere in the journals had her father mentioned this man. She stepped back, allowing the assault team to bundle the Commissioner away to an awaiting van, leaving Jake and Leigh with a visibly shaken Swayne.

"Is this what you couldn't tell me about?" she demanded of Jake, and he nodded, his cold and seemingly heartless demeanour frightening her. She thought she knew him, thought she'd seen into the depths of him, but she hadn't anticipated this, this callous man, and the reality of who and what he was hit her. He was a trained killer. Even the cool exterior of Leigh seemed to radiate warmth in comparison. "At least tell me what he was involved in," she demanded.

"The visas." It was Leigh who answered.

"Impossible," Swayne turned that anger on the young woman.

"Senator, I asked you to trust me," Jake's voice was as hard and cold as their surroundings. "We wouldn't be here if we didn't have the evidence to back it up."

He took hold of her arm and led her to the vehicles waiting to return them to Huntington.

Chapter 40

The explanation never came, not to Swayne's satisfaction. Denied access to Jonathan, she became less assured when Jake also failed to secure answers. After a tense drive back to the house to collect her things, and a bumpy helicopter ride to Huntington, tempers flared. Even with her attempts at a brave face, Swayne was shaken by the experience. Jake offered her reassurances, but she'd seen his true and predatory nature. If she thought she'd learned how to read people, this latest misadventure proved how much she'd been kidding herself. She felt betrayed by him, but she knew that sense of betrayal lay within herself.

Leigh remained a mystery to her. The younger woman remained silent on the journey back, not that conversation was desirable, or even possible, above the noise of the rotors and engine. Leigh glanced at the Senator every so often, receiving an angry glare in return. Even the glaring seemed not to faze this girl, and Wilma wondered if her instincts were also off there.

Safely inside Huntington, the Senator had time to rest and freshen up before meeting Lantry, and there she learned the awful truth of Jonathan's crimes. While she found Lantry clinical in his approach to the facts, something remained amiss, and Wilma sat in silence as he casually read through the list of offences. How could she have been so off? How could she have been so wrong about this man? To make matters worse, Jonathan wasn't even at Huntington. At least that was also news to Jake, and Wilma had a childish sense of satisfaction knowing he was just as surprised. She wanted to face Jonathan, to question him herself, and now even that was denied her. He was being held in custody in London, and miles away from her.

She felt powerless. It had been a long time since she'd felt that way, and she didn't like it. Lantry explained how the British Home Office intervened, taking over the case on account of Medlington's position and political persona within the EU. Such scandal reflected badly on the

British political system. Swayne asked to see the file, but Lantry flatly refused, the finality of his tone surprising even Jake, who sat forward to argue for access to the information, and Swayne saw that predatory look again. Unlike with her, that look didn't faze Lantry, but then she doubted this man could have achieved his position if a dangerous look threatened him. The two men squared off, but Jake knew from experience just how far he could push this man. He sat back knowing if he pushed too far Lantry wouldn't hesitate to push back stronger, and harder. And there was still the question of where Jake got his information. Push Lantry too hard, and Jake put himself and Leigh in the firing line. Jake began to understand the depths of Leigh's hatred and mistrust of this man, and he allowed that to guide him now.

He tried to warn Swayne about Lantry before this meeting, but she remained angry, and Jake let the snippy comments slide, knowing the woman was still in shock, though he expected her to handle the situation better than she did. If her behaviour concerned him, then her request to speak with Leigh came from left field. He hesitated, weighing up whether to question her about it, but she gave him a look that told him she was in no mood to have her motives quizzed by him. A short while later she answered a knock on her door, half-expecting Jake on the other side. Lantry hinted at Leigh's anarchic tendencies, so Swayne was a little surprised to find her standing on the other side of the door. Without exchanging a word, Swayne stepped aside, allowing Leigh in. Leigh sat, relaxed, and if Swayne expected nervousness, she was disappointed.

"You're wondering why I asked to speak with you?" Swayne began.

"Jake?" Leigh guessed, a little surprised when Swayne shook her head.

"No, but we'll get to him later," the Senator answered, handing Leigh a file, and sat to watch her reaction, but Leigh continued to disappoint her.

"Where did you get this?" Leigh asked.

"Jonathan had it. I took it when I collected my things," Swayne answered. "I thought you'd appreciate knowing how he knew your father. It seems he was having an affair with Jonathan's wife." At last a reaction, a look of surprise, but Leigh shook her head as she held up a photo, one of the pair in a compromising embrace.

"I have plenty of photos at home of my mother and father, so I can say with some authority that that is not an affair. His look is predatory. She was either a target, or an asset," she told Swayne, who refused to believe her, dismissing her claim as a misguided attempt to maintain her father's good image. "I'm under no illusion about the kind of man my father was," Leigh went on. "He could be ruthless, and devious, capable of using everyone and anyone he needed to. This picture tells me she was more likely an asset, which means Medlington was the target."

While Swayne liked the bluntness, she didn't like how Leigh now targeted Jonathan. She knew she needed to get a grip of herself, she continued to allow her emotions cloud and dictate her reactions, but it had been a long time since she'd allowed anyone in. It was natural to feel this hurt, but she knew she needed to grab hold of her senses again.

"I'm sorry," Leigh went on. "It's not my intention to upset you." As cold as this girl came across, Swayne heard the sincerity in her voice.

"Did losing your parents so young make you this hard?" Swayne asked, and to her surprise Leigh laughed.

"Honestly?" she asked, and Swayne nodded. "I'm not hard," Leigh admitted. "It's chronic shyness, which others interpret as hard, or aloof. Their deaths made me rebel, a lot."

"That's a very honest answer, for someone so shy," Swayne said, trying to keep the sarcasm at bay.

"Jake advised on openness and honesty with you."

"Oh, he did, did he?"

Leigh studied her closely.

"You hate him right now, don't you, for what he had to do, and how it came about?"

"You're not just a pretty face, are you?"

"As many have learned, to their cost," Leigh answered in that cool, matter-of-fact tone, and the old Swayne returned. The bullshit detector was back online, and she saw Leigh with a fresh look, finding a mask of respectability, technical expertise and indifference protecting a lost and lonely child. No wonder Jake fell for her. He'd found his kindred spirit, both growing up amid adversity, and both with the ability to switch off any, and all, emotional attachment out of self-preservation. Both of them survivors.

"Jake tells *me* you're the woman to go to if I want information," Swayne said.

"What do you need to know?" Leigh asked. Swayne shrugged, unsure herself.

"Lantry told me…," she started.

"No doubt a load of bullshit," Leigh finished.

"You really don't trust him, do you? Neither does Jake."

"He doesn't make it easy to trust him."

"We're all in agreement on that then. But he said Jonathan's been involved in illicit things for a very long time," Swayne said.

"There's nothing on the records here," Leigh told her, and it was Swayne's turn to look surprised. "I already checked," Leigh went on. "There's also no official record of my dad's involvement with his wife either."

"So how …" Swayne mused to herself.

"How did Lantry know what Medlington was up to?" Leigh asked, and Swayne nodded. "That's what Jake, and I, have been wondering." Leigh flipped back through the file again, concentrating on the details, but the file was too staged. If it was sent to Medlington instead, it would have served as a threat to either pull the man back into line, or as a deterrent to prevent him from betraying whoever pulled his strings.

"Possibly it was a black op," Leigh volunteered, which would explain the lack of available information. "I can tell you where they're holding him," Leigh said, offering Swayne some token of hope.

"He's at their HQ in London," Swayne answered, but her confidence dropped another notch as Leigh shook her head.

"He's being held in Manchester," she answered.

"Are you sure?"

"Of course I'm sure." That cold aloofness returned. "Would you like to pop down and say hi?"

"Lantry's just going to let us drive down?"

"Who says Lantry needs to know anything about it?"

"And we can just requisition a car like that?"

Leigh laughed at that.

"You really don't know anything about me, do you?"

"Only what Jake has told me," Swayne admitted. "Why?"

"Acquiring a car will be not a problem for me," Leigh answered.

Chapter 41

Operations Centre, Home Office, Manchester, UK

Jonathan Medlington sat handcuffed to the metal table before him. This unwarranted level of security and captivity felt demeaning, as did the interrogation he'd been subjected to. This shouldn't have happened, shouldn't be happening. His status within the intelligence community should've ensured him immunity from this kind of treatment, and safeguarded his freedom. He couldn't explain where it had all gone wrong, but he had a fair idea where to point the blame. Somehow his target turned the tables on him. It was the only conclusion he could come to, based on the evidence he'd been presented.

It was damning against him, but he'd done everything right, followed all the subtly worded orders and instructions issued to him from Head Office, and during meetings with his Intelligence Liaison Officers. So what the hell had gone wrong? He'd been on the verge of catching that arrogant German red-handed, ensnaring him in a three-way trap, using Swayne's US agent with Lantry's operatives to tighten the net and push the man into making a rash move. However, this was not the move any of them anticipated him making. Had Gouderhoff known? Had he suspected? Turned the tables on them all?

The inclusion of Lee Harte's child disturbed him even more. Now there was another arrogant prick Jonathan loathed with a passion. What was Christopher thinking by including her? How had that even come about? And that same arrogance as her father, Jonathan thought. He'd already demanded that he speak with Christopher, the only man who could explain and secure his freedom, but so far it proved to be a long wait. Amongst everything else, he thought about Wilma, and he hoped he'd have the opportunity to tell her everything, that he was not some heinous felon, but a man who still cared deeply for her. He'd seen the horrified look on her face, and he regretted his actions, regretted not having the opportunity to tell her everything.

The door opened, and he looked up, somewhat relieved to see one of his ILO's, but his hope of a swift resolution died as the man dropped a thick file onto the metallic table top, allowing the resounding thud to reverberate around the unadorned room. Paul dragged the vacant chair out, the legs grating against the floor creating a hideous noise. Jonathan knew it as another interrogation ploy, and realised this nightmare wouldn't come to an end anytime soon. The waiting game commenced but Jonathan held out, remaining silent. He'd already told them everything he knew, several times, and his story hardly varied. He knew that without Christopher's intervention he was damned anyway. He waited Paul out. Years dealing with politicians and bureaucrats gave him an edge in playing this game, but unfortunately he'd already played his only hand, he had nothing else to offer, to bargain with.

"It's not looking good, Jonathan," Paul finally said. Jonathan continued to watch him, refusing to answer. He had nothing left to say, nothing left to argue. "This whole thing with the visas, it all points right back to you, and that new designer bomb that killed the American....? Your EATA agent turned out to be not as wholesome as you reported. It's not looking good at all." Again Jonathan held his peace. "Tell me about Rachel's death," Paul said. That was enough to shake Jonathan.

"Rachel? What's she got to do with this?" he demanded.

"Maybe everything," Paul answered.

Jonathan shook his head.

"She had nothing to do with it, with any of it."

"That's not what her file suggests," Paul commented, flicking through pages. "A sniper's shot while she was driving. Now that's impressive."

Jonathan knew Paul was trying to goad him into making a rash move, but the only sign of unease and discomfort he showed was to shift in his seat, as much as he could with his restraints. "She was under direct monitoring from the Home Office Terrorism Unit. Now why would they need to do that?" Paul pressed. The malevolent look Jonathan gave Paul showed his level of hatred and told Paul he'd hit a nerve.

"Or you were the target that time, and she was used to get close to you," Paul continued to press. "Still, it doesn't look like she minded the attention." He threw an old photo onto the table, in Jonathan's line of sight, one he hadn't seen before, more sexually explicit than any of the other surveillance photos he'd seen, and the first hard evidence proving Rachel had a physical affair with that bastard Harte.

"I want to talk to Christopher Lantry, now," Jonathan answered, his rage starting to bubble to the surface. Even after all this time the betrayal still ate at him. Paul shook his head.

"Director Lantry is a very busy man," he answered.

"Listen, you little prick, you get Lantry here, now," Jonathan demanded, standing as best he could despite the shackles, but Paul appeared unperturbed by the reaction.

"Director Lantry is unavailable at this time," he answered in that pedantic tone that irritated Jonathan.

"I've already explained myself to you. Lantry was one of my handlers, and he can explain everything just as I have. Now get these fucking cuffs off me."

"Did you have your wife terminated?" Paul asked, ignoring the last statement. The Commissioner fought against his restraints at the question.

"How dare you?" he growled at his interrogator.

"I dare, *sir*, because it seems history is repeating itself. You were investigated back then. You'd been implicated in illegal arms transactions."

"I was an operative at the time," Jonathan answered. "That should be in my file."

"Oh it is, but you have a tendency to blur the boundaries."

"There was no blurring of boundaries."

"Sit down Jonathan, you'll break a wrist if you keep that up," Paul offered as Jonathan continued to wrestle with the cuffs. After a moment's consideration, Jonathan sat.

"Listen to me," he started. "All orders that time came from Lantry. Someone high up in government was involved in those transactions, and I was the inside spotter back then while I held a ministerial post. You and I are on the same side, working for the same people."

"So why was Lee Harte assigned to watch Rachel?"

"I don't know."

"Really? No idea at all?"

"None."

"Were you using her? Getting her to dead-drop information to your terrorist contacts?"

"You bastard."

"Maybe she was using *you*, and Harte was her agent provocateur, drawing her in, leading her to incriminate herself."

"Are you telling me he was the one who assassinated her?" Jonathan demanded.

"He would have been one of the few men capable of taking that shot, but no, he was already dead at the time. Did you turn him?"

"Turn him? To what?"

"Use him for your own purpose, have him deflect attention from you to Rachel."

"I hated the bastard. He was having an affair with my wife, why would I have anything to do with him?"

"Still, it's strange he was shot while investigating you and Rachel. Did he get too close to uncovering you?"

"Listen to me you little prick," Jonathan snapped back. "I had nothing to do with either of their deaths. I had nothing to do with any illegal arms trade, except to find out who it was at a high level."

"It's very strange that you never found them, just as you failed to capture this so-called German you allege is behind this latest operation."

"That so-called German used to be one of ours that went rogue," Jonathan argued back.

"So now you're claiming you were on a mission to catch him?"

"That's exactly what I'm claiming, and Lantry will back me up on that." Paul shook his head.

"Unfortunately for you, the Director is doing no such thing."

"What? Impossible. You and I have worked together. You know the operations we've been engaged in."

"More liaised than worked," Paul said, causing Jonathan to wonder even more where all this was leading. Had he just been burned?

"What do you really want?" Jonathan asked after a lengthy silence between them.

"Just the truth."

"Or a confession?"

"Whichever suits."

"I have nothing to confess, I've done nothing wrong."

"A jury won't see it that way, not that it would make it to trial."

"Are you threatening me?"

"Is there a reason you'd feel threatened?"

"I'm sure a review and analysis of this interview would show that."

"What interview?" Paul asked, confirming the inevitable to Jonathan as Paul gathered back up all the documentation and photos, and made a show of closing the file with a web-strap. Jonathan stared as the prongs of the strap bit into the cotton strip to hold the file closed, knowing it to be now a close parallel to his own life. Paul stood, picking the file up, pushing his chair back into place.

"Am I going to be black-flagged?" he asked.

"You already are," Paul answered, the silencer on the gun deadening the sound of the shot.

Chapter 42

Swayne had to admit she admired how well the pair worked together, and with military precision. While the time and weather conditions were far from ideal, the lateness of the night, combined with dense fog served them well, concealing their departure. Leigh procured a car, arriving at the designated side exit.

"Couldn't get anything more conspicuous?" Jake commented as he sat in the passenger seat. Swayne sat in the back.

"What?" Leigh shrugged.

"A Jaguar? Really?"

"We have a very important person on board," she said, trying to defend her choice of car.

"Bullshit," the very important person said from the back.

"It's the only car without a Lo-Jack tracker on it," Leigh explained.

"Why, whose is it?" Jake asked, suspicion mixed with curiosity.

"Lantry's," she answered, and Jake groaned in despair, while Swayne couldn't help smirking at the audacity of the agent. The conversation dropped to a minimum as Leigh concentrated on driving in such difficult conditions, but she still did so at speeds that were utterly dangerous in the hands of a less experienced driver. What should have taken them over four hours, she achieved in just over three, despite the fog that thinned and thickened at random.

The preprogrammed Sat-Nav led them to their destination, but it took persuading, threats and ID checking before sanction was granted, allowing them to enter. Leigh stayed in the car. The drive took its toll on her, and after finding a suitable place to park up, she promptly fell asleep in the driver's seat.

That a US Senator demanded access put the entire facility on alert. That she was connected with the detainee was of greater concern. That there was just no bullying her into backing down set tensions running high, and Jake knew Swayne was bouncing back to her old self. Having something to fight for restored her confidence and drive.

No doubt Lantry now knew of their whereabouts. After all, he'd sanctioned the initial operation, but he'd told Swayne that Medlington was in London. Had he deliberately misled them, or had he genuinely not known either, assuming the London office had the Commissioner in custody.

Somewhere along the chain of command, permission was granted as they were allowed past the reception area and into the inner sanctum. Swayne insisted on speaking with the Commissioner, to the point of being downright belligerent, and the clerk ceased trying to put up an argument. Swayne swept all arguments aside, so instead the clerk led them down to the holding rooms, crashing into another member of staff as they rounded a corner, causing the other man to drop the large file he carried. Jake reached the file first, picking it up, trying to read the file name as he handed it to the man, not surprised to find the words 'Top Secret' emblazoned in red, but in the handover Jake noticed the holstered gun beneath the man's jacket, puzzling Jake, as he'd been required to relinquish his own weapon before entering. He let it go and caught up with Swayne.

"I'll watch from the obs room next door," he said and Swayne smirked, that even in this secure place he wasn't allowing her to get far out of sight. Swayne gave Jake a look that said she'd be fine without him.

"You're worried he's going to try something?"

Jake shook his head.

"Actually, I'm thinking I'll have to save the poor bastard from you."

"Cheeky pup," she said, opening the door and froze, stifling a scream. Jake moved her out of the way and entered, seeing Medlington's body arched back over the chair though still shackled to the table. Jake went to the body, knowing it was pointless, but still checking for a pulse and getting a look at the wound. It was a clean and professional shot. Medlington would have died instantly with no pain, but the scratched

230

red skin around his wrists showed he'd struggled for a bit beforehand, and the horrified expression on the man's face said enough. Swayne entered, but Jake shook his head and ushered her back out, allowing the British in, fetched by the clerk who'd raised the alarm.

After a lengthy interview, recalling the man Jake bumped into, and who subsequently couldn't be found on the premises, Jake phoned Leigh. Her soft mumbled answer said she'd been asleep. How well rested was she, he wanted to know. He told her of Medlington's assassination, and a message from Lantry said to return to Huntington. Chris also made a snide remark about his missing car, but Jake didn't feel the need to tell her that. Leigh recognised the tone and didn't push, knowing he'd fill her in. If the conversation during the drive to Manchester was at a minimum, it became more sombre and subdued on the return journey, as did the pace, the sense of urgency now gone.

She returned the car to the garage and went to her room, finding Jake dozing on her bed, shoes off, but still dressed. She covered him with a blanket and while he stirred he didn't wake. She was too keyed-up to sleep, the earlier nap was enough of a rest, and it also knocked her off her normal rhythm. While she was physically tired, her mind refused to quieten, and she went in search of somewhere quiet, out of the way, to just sit and think undisturbed.

Those requirements led her back towards the guest quarters, towards Swayne's room, but Leigh by-passed it. While Leigh saw why Jake liked the woman, she found her too forceful, domineering, and intimidating. But Leigh knew herself to be easily intimidated by others, and therein lay the real reason she remained so much alone and shut off from other human interactions.

The only time she'd ever overcome that was through drugs and alcohol, among other things, gaining a sense of power and control. While the more mature part of her knew it was a completely false sense of control, a part of her still missed that sense of power, of no longer feeling scared all the time. Tom's harsh lessons knocked most of that out of her, but he didn't completely stamp out the rebelliousness that still lurked in the depths of her, only to resurface when she went to college.

In Germany though, she learned that control, finally getting clean, and living without drugs. She learned to hide her fear behind a mask of nonchalance and indifference. The fear of losing control again scared her the most, and Huntington pushed her to the point where that self-control cracked, when she'd shot Isobel at point-blank range, then threatened to shoot her in the head. Strangely though, it was only when that self-imposed control shattered, that she felt more powerful, calm, and in control.

That she was turning into her father gave Leigh some comfort, though he never displayed these characteristics when at home. But who was the real Lee, the cold, calculating agent, or the family man? Was it possible to be both, and if so, how? She wanted to know, needed to know. If it was possible, then how could both aspects be reconciled? Maybe they couldn't. Maybe they would forever remain two separate entities, and that self-control would always be required to keep them apart.

Leigh found the room she sought, having hidden there before; the library and music room. She sat by the window watching the day grow brighter, staring out at the woods beyond, and mulled life, and everything else, over in her mind. She hated these moments, these bouts of melancholy, and the accompanying emotions of feeling lost and alone.

This was what sent her into the sweet embrace of drug-induced ecstasy in her teens, and to more extreme pleasures in her early twenties. Even now the desire to indulge, to be rid of these feelings, grew strong, almost overwhelming, even after all these years of staying clean.

Swayne accused her of being hard, but nothing could be further from the truth. She'd answered Swayne honestly when she said her cool demeanour hid who she truly was. Not just the shyness she'd spoken of, but the moments of fear and panic before logic kicked in.

That hard shell served as a very successful defence mechanism, again courtesy of Tom. If she failed to show a reaction, emotional or

232

otherwise, others found her difficult to read, manipulate, or push her buttons. With another sigh, she took a deep breath, stretching to unknot her shoulders and upper back.

The baby grand piano, in the far corner of the room, drew her attention; the keyboard lid closed, yet a music book sat open on the music stand. She sat at the piano, thumbing through the book, finding it to be a collection of Beethoven Sonatas. Most of them she'd learned for exams, or used as sight-reading practice, and just like computer code, the dots on the lines made perfect sense to her.

She smirked as she remembered a conversation between her parents and her English teacher, discussing her as though she were invisible, but on the topic of her inability to spell correctly, and the regularity at which she mixed letters up. Her teacher accused her of laziness, and at the time dyslexia wasn't much heard of. A test much later in life proved she had a mild version of it, yet it worked to her advantage, computer code and music notes making perfect sense, and those codes came to life for her.

Now she looked at one of the sonatas, remembering how it sounded, rather than interpreting the written notes. That was how she'd always learned; reading the notes at the start, but then sound and memory took over. That she never looked at the music after that drove her mother to despair, knowing examiners preferred kids to look like they knew where they were in the music. Leigh could never do that. Looking at the sheet music distracted her, disorientated her, and if she had to resort to reading the score after already learning it, it had an adverse effect on her fingers. Engaging one aspect, disengaged the other.

Her mother could never figure it out. Her father found the conundrum amusing. Leigh never questioned it, just learned the notes, and then played without looking at the music. This particular sonata she remembered, she'd played it as part of her last graded exam. But that had been well over a decade ago, and whilst the written notes helped her remember how the melody went, her fingers seemed to have forgotten some of it. She played the opening chord, the action on the piano light, making the chord sound louder than she'd intended. She played through the next few bars, finding her left and right hand coordination not to be as inline as it used to be. Typing maintained the dexterity of her fingers, but she had to admit, playing the piano was much different, and she was rusty.

Nevertheless, she ploughed on through most of the first movement before flicking through the book again, finding another one she remembered, and began to play it. A couple of bars in she stopped, startled as old memories resurfaced, slamming into her as they smashed through the barriers she'd erected long ago.

She stood abruptly, fighting the tightness in her chest as she tried to breath. In her mind she saw a much younger Karl sitting beside her, both of them jostling for room on the piano stool, pushing and elbowing each other. All good natured fun. He'd been a good player, but he relied on the music more, following her mother's direction better than she did.

He taught her German. How could she have forgotten that? Was this why she'd avoided the piano and the music room for so long, fearing it would unleash so much, unlock the archived past. He hadn't been such a heinous character, more like a big brother.

The drugs, Tom and Germany served their purposes well in locking all this away, but now she wanted answers, and only one person could give them to her.

Chapter 43

Karl received the message he'd been waiting for, and dreading. Leigh wanted to talk. The text message gave the name of a hotel in London, and the time she planned to be there. He tried to send a reply, but it bounced back, meaning she'd turned off her phone, making it harder for anyone to track her.

Karl arrived at the hotel before her, watching from a quiet spot as she entered and requested a room for the night. While waiting for the paperwork to print out, she looked around the lobby, a measured scan of her surroundings. She spotted him, but returned her attention to the booking form requiring her signature. She paid in cash, despite being asked for a credit card. Her acting skills were flawless as Karl overheard her story about a stolen wallet. Karl laughed to himself at hearing the creative touches, such as the sympathetic, but ineffectual, cops. Yes tragic, but not uncommon, and really, she should have been more careful.

She dropped her backpack in her room before returning, and he followed her as she left the hotel, catching up with her outside. He knew of a quiet pub a short walk away, with a warm fire, and decent beer. Conversation was kept to a minimum as they walked, their breaths misting in the frosty air. The bar was quiet, and Karl found a vacant table by one of the fireplaces. A fresh shovel of fuel dampened the fire down for the moment, but fingers of flame snaked up, giving the promise of a roaring blaze soon. He ordered two beers for them, and then sat at the small table beside her.

"How did you escape so easily?" he asked.

"Got the train down," she answered.

"And no possibility of being tracked?"

"Left everything behind, mobile, e-pad, wallet..."

"So that yarn you spun the receptionist?"

"A bit economical with the truth, but true, I have no wallet."

"Good thing you had enough Sterling."

She sniggered at that.

"What?" he asked.

"Lantry's going to find his petty cash a little short."

"You didn't?" He didn't know if he was more pleased or shocked by her actions. A mixture of both perhaps. "Somehow I don't think your dad would approve."

"It's Lantry, so I really don't give a shit," she answered. "I took his car last night." As the information sunk in, he burst out laughing.

"Your dad made a point of antagonising Lantry, but he never stole his car. Which one?"

"The Jag."

Karl let out a low whistle.

"And you didn't get your ass handed to you?" he asked.

"Not yet," she said, sipping her beer slowly. They both fell silent for a moment, and to him she seemed to slip away as she stared into the fire. He waited her out until he feared he was losing her completely.

"What happened?" he asked, startling her.

"Medlington's dead," she told, him but only the tightening of his lips gave any indication of a reaction. "You don't seem surprised."

"I didn't do it," he said.

"Never implied you did," she replied. "But the information you gave Jake was enough to sign his death warrant."

"That, unfortunately, is the price for what we do."

"Did you know he was supposed to be MoD?"

That he nodded surprised her.

"And that dad was involved?"

Again he nodded.

"Lee wouldn't talk about it, and he sent me back to Germany at the time, said it was for my own safety."

"There's no file on it, that I could find," she told him, and he knew if she couldn't find it in cyberspace, then it couldn't be found.

"But what's happened?" he asked again.

"What do you mean?"

"I don't think you're the kind of person to jump at shadows, or get freaked out over a missing file, and certainly not reckless enough to risk meeting me so openly." She gave him a cold hard stare, almost a replica of Lee's.

"I played the piano," she started.

"That's what I remember the most about you," he answered, thinking it was an unusual statement for her to make, but she shook her head.

"I haven't really played since they died," she said, and then he understood. She associated the piano with that part of her life. By not playing, she shut everything away, but now it unlocked a door.

"What did you play?" he asked.

"Moonlight Sonata," she answered.

"Your dad's favourite piece. I remember, at the end of an assignment, he'd put on a recording of it. Drove me insane at the time, listening to it constantly, but I think he used it as a sort of meditation, to clear his mind."

She nodded slowly, that lost, faraway look returning.

"Bianca, or Melanie, whatever her name was..." she said, and he gave her a wary look, wondering where this change of direction would lead.

"What about her?" he asked.

"She was with you, wasn't she, just before I shot her."

"You took her out?" He sounded surprised, having assumed Jake did the deed. The look she gave him told him he'd focused on the wrong point. "What makes you think she was with me?" he asked.

"Your shower gel," she answered.

"And?"

"The items in your bathroom are not off-the-shelf generic stuff, they're designer, and I recognised the scent of the gel."

"And?" he asked again.

"So she *was* with you before I shot her."

"We didn't have sex, if that's what you're getting at," he answered. "And I would never have considered you the jealous type."

"I'm not," she answered, but the sharpness in her tone left him wondering. "I'm more concerned about who's playing whom."

He leaned in closer.

"You think I'm playing you?"

She mimicked him, leaning in so they were almost nose-to-nose, but with the same glare as her father. It was a dangerous expression on him, but it looked fierce on her.

"Someone is pulling the strings."

"It's not me," he answered, and sighed, sitting back. "Besides, Bianca came to me through Medlington."

"You didn't know her from Huntington?"

He shook his head, surprised.

"But you're correct; she'd been at my place before returning to Shannon. Well, one of my places. She didn't know about Waterford, nobody does." The pointed remark was not lost on her. "She arrived in a rage over you and Jake. Actually, it was mostly you. She was infuriated, jealous…"

"Jealous?" she asked, and to her surprise Karl blushed, and looked away. "Why would she be jealous? Karl?" she pushed when he wouldn't answer.

"I made a promise to your father, a long time ago, and one that I haven't been able to keep," he answered.

"Which was?"

"To keep you safe, to take care of you."

"It wasn't your fault you couldn't keep it."

"I still should've tried harder."

"Is that why you sacrificed her? Sent the information to Jake?"

"She hurt you, badly, and for no reason except …"

"Except what?"

"She seemed to instinctively know how I felt, about you. I suppose I asked too many questions about what you're like now, focused too much on you during my meetings with her." He still didn't look at Leigh as he spoke.

"I still don't understand what she had to be jealous about," she pushed again.

He fiddled with a beer mat from the table, tearing the corners, but a haunted smile grew on his face.

"When I first arrived in Ireland, I was so horrible to you. I was horrible to everyone really; I was a very angry boy. Your mother thought it would be good to take in an exchange student, and good for you, but she was wrong on both counts, and unfortunately she took the brunt of my temper back then. I took it out on her because I was angry at my own mother, for dying, for leaving me.

"But you... you I hated, and feared, the most. You were this shy little thing, but they loved you so much, and in a way I'd never known, never experienced, and I hated you because of it. Your dad wasn't shy about giving me a slap when I deserved it, and to be fair, I deserved everything I got. But one day, I'd been particularly nasty to you, and you finally lost your temper at me, and lashed out. I remember you wore this beautiful pink dress, and black patent leather shoes with little straps. I remember the shoes well, because they hurt when you kicked me in the shin, and then you punched me in the balls. Then, you told me exactly how I made you feel, how much I'd hurt you, and how much you hated me," he chuckled at the memory. "Your dad witnessed it, but he never said anything, to either of us, but of all the lessons, yours hit home the most. And I fell in love with you in that moment."

His voice was barely above a whisper, but he dared to raise his eyes to hers, hoping not to find loathing, or disgust in hers. Relieved, he found neither, but she'd paled, and seemed to struggle with maintaining her cool expression.

"I'd locked all of that away," she said.

"But?"

"When I played this morning, I remembered you sitting beside me at the piano. I remembered you teaching me German, and you loved Beethoven," she said, and he smiled.

"Your mother preferred Bach and Scarlatti. She gave me a hard time about my technique on the preludes."

"She gave everyone a hard time," she said. A frown crossed her forehead, deepening as she stared into the fire, but it wasn't the lost expression from earlier, more concentration. She turned to look at him.

"Moonlight Sonata," she said.

"What about it?"

"Dad's favourite piece of music."

"Yeah, and?"

"Dad's favourite piece of music." This time was a statement.

"What about it?"

"What if that's the key, to the journal."

"But there's five different encryptions in the book," he said, and she nodded, but a smile grew.

"I had the right idea, just the wrong starting point," she said, more to herself than answering him. He did a quick internet search on his phone for the musical key of that piece.

"It's in C sharp minor," he said, and she nodded again.

"It's got four sharps; F, C G and D," she told him, listing them off in their sequential order.

"That's still only four," he answered.

"All sequences, whether for sharps or flats, start at the same point, but…" She was lost in thought again. "That would put C in it twice so… Maybe it's the progression of key signatures, not the actual sequence of sharps."

"So what's the code?" he asked.

"The music is in a minor key, so it would start in A minor, then move to E minor, B minor, F sharp and then C sharp minors."

"You know, that never entered my mind as the code."

"You didn't decipher the other ones, they all had musical references," she told him.

"So he coded them with you in mind," he said, startling her.

"But you said he didn't want me in this world."

"That's true, but who else would he trust?" It was a strange comfort to her, that her father had such faith in his own child.

"I have to get back to Huntington," she said. "My e-pad has a secure connection to my systems at home where the scanned copy of the journal is saved. When I have access, I can enter the code, and see if I'm right."

"Is there a train back tonight?" he asked, relieved and happy when she shook her head.

Chapter 44

She sat in an empty carriage on the train back to Edinburgh, departing London much later than she intended. At this rate it would be almost midnight before getting into Edinburgh. Earlier, using an internet café close to King's Cross Station, she logged into her mobile phone account, and sent a web-text to Jake, asking him to pick her up, but with no phone she couldn't be sure he'd be at the station. More likely he would, just to give her a bollocking for disappearing without telling him.

She dozed for most of the journey, darkness making it impossible to view the countryside passing by, and she hadn't gotten much sleep earlier. If the Germans had a reputation for being reserved and aloof, that certainly didn't apply to Karl. Maybe his earlier admission fuelled his passion more.

And what of Jake, she wondered. Was it fair to compare the two? They were completely different men, so why was she even considering this, she questioned herself. Despite all efforts, she felt her emotional barriers crashing down when she thought of the two of them.

She invented a cover story about a rugby match at Twickenham, checking the scores and who'd played. And her ticket to the game? Well, she couldn't get one; the touts were being extortionate, so she resorted to watching the match in a sports bar. Before leaving the café she printed off a commentary of the game, and read through it enough times to talk about it convincingly. That she was perfecting her ability to lie so well concerned her. Where would she draw the line of what she was capable of doing, of what she was prepared to do? Was there even a line anymore? And to top it off, she now seemed to have gotten herself into a relationship with two men, who were at odds with each other.

During their lengthy talk in the bar, Karl's questions became more personal, more intimate, as he tried to catch up with the life he'd missed out on. He was just as open and frank about himself when she put the questions back to him.

More memories of him came back to her, silly little things like practical jokes going wrong, and then being punished for it. Karl's aunt didn't want him back, but by then Karl didn't want to return. He'd found the family he'd been missing all his life, and under the threat of losing it all should he step out of line, he agreed to Lee's terms and conditions just to stay with the Hartes.

All went well until that fateful day when he'd followed Lee into town, and fell into the clutches of Lantry. That much Leigh knew about, having read it in the journals.

After a late breakfast they spent the day no differently than any other couple in the city for a romantic winter break, and the romantic aspect of it hadn't bothered her in the slightest, the hand-holding, the spontaneous embraces and kisses from him. Sitting alone on the train however was a different story. It almost felt like she'd been cheating on Jake. This was getting ridiculous she told herself as she stepped off the train, and headed for the exit, finding Jake waiting for her, looking relieved, but not pleased, to see her.

"What the hell were you doing in London?" he demanded. She wasn't surprised he'd worked out where she was. If the origin of the train hadn't given it away, she knew someone, somewhere, within Huntington's cyber unit, had.

"Rugby match."

"Bullshit."

"Leinster against Harlequins. It was epic."

"Now I know you're lying."

"How can you be so sure?"

"You've never expressed an interest in sports."

"And you've known me for how long?" The question threw him and now that she mentioned it, he had seen sport-like jerseys in her wardrobe. He hesitated.

"So who won?"

"Leinster," she said, as though there'd been no doubt of the outcome.

"Lantry's been looking for you," he said, a little more pleasantly.

"His car?"

"Among other things."

"What other things?"

"Like why you didn't take your mobile phone, or your wallet? You left them in your room."

"That's where my wallet is. Thought I'd been pick-pocketed."

"And your mobile?"

"Didn't want it pick-pocketed." She sat into the passenger seat, using the effort of fastening her seatbelt to steady her nerves, and take a breath. How the hell had her dad managed to pull off this double life, and keep his nerves intact, she wondered.

"How's your Senator doing?" she asked, changing the subject.

"It looks like she's back to her usual self, demanding answers, then demanding explanations when she does get answers."

"Glad I'm not on the receiving end of that."

"You might be soon. I told her about the journals," he said. She looked at him in fury, but he held his hand up. "Look, she already knows my history, my real history, and the reason I've been fixated on catching Karl. But the journals, they've thrown everything I believed in to hell. She's the one person I had to talk to."

The mention of Karl reignited her confusion, and even though it had been hours ago, she still felt his powerful and deep kiss on her lips as they said goodbye. What the hell was going on with her, she wondered. She caught Jake's questioning stare.

"What?" she demanded, sounding more defensive than intended.

"I just admitted something about my past, and you haven't said a thing," he said. "What's with you?"

"What? So your dad was a psychotic sociopath? Like that's news to me," she replied. Trying to keep his focus on the road, he still managed to glare at her.

"You knew? How the hell did you find out?"

"You checked me and my dad out, so I did the same. I'm guessing yours made for way more interesting reading." This argument was good, she thought, and it felt good as well. It re-established her emotional indifference towards him.

"Those files were sealed."

"Yeah, right. With the proper software, everything and anything's well within the bounds of possibility." He drove the rest of the way in silence, but every now and again, he glanced across at her, though it was clear she paid him no attention. Her mind was elsewhere, and she thought about the key to the last journal.

While she could access her systems using her e-pad, she now found herself reluctant to do so. Jake easily accessed that very same e-pad while in Shannon. Until she was sure the code was correct, and had a chance to read the contents, she didn't want it accessable by anyone, and Huntington was too dangerous, its cyber unit employing some of the best in the field. No, she decided, she needed to return home.

"I want you to bring me to the airport tomorrow," she said, breaking the silence just as he turned into the entrance of the estate.

"What? Why?"

"I'm going home."

He stopped the car, the tyres skidding on the gravel.

"Like hell you are. There's still the whole mess to sort out with Karl's info, and Medlington."

"It's your mess, not mine. It's *your* Senator who's involved and Karl gave the file to *you*." The venomous look he gave her spoke volumes. "Besides," she said, deciding to play fair. "I think I have a lead on the decryption." It had the desired effect.

"The last journal?" he asked, and she nodded. "Is that what you were really doing in London?" She shrugged, which he took to be a yes. If that was the case, it also explained why she hadn't taken any items with the potential to GPS her location. "But how?" he started. "Wait, who?" he changed the question. She looked away, and his mind raced at all the possibilities. Did he really want to know the answer?

"I thought I could find the answer in London," she said, returning her gaze to him. He seemed to accept the explanation, and again she wondered why she spared his feelings. She had her own reasons for not revealing she'd spent the night with Karl, again, but they were all for self-preservation. Consorting with a known terrorist was treason, no matter which way she tried to rationalise it, and prison didn't appeal to her. Jake put the car in gear and drove on.

"You realise that if you enter that house the chances of you getting back out soon are slim," he said.

"I'm aware of that."

"And you're still going to take the chance."

"What option do I have?"

"Climb into the back and hide. I'll say you weren't on the train, that you sent another text to say you'd missed it."

"Why?"

"Because I need to know what really happened."

"Take the car around to the left side of the motor pool. Slow down just enough for me to jump out," she said.

"I'll grab your things."

"Just get my wallet and mobile, I already have my passport."

"And you didn't think that wouldn't be pick-pocketed?" he retorted. She shrugged at him. Taking his foot off the accelerator, and dropping gears, the car slowed itself down without the need to apply the brake.

"I'll be back as soon as I can," he said as she opened the door.

"I'll wait just inside the tree-line," she answered, then disappeared into the darkness.

Chapter 45

Leigh's unexpected arrival at Shannon startled everyone. The rumour mill kicked into overdrive when the visa team were refused entry following Matt and Danny's arrests. With Isobel's death, the facility turned into a crime scene, and the remaining team members were subjected to intense questioning. With everyone passing scrutiny, and renegotiations with the Americans on the visas ending successfully, the facility reopened for business, albeit under even more restrictions from the EU. Each day saw the arrival of more refugees from the States.

Leigh hadn't intended staying for as long as she did, just a quick check that her systems were holding up, and all modules were interacting as they should, her sense of professionalism in her work kicking in. Matt's direct supervisor had a string of questions that went largely unanswered by his own department, and with her on site, he took the opportunity to put those questions to her. Showing her British Intelligence ID shocked him, adding credence to what she said. That his own people were involved, whom he'd vouched for at the start, stunned and disturbed him in equal measures. Leigh gave him the barest of details, refusing to be drawn into divulging more than she deemed necessary.

Her car was still in the employee's section of the car park, and after putting an end to the questioning, she retrieved her keys from her office, and returned home in the early hours of the following morning. Having had no decent sleep in the last few nights, fatigue battled curiosity, the need for sleep fighting against her desire for answers. She made herself a compromise, entering the code first, waiting to see if the program would accept it, and on seeing the runtime-status bar slowly progressing, she left it to run its course, the curled up on the sofa in the den. She pulled a throw over herself to keep warm, and promptly fell asleep. The decrypted document awaited her when she awoke, sleeping longer than she intended, and as with the first journal, she also printed this one out, settling down to read it. The style of writing in this one was different, more clinical and technical. Though a shorter document than the others, the detailed content made speed-reading impossible, and she had to reread it several times.

During this time she received texts from Karl and Jake, both looking for updates. She had to text back to say the decryption was still ongoing, and warned them to back off. The phone calls from Lantry she ignored outright. Despite how tired she felt, she read through it once more, flipping back and forth through the pages to cross-reference and verify one significant discovery. Using the number of the disposable mobile phone he'd used to text her, she located Karl, finding him to be back in south-east Ireland, though she was unable to pinpoint his exact location. The last text he'd sent placed him at Waterford train station.

She toyed with the notion of texting him, but dismissed it outright. Chances were he was back in his lair, and his electronic security mechanism would prevent him getting the text. Besides, what she had to do required face-to-face interaction, and she drove to him instead, disabling the tracker on her car first. Whomever installed it, didn't reckon on her having intimate knowledge of her car. She ripped the device out before tearing out of her drive, and onto the Kilkenny road. She thought about what she'd read as she drove, knowing tiredness also fuelled this rage and need for action.

As with the last time, she let herself in, finding the codes still working for her, and descended in the lift to his living area. It was obvious he wasn't expecting her at that hour, but she found him on the sofa, waking up as his perimeter alarm beeped. He stretched before turning to face her, but only managed to turn half way, before he felt the barrel of her gun against the back of his neck.

"You bastard," she growled at him, clicking the safety off. He held his hands up in a gesture of surrender, startled at her action, and not knowing what caused it.

"Leigh?" he questioned, but felt the gun digging deeper. "What's going on?"

"You sold them out," she said, and he heard a cold tremor in her voice. He shook his head.

"I have no idea what you're talking about." He rose slowly, feeling the pressure of the gun ease from his neck. His mind raced, trying to figure out what happened, but no answers came.

He turned around to face her, finding the same look of fury as he'd seen in Lee before, that same dangerous expression, and he knew she believed he'd done something. Had Lee implicated him in something? Had she deciphered the journal then? But what could Lee have written to have enraged her so much, that she came all this way to confront him.

He moved cautiously around the sofa, towards her, but she took a step back, her weapon still trained on him. No tremor, no shaking in her hands, he noticed, scaring him all the more.

"Leigh, talk to me. Tell me what's happened." He moved closer.

"The code worked," she told him.

"And?"

"All this started because of you."

He shook his head.

"How?" he demanded.

"You sold dad out. You told someone that dad started his own investigation into the Medlington thing." She saw the puzzled look on Karl's face, and it seemed genuine.

"I never sold him out, you have to believe that." He continued to inch closer, his movements almost imperceptible until he was within arm's length of her, and attacked her, knocking her gun to the side.

The unexpected move pushed her sideways, and he stepped behind her, grabbing her arm, but she retaliated with her free arm, reverse elbowing him in the jaw. He didn't expect her to react as quickly, and let her go. She continued to spin around and caught him on the same side with a punch, using the butt of her gun, but he rolled with it, catching her hand in a wristlock, knocking the gun from her grip, hurting her in the process. The gun fell to the floor, and he kicked it away, sending it sliding on the tiles, and out of reach. She half-turned again, reverse kicking him, her heel impacting with his knee and he let out a roar in pain. He still held her at the wrist, and he twisted her arm up behind her, causing her to cry out, but it still didn't stop her from trying to break free. He grabbed her free arm and propelled her forward, slamming her into the wall. It knocked the wind from her, and the only sound she could make was a grunt. He used his own body to pin her against the cold stone wall, the rough stone grazing her cheek.

She continued to struggle against him, but couldn't push away from the wall. She tried to kick back, but being taller, his knee reached higher than hers, and in spite of the pain she'd inflicted, he pounded his knee into the back of her thigh and pressed in hard, immobilising her even more. That she continued to put up a fight surprised him, as did her strength, but the level of her anger and hatred wasn't lost on him. Pressed against her, smelling her perfume he couldn't help the arousal he felt. Pressed against her as he was, she felt his hardness, and in spite of the holds on her, she renewed her fight, partly out of disgust at his physical reaction.

"Stop," he said into her ear. "Stop struggling, and just tell me what's happened, explain to me what you think I've done." She struggled to breathe, and he loosened his grip a little.

"Dad found out what was going on with Medlington, and that so-called arms trade investigation, and he found out who pulled the strings."

"But Lee never told me."

"It didn't matter, you told them anyway," she growled. He let her go, and moved out of her reach, but shook his head at her accusation.

"How could I tell what I didn't know?"

"Who did you talk to?"

"No one."

"You damn well did." She took a step towards him, her fists clenched at her side. He retreated a step from her, and frowned as he tried to think back all those years ago, trying to recall what happened.

"Lee said it was too dangerous to tell me, and then he sent me away, back to Germany."

"Who did you talk to before he sent you away?"

"No one," he repeated. "I never spoke to anyone outside of the Ministry." A strange look crossed her face that gave him pause. "Someone in the Ministry?" he asked. "But," he hesitated. "The only person I talked to, whom I was summoned to... was Lantry."

He stopped as what he said hit home.

"Nein, nein, mein gott," he said, over and over.

He ran his hands through his hair. Strangely she remembered a similar action when he was younger. Her own anger, while it still raged within her at his seeming betrayal, started to abate, at witnessing his reaction. He truly didn't know anything about this, about his part in the whole sequence of events. The journal didn't reveal everything. Some things couldn't be entrusted to a paper, no matter how clever Lee thought he was being with his codes. However, Karl was still part of the puzzle, and the solution. He continued to talk to himself.

"Sprechen Englisch, bitte *(Speak English, please)*," she said to him, more civilly this time. "Sie haben etwas anderes gehört zu papa *(You have something else belonging to dad)*," she added.

"You said you'd forgotten your German," he accused, and she just shrugged. He rubbed his jaw, feeling the growing swelling and went to his fridge-freezer, taking out a bag of frozen veg, holding it to his face. She retrieved her gun from the floor, resetting the safety.

"You really had no idea?" she asked.

"About your dad? No. I do remember Lantry hauled me in for one of his status reports, you know the ones where he does his nit-picking of every minute detail?" She nodded. "He asked me for a status update on

Lee and his current case. I just assumed he knew what Lee was up to. He sounded like he knew."

"He must've guessed dad was up to something." She pulled the folded printout from inside her jacket, and handed it to him.

"Is this it?" he asked, and she nodded.

"Dad wrote that you were the one who compromised him. But he also said he sent a key. There's a set of numbers at the end." He flipped to the back page and looked at the numbers.

"The first set of numbers are a German telephone number," he said.

"I know, and to whom," she answered. "It's the second set I haven't worked out."

"It looks like an old bank account number," he said.

"You're sure?" she asked. He nodded.

"Safe deposit box, I think. I'd have to check, but one of these look like a bank's old national sort code."

"And the key?" she asked, that cold hardness returning.

"I gave you everything he gave me. The journal was the last item."

"Maybe there's something in the boxes I overlooked," she said, talking more to herself than to Karl. He sat down, pressing the frozen bag to his face again, and began to read.

It didn't take him long to get through it and he now understood her reaction. Lee stated he knew Karl spoke to Lantry, revealing what Lee was up to, and it pushed Lee into taking more drastic action than he wanted to. There was a brief mention of packing Karl off to Germany, but Karl's recollection of it was far from the 'let's take a trip' impression the document gave. Lee roughly hauled his ass out of bed in the middle of the night, made him pack his things with the barest of explanations. He put the document down, and found Leigh watching him intently.

"If I was responsible, why would Lee continue to protect me?" he asked her. She shrugged; it'd been a question that bugged her too. She knew her dad wouldn't have hesitated in eliminating Karl. She knew she'd acted rashly, and out of character for her, but that was the beauty of the attack; it was unexpected, and it yielded a result. And the attack was also fuelled by the emotional upheaval Karl stirred in her, his passion for her, making his seeming betrayal all the more insidious.

"This code is the location to where Lee hid his proof," he said. "This says Medlington was a soft target, he was bait." She nodded.

"According to Jake and that Senator, the man believed he worked for the greater good, but according to dad's journal Medlington was used to unwittingly supply false information. The file on his wife and dad looked... wrong."

"Wrong? How?"

"Staged," she answered. "Like it was meant as a threat."

"But by who? Lantry?"

"Who else?"

"So Lantry was behind his death?"

"I can't be sure, but you've read the journal just as I have. Medlington was dad's target, but he knew something was wrong with the set up."

"That it *was* a set-up," Karl concluded. She nodded.

"I'm starting to think so. Sorry about your jaw," she said, but it didn't sound entirely sincere, and he gave her a sour look, his face now aching from the cold.

"When's the last time you had a decent night's sleep?" he asked.

"Not since before meeting you in London."

"Then stay here and rest. Tiredness is making you irrational, not to mention grumpy, and it's too dangerous for you to drive back when you're like this."

"Yeah? Well you should see me when I have something to be grumpy about," she countered, but he was right. She left the document with him, and he reread it a few more times, but something was amiss. He guessed pages were missing, and he couldn't figure out if it was Lee's transcription, or if Leigh removed them. If so, why? What did they contain? She'd already allowed him to see the part that enraged her so much, so what other reason was there.

He left the document on the coffee table along, with the now defrosted bag of veg, and followed her into his bedroom, finding her under the covers, stripped down to her smalls, and asleep. He undressed and slipped in beside her, cosying up to her and while she stirred, she didn't wake. That alone told him just how tired she'd been. She'd always been a light sleeper, ever since she was a child, and he knew from watching her, when he could, that during her late teens she hardly slept at all. Granted, most of that was drug fuelled, and nothing he could do to help her. Besides, Tom was a permanent feature in her life at the time, eliminating any chance for Karl to get close to her. Tom intervened when and where Karl couldn't. Would he have been able to deal with her as Tom had? Karl didn't have the answer to that one, but he suspected not.

She disappeared again while he slept, taking the document with her, and he mulled everything over in his mind as he made tea, finally knowing who set the bomb for him, and why. He'd always had his suspicions, and they always led back to Lantry, but he'd felt he was wrong, that he'd overlooked something important, something significant. Another question popped into his head. Had Leigh shared any of this with Jake? Karl doubted it, based on her reactions. She wanted to confront him on her own, and knowing what a guarded person she was, he knew she wouldn't have shared this with anyone else just yet. His jaw ached, and bruising began blossoming, but by god, could that girl throw a punch. Lee would've been proud.

The bomb, he thought. Pertinent details leading up to it were missing. Why had she left it out? Delving into his past brought back memories of that time, and he thought he knew of another reason why she could've been angry with him.

Chapter 46

Swayne overheard the rumour and went to find Jake. Tom Barnett's arrival at Huntington made Jake hurry even more. Leigh had been returned to Huntington. That fact alone had an ominous overtone to it, and information on what happened was sketchy and slow in coming. Even Swayne failed to get answers, but the woman's persistence won out, and the Site Operations Manager released details to them that Jake could scarcely believe. That Leigh allegedly pulled her weapon on Tom was believable, knowing how she felt about the man, but it remained unexplained what the circumstances were leading up to it. She wasn't in the usual interview rooms, but segregated from the main building. That had serious implications, and he knew she wasn't under regular questioning, more like intense interrogation.

Jake got his hands on a copy of Barnett's version of events, but he found it hard to accept Leigh acted in the way Barnett claimed. More than likely she'd reacted, but his allegations still beggared belief. From the time Jake dropped her off at the airport he'd only received one text from her, and not what Jake hoped for. His understanding of what really happened to him in Germany lay in her deciphering that journal, and it had been four days since he'd last seen her. Her three disappearing acts from Huntington set off alarms, and Barnett's capture of her amounted to the equivalent of an arrest.

Barnett's report said she'd resisted with force, but the man arrived at her house with back up, obviously expecting trouble from her. Had Barnett found anything else, Jake wondered, but nowhere did the report mention any documents being on her at the time. Barnett's report also went on to describe how he had set up a surveillance team to monitor her home, and alert him to any signs of her returning. Only on rereading that part did it register with Jake. She hadn't been home. So where the hell had she been for four days, if not deciphering the journal? Swayne understood his concerns, he'd already confided in her about helping Leigh return to Ireland, and the reason behind doing so.

When the operations' manager caved in under Swayne's relentless onslaught and told them where Leigh was being held, Jake's stomach sank. She was in a bad place. The stone building, used as the armoury, contained a deep basement, converted into holding cells with stone walls thick enough to muffle screams for when detainees were subjected to physical forms of interrogation. It was mostly used for training purposes, and Jake knew the place. He'd been subjected to late night *snatch'n'grabs* as part of his rehabilitation and retraining, held in these cells for hours on end; harsh teaching methods in survival and resisting torture.

They weren't just used for educational purposes. They were also used for brutal information extraction. While the walls muffled Leigh's screams making it harder to pinpoint her location, they didn't deaden all sound, and he needed her to continue screaming so he could find her. That she screamed was an indication of the severity of her treatment. He found her, barrelling his way through the heavy door, hurting his bad shoulder, but ignoring the pain. Her interrogator, not expecting anyone, was slow to react to Jake's assault. Jake caught hold of him, slamming him into the wall behind, knocking him unconscious.

Releasing his grip on the man, Jake turned his attention to Leigh, kneeling on the rough stone floor, shackled to a thick metal post in what he reckoned was an extremely painful and restrictive way. She'd been stripped to the bare essentials, but even they were torn from where she'd been struck with something sharp. Various whips, and other painful implements, sat on a long narrow wooden table nearby. Before unshackling her, he checked for more injuries, brushing her matted hair from her face, finding cuts on her lip, over her eye and a bloody nose. Most of the bruising on her torso was nasty, but superficial, her arms and legs bore the brunt of the torturous regime. She'd been restrained so that the sensitive inner parts of her limbs were accessible for inflicting pain.

"Use the riding crop," she muttered through staggered breath, "It's got a better sting." Jake smiled at her continuing defiance, and with one hand holding her head, he reached around to undo the bonds holding her by the wrists.

"It's me, I've got you," he whispered in her ear, catching her as she fell forward, unconscious.

The overhead light hurt her eyes as she opened them, but the sight of Lantry hurt them more.

"You need to put that man on a leash," she said, rolling onto her injured side, but regretted the action.

"Funny, that's exactly what he said about you," Lantry answered.

"Yeah I bet he did, but I'm guessing he forgot to tell you he struck first," she shot back.

"I've never had a reason to question the voracity of his reports before, whereas I've always had to question yours," he answered. He loomed over her. "So who do you suppose I'm going to believe?" She tried shifting again, wondering why her movements seemed hampered, then realised one wrist was cuffed to the infirmary bed.

"What? Don't you trust me?" she asked, and he heard the sarcasm in her voice.

"Tell me where the hell you've been, and I'll consider removing them," he answered.

"You know where I've been," she said.

"Not everywhere you've been, and certainly not why?"

"That's not what you originally asked. Now you're just amending the parameters of this conversation." She saw his fists clench in annoyance. In truth, if he hated this trait in Lee, it vexed him no end with her, and she knew it. But something else was amiss with her. While he knew she hated him, and that hatred was good, allowing him to control her, push her in the direction he wanted, this defiance was different, hardened somehow, and he didn't think the cruel interrogation had anything to do with it.

How well she took her punishment continued to impress and disturb him, but it was the transcript of the interrogation, which recorded her suggestions to her punisher of where best to hit her, and with which implement, disturbed him the most. Was it just pure defiance, he wondered.

And no, he hadn't believed Tom's version of events. He never did. Tom was an instrument, albeit a blunt, but powerful, one. Of the team of Lee and Tom, Lee surpassed his mentor, being far more subtle, a precision tool. Like her father, young Leigh was also meticulous and calculating in her actions, and he knew Tom would never have seen an attack by her coming.

Lantry watched over her training, taking more interest in a raw recruit than a Director should, but considering who she was, considering whose progeny she was, she required watching and as it transpired, deserved watching, even if it was simply to discover new ways she could fuck up his day. He straightened back up, knowing looming wasn't intimidating her.

"Where were you?" he asked again.

"I checked my systems in Shannon and I went home," she answered.

"Why?"

"You sent me to do a job, and that's what I did."

"But Jake put an end to the visa corruption."

"Did he? Really? And what about Gouderhoff?"

"What about him?"

"He's still out there; possibly still involved in Shannon."

Lantry tried not allowing a smirk to show.

"Is that what you were doing, chasing him?" he asked.

"Of course," she answered, knowing she needed to temper this performance to make it convincing. So why did she find it easy to speak passionately about Karl, she wondered. If Lantry wanted to interpret that passion as hatred, then all the better.

"And what did you find?"

"I found his safe house in Limerick. Apparently Bianca would rendezvous with him there."

"What else?" he pushed. She shrugged.

"That's as far as I got before your pit-bull struck."

"And I thought Tom was your guardian angel."

"My what?"

"If his report is accurate, he's the reason you're still alive."

"Is he?"

"He got you clean."

"Did he?" She answered adamantly enough to give him pause.

"Didn't he?" he asked.

"He's not the one who got me completely clean," she answered. That stopped him, she noted with smug satisfaction, that huge and significant chunks of her life remained unknown to him. This boded well for her, once she figured out her escape from Huntington.

Chapter 47

Jake returned to Brussels with Swayne, not that he'd had much choice. Lantry gave him no option. With the reinstatement of the visas for Americans, the Senator was needed back at the Commission. He'd been reluctant to leave Leigh behind, not just because he desperately needed to know if she'd deciphered the journal, but because she hadn't regained consciousness following her ordeal. Lantry had been determined in keeping Jake away from her, also refusing to answer why such a level of violence was required on her. It frustrated him but he couldn't keep pushing without Lantry asking questions, and his text messages to her continued to be blocked.

Jake was reassigned to the Embassy as an ad hoc Intelligence Officer. Another reason to feel frustrated, but mercifully Swayne stepped in, and had him assigned as her Intelligence Liaison Officer. It freed him from a pompous, overbearing supervisor, who had limited experience in the field, but who unfortunately believed he knew more than he actually did. People like that never got killed. They just got everyone else killed instead.

Swayne did have a task for him, to continue his monitoring and checking of the US numbers, given his former experience in the area, but it served to remind him of Leigh. It ached, but he blocked it out as best he could, until the day a business card arrived in the post for him, the card doubling as an appointment card, and it contained a date and time. Swayne looked over his shoulder as he frowned at this new puzzle.

"You're getting a tattoo?" she asked, looking at the card.

"No," he answered with a growing smile. "But I know who might."

Chapter 48
Frankfurt, Germany

"You're sure you want to be here?" Jake asked her, and Swayne nodded. She was nervous, and wasn't sure why. It wasn't her past they were chasing up, but she found all this intrigue exciting. Jake assured her it wasn't all like this, dashing across Europe, chasing leads, infiltrating the enemy's lair. More often, it was boring surveillance, stuck in the same spot for hours on end, watching nothing happen. Television, he told her, filled her head with fast-paced thriller action. Yet here they stood, outside a grubby basement shop front, on a side street, in Frankfurt. He pulled his coat collar back up over his face to protect against the bitter and biting cold, and descended the steps to the tattooist, stepping into a tiny reception area. At least it was warm. Swayne closed the front door behind her as the door in front of Jake opened.

"Haben sie einen termin? *(You have an appointment?)*," the man asked.

"Wir haben einen termin mit Jürgen *(We have an appointment with Jürgen)*," Jake answered, taking the appointment card from his wallet, and handing it over. The man checked it, giving Jake and Swayne a once-over look that bordered on puzzled, or bored. Jake couldn't decide which.

"Hier warten *(Wait here)*," he said, and disappeared into the rear.

"Now what?" Swayne asked.

"Now we wait."

"And the appointment card he took?"

"Consider it the same as handing in the invitation card at one of your charity gigs," he explained to her.

"So whoever sent it will know it's us?" she asked, and he nodded. "And they're not *gigs*, they're very important fundraising events." He smirked at her mild indignation, but it was short lived, as the door opened again.

"Kommen ein *(Come in),*" he said allowing them entry The unflattering lobby hid a clinical and meticulously maintained interior. A mild scent bugged her that she couldn't place.

"What is that smell?" she asked Jake, as quietly as she could.

"We just finished with a client, and cleaned the room. What you smell is disinfectant," the other man answered in perfect English. "American?" he asked. Swayne nodded. "Einfuhr *(import)*?" he asked, referring to the recent influx of Americans into Europe. She shook her head, not understanding what he asked, but she didn't think it was good when she saw Jake's features harden.

"Nein," he answered for her.

"And tattoos, do they hurt?" she asked, curious by it all.

"Depending on what you get, and where you get it, yes, it can hurt, very much," but the smile on his face belied what he told her. "This appointment, it is for you?"

Swayne laughed uncomfortably.

"Eh, no," she answered. She'd been fascinated by the concept of tattoos, but could never understand the need, nor the desire, to get one. The guy handed the card back to Jake, and opened another door for them, gesturing for them to enter.

With her eyes closed, earphones in, and the buzz of the tattooist's needle going, Leigh neither heard them enter, nor registered their presence, but Jake felt a pang of longing as he watched the expression on her face, a mix of pain, and pleasure.

"Is that...?" Swayne asked, trying to take the scene in, and the semi-naked girl in the seat. Jake nodded, but smiled. "Are her...?" Swayne still struggled. "Are those...?"

"What?" Jake asked, trying to rein his grin in at her growing indignation.

"Those metal pieces?" Swayne asked.

"Yes," Jake answered. "Her nipples are pierced, amongst other places." He did his best not to laugh at the Senator's reaction.

"But she seemed… so…"

"Normal?" Jake asked.

"I *was* going to say respectable," Swayne defended herself.

"It just goes to show you can never judge a book by its cover, or a person by the well-tailored three-piece suits they wear," he said.

"But that's just it. She dressed so well, so… respectable," Swayne repeated.

"Believe me, tattoos and piercings are the least of her deviances," he said, sounding as though he spoke with authority. Swayne wasn't sure if she wanted to know more. The door opened again behind them, and the latest arrival looked startled to find them there.

"Was machst du hier? *(What are you doing here?)*," Jake growled. Karl looked past him at Leigh, finding her to be still ignorant of their presences. He held up a business card, identical to the one Jake received.

"I have an appointment," Karl answered, in German. "You?"

Jake held up his own card.

"Same here," he answered.

"And you are?" Swayne asked.

"The man responsible for Jonathan's death," Jake answered in English, wanting her to know exactly who this man was, and she paled.

"Play fair, Jaran. All I did was hand you the evidence," Karl answered. "That makes you just as responsible as me."

The room went quiet as the needle stopped. They watched as Leigh opened her eyes, and pulled the earphones out before inspecting the latest addition to her collection. Only then did she register them in the room with her, and in no way displayed any sense of self-consciousness at having her body on display. The inclusion of the Senator surprised her though, and Leigh found the woman's attempt to restrain her jumble of horrific disgust and fascination, amusing.

"Hi guys," she said. "Glad you could make it."

Chapter 49

Karl reacted first, nudging Jake out of the way to reach her, kissing her with as much force and passion as he could muster. Not to be outdone by his rival, Jake made his kiss longer, deeper, until Leigh had to push him back to catch her breath.

"Wow, I'd almost think you two missed me," she said. "Senator," she acknowledged the other woman. "I'm surprised to see you here."

"I wanted to see this through to the end," Swayne answered, and Leigh gave a nod in understanding.

"What happened after I pulled you out of that torture?" Jake asked.

"Torture? What torture?" Karl pushed his way back in. "What happened? You disappeared with the copy of the journal, and then I didn't hear anything from you for weeks."

Swayne saw Jake's jaw clenching, the muscles rippling as he glared at his nemesis. Leigh held her hands up.

"Boys, back off," she said, her authority in no way diminished by her still semi-naked state. If anything, Swayne thought, standing on the side-lines, with an optimal view of this triangle, her nakedness and artwork lent her more authority.

Both 'boys', as she'd called them, gave her some room, and she reached for her shirt. She dressed slowly, oblivious to the effect she had on the men. More likely Leigh's movements were to avoid adding to the discomfort of getting a tattoo. Judging by the grimace on Leigh's face, her actions were not intended to inflame the men further.

"Do you get an anaesthetic before getting those done?" Swayne asked, burning curiosity compelling her to ask. Leigh looked at her curiously before shaking her head. No anaesthetic? Dear god, why did people put themselves through that?

"So you deciphered the journal?" Jake asked.

"Yep."

"And?" he pushed, but her glare hardened, enough to halt him.

"It's not here," she told them both. "I figured the best thing to do was get it somewhere safe, until I figured out the numbers."

"Numbers? What numbers?" Jake asked.

"There were numbers at the end, that I thought referred to a German bank account," Karl told him.

"You let him read it first?" Jake demanded, but her arched eyebrow at his outburst made him back down.

"Huntington was too dangerous, I couldn't bring it there. He was closer, and it affected him more than it affected you," she told him.

"But..." he began, but she stopped him.

"You'll get the chance soon, but for now, just shut up, and stop asking questions until we get there."

"Why, where are we going?" Jake asked, and she looked at him incredulously.

"Which part of 'stop asking questions' did not compute with you?" she asked before turning to glare at Karl for sniggering.

This was not the same little girl they'd left at Huntington, Swayne thought. Whatever happened to her since their return to Brussels hardened her, changed her. Even though she was the smallest person in the room, she dominated it, radiated a force that was almost tangible.

The two men backed down, but Swayne saw the rivalry between them, and not just from the attempt on Jake's life. A new complication entered the mix. That complication was Leigh. If they managed to uncover what really happened with that bomb, then their rivalry over Leigh would continue to keep them at war. If the young lady in question was aware of this, then she gave no sign of it, but Swayne suspected she already knew by her efforts to treat them equally.

"So who's Jürgen?" Karl asked, and Leigh glowered at him. Apparently the 'stop asking questions' rule also applied to him.

"You already know Jürgen," she told him. "He was an old contact of dad's."

"But he had a... oh," he started, but quietened on realising where they were going.

"Yeah," she answered, smiling as she pulled on her coat, and led them back out onto the street, walking about half a block before descending steps again and knocking. As the door opened, Leigh showed the woman the two stud piercings she had on her right hip, and the door opened wider.

"Domina, willkommen, bitte kommen *(Mistress, welcome, please come in)*." The opening term confused Jake, but Karl groaned, and Jake heard him mutter an 'oh nein' under his breath.

"Danke, Kleiner. Wir sind hier um Jürgen sehen. Sie haben Terminkarten *(Thank you, little one. We're here to see Jürgen. They have appointment cards)*,"Leigh answered.

"Yes Mistress, you're expected," she said. There was that term again, Jake thought. As they followed her into this new place, Jake leaned closer to Karl.

"Do you have any idea what that was about?" he asked, automatically conversing in German.

"Yes, unfortunately," Karl answered.

"And?"

"I was only ever here once, it was a BND drop box."

"This place is German Intelligence?"

"That's one of its uses."

"And the others?" Jake asked. The long narrow hallway opened into a large room and what Jake could only describe as something from a dungeon torture scene in a medieval movie. "O weh süßen Gott *(oh dear, sweet god)*," he uttered, and Karl nodded.

"Yep, it's a fetish club, specialising in bondage and dominance," he confirmed. Behind them, Swayne was too shocked for words.

"Why did she bring us here?" Jake wanted to know.

"I don't think we want to know the answer to that, but I'm seriously hoping it's the Intelligence side," Karl answered.

"There's no way she's doing that to me," Jake said, indicating towards the scene being played out in the room.

"Oh, I don't know, I think it would suit you. I like the idea of you being shackled and beaten," Karl told him, before catching up with Leigh, without waiting for Jake's response.

They entered a large bright office that could have been at home in any normal working environment. A heavy set man greeted her, gesturing towards the seats in front of his oversized desk. Jürgen acknowledged Karl.

"Word is you were the one who killed them," he said to Karl.

"Word is wrong," Leigh answered for him.

"And him?" Jürgen asked, indicating to Jake.

"Another interested party," she answered. "You have the package?"

"So you're not here for a little fun?" he asked.

"Package first."

"So like your father, business before pleasure." He went to his safe and retrieved the large envelope she'd sent to him, after she'd called him some weeks ago.

"And the key?" she asked. Jürgen handed her a narrow metal bar, rounded at one end and pointed at the other.

"That has been sitting in there for almost fifteen years," he said. "He knew he was in danger. I'm just surprised he entrusted it to me."

"He knew you were reliable," she answered.

"I never expected you to be the one who came looking for it. I always assumed it would be him," Jürgen nodded in Karl's direction. "When you showed up all those years ago, looking for a tattoo, I thought you knew then."

He left the rest of their history, her history, unsaid. She felt the weight of the metal key in her hand. For a moment she was lost in thought.

"As for playing, are you available?" she asked Jürgen.

"Are you still clean?"

"Of course, I'd know better than to ask otherwise."

"When was the last time you played?"

"The last time I was here," she answered.

"It *has* been a long time. Then I think I can make time for one of my favourites," he answered.

"Give me ten minutes?" she asked, indicating to the others and Jürgen nodded.

Back on the street, she tore open the package and removed the two envelopes. The smaller of the two she folded, and tucked into the inside pocket of her long coat, the larger one she gave to Jake.

"You, read this," she told him. To Karl, she handed the metal key. "You, take care of this." She took another key from her pocket and held it out, waiting for one of them to take it. "This is the key to a secure location. Not yours," she said to Karl, about to speak. "Your safe house here is compromised, its location has been known for years." Jake took the key, and she gave them the address, not wanting to commit it to paper. She turned to descend the steps again.

"You're not coming with us?" Jake asked.

"I'll catch up with you later," she told him.

"Why are you going back in there?" he asked, and wished he hadn't, seeing a smile grow on her face, mirroring a brightness in her eyes.

"I've got a session under Jürgen," she answered.

"When you say session?" Jake pressed. She found his expression of bewilderment delightful. Karl grasped what was happening, and he looked concerned, but remained quiet.

"You have your kicks, and this is mine. Don't wait up boys, I may be awhile." She disappeared back inside.

"She's …?" Jake looked to Karl, who just nodded. "When she said under, did she mean like that guy we saw?"

"More than likely," Karl answered. Something else registered with Jake.

"She spoke fluent German," he said.

"Yeah, I wondered how long it would take you to twig that," Karl taunted. "And I thought she liked intelligent boys."

"What's she doing with you then?"

"Obviously upped her game after she met you."

Unable to understand what they were saying, and still in shock at what she had just seen, Swayne hailed a taxi, giving the boys a whistle to get their attention and stop their bickering. Leigh's description, calling them boys, was accurate at this point. Perhaps she'd also use it from now on.

Chapter 50

They were still up when Leigh returned to her apartment, feeling more relaxed than she had in a long time. Swayne had gone to bed, leaving the two men to discuss the document, among other things.

"How the hell did you get involved with Jürgen?" Karl asked, genuinely concerned.

"Long story," she answered.

"We've got the rest of the night," Jake said. It was clear the category of 'other things' included her.

"Jürgen's not exactly known for his soft touch," Karl added, and she laughed to herself.

"Oh, you don't have to tell me," she smirked.

"What possessed you to get into that lifestyle?" Jake asked.

"Stop. Both of you, just stop. I'm feeling pretty good right now, don't ruin it," she answered. Karl leaned in closer.

"Are you high?" he asked.

"A little, but on endorphins and adrenaline, nothing chemical. Jesus, you're not my dad, back off," she told him.

"But with Jürgen? How?" he said. She pushed him away.

"You know, you're not exactly in a position to be making judgements about my lifestyle choices. Either of you." She caught the quick glances between them, and knew it was also something they'd been discussing, reminiscing perhaps.

"Just explain this thing with Jürgen, please," Karl begged.

"It started because of you," she told him. He shook his head, denying it. "We were here on vacation, and dad had to pick up something that you were meant to collect. I remember it because he warned me not to say anything to mum."

"He brought you on a pick-up?" he interrupted her.

"He had to. We were sightseeing, just us, when you called him."

"I can't believe he brought you there."

"What choice did he have? It was obviously important, and you couldn't make it. At the time I thought he just didn't want mum to know he'd brought me to a tattoo place. Later, I discovered the only way to get to Jürgen, was through the tattoo place, and it's where I got my tats."

"How did you think of going there? There are plenty of places in Ireland," Karl put to her.

"He gave me his card at the time, and I kept it thinking it was really cool. Years later, I found it again and decided that was where I wanted to get them done. That time I *was* stoned. But whatever you think of him, and yes he can be a very cruel man, he's still the reason I'm clean. He's the reason I'm alive, not Tom.

"As soon as I went to college, I fell right back into drug use, but Jürgen wouldn't touch me until I was clean and sober. As for the lifestyle? I needed that discipline at the time. Now, it's something I get a release, and the utmost pleasure from."

She knew of Jake's past with his own father, likewise Karl's early upbringing hadn't been pleasant, so she didn't expect either of them to understand the sense of freedom and power that the physical infliction of pain brought. Nor was she going to try explaining it further. She had her own arrows to sling at them, and took the folded envelope from her coat pocket. Their discussion woke Swayne, and she re-entered the room.

"Dear lord, are they still bickering?" she asked Leigh. "It's worse than a lover's tiff." A dangerous grin grew on Leigh's face.

"Senator, you're not that far from the truth."

"What?" Swayne answered, glancing from one man to the other. Leigh held the envelope up, still sealed.

"The missing pages?" Karl asked.

"Oh yes," she answered. He reached for it, but it was Jake who snatched it from her hand, tearing it open.

"What exactly did you mean by that?" Swayne said. Leigh didn't look at her, but focused on Jake.

"Dad knew exactly what you were up to, but he wasn't sure who you worked for. You took advantage of Karl's vulnerability at the time."

"I wasn't vulnerable," Karl defended himself.

"You'd been abandoned in a strange place, with very little explanation, and no one to talk to. You were vulnerable, and Jaran used that to get close to you. Well, a little more than just close."

"I had an assignment," Jake answered.

"And you used every advantage." She shifted her attention to Karl. "As for you, you ignored dad's advice to stay away from him."

"I thought letting him get close would help Lee, would help find out who was behind it all," he answered.

"And you two got really close," she said. Swayne had a sinking feeling she knew where this was headed. "Well, well," Leigh went on. "This has turned into the ultimate three-way triangle."

"Are you saying that they...?" Swayne began.

"Let's just say what goes on after lights-out in an all-male barracks..." Leigh left the rest unsaid. The glares from both men said it all. "Don't look at me like that," she said to Karl. "It's not like it was your first gay encounter. In fact it's starting to seem a little incestuous, but you lied to me about not having a relationship with my dad."

"I didn't lie to you," he argued back.

"You posed as a gay couple to get close to a target," she shot back.

"Posed being the operative word," he said.

"The Scene's too small and intimate, especially back then. You would've had to do a little more than pose to be convincing." To her surprise, he blushed furiously.

"Why are you doing this?" he growled at her. Her smug grin dropped in a flash, and they saw the hardened look that lay beneath it, glimpsed elements of Lee Senior in her.

"To prove a point, that neither of you are in a position, nor have any right, to question my lifestyle choices," she told them.

Despite the freezing temperature, Swayne found Leigh sitting out on the small balcony, staring out across the city's night skyline, lost in her own thoughts, well wrapped up and huddled into an oversized coat.

"I have to ask," Swayne started, startling Leigh. "How can you do that?"

"Do what?" Leigh asked, but knew what Swayne was getting at.

"Jake says the tattoos and the piercings, they're called body modifications?" Leigh nodded. "Why would you do that to your body? And that... place..." she trailed off.

"What about it?"

"It's so... wrong. How could you allow someone to do that to you?"

"Because it's pain I can physically experience, pain I can feel and deal with," Leigh answered. "If I feel pain, real physical pain, then I know I'm still alive. It's how I learned to deal with the grief, with everything, without resorting to drugs. Instead of dulling and numbing the hurt, it... enhanced it, made it something tangible."

"So you substituted sex for drugs?"

Leigh shook her head.

"No, often there's no sex involved."

"So what is it then?"

Leigh paused for a moment, figuring out the best way to describe it.

"Have you ever had something so pleasurable, but after a while it started to become painful?" Swayne gave the question consideration before nodding, though compared to this kid before her, she felt her experience to be somewhat lacking, and naïve in her understanding and expectations. "Well, this is the reverse."

"Pain is pleasurable?" Swayne asked, and Leigh nodded, but Swayne still didn't get it.

"Pain or pleasure, it's how we physically perceive the world."

"But it's physical abuse." Swayne was horrified that anyone would put themselves through that, allow themselves to be restrained and beaten.

"It's not what you think," Leigh tried to reassure her, but she recalled what Jake told her of this woman's past, and understood the revulsion. "It's not abuse. Neither party is acting out of malice or hate. With the right person, in the right hands, and for the right reasons, it's an emotional release. That's why Jürgen wouldn't tattoo me, pierce me and certainly not play, until I got my act together and cleaned myself up. In the wrong hands, yes, it can be very dangerous, and a Sub on drugs is unpredictable, making the situation potentially lethal."

"A ... sub?"

"A submissive, someone who surrenders."

"You never struck me as the surrendering type," Swayne said, curious at the smirk appearing at the corner of Leigh's mouth.

"Obviously no pun intended," Leigh quipped before Swayne realised what she'd said.

"But you still handed over that control, you physically put your life in someone else's hands?"

"It's a misconception that the Dom has all the power and control. They can only push their Sub to the limits the Sub's prepared to go."

"So you still have limits?"

"Of course, but at the start I did it for very different reasons. I believed I deserved to be punished. I welcomed it, and it gave me a greater emotional release than drugs ever did."

"Why would you think you deserved to be punished?"

"Guilt. I was also supposed to be in the car, the day they were shot."

"Survivor's guilt," Swayne said. At last, an aspect she could finally understand. Leigh's manifestation of dealing with it continued to confound her though.

"And your miscarriage?" Swayne probed.

"What about it?" That coldness, that hardness returned, but Swayne now saw through it, saw the hurt that still lay beneath that exterior.

"Was that a result of one of those sessions?" Swayne asked, regretting the question as soon as it was out there, seeing an uncharacteristic flash of fury crossing Leigh's face. Leigh took a deep breath, calming herself.

"No," she answered, "but again, it's where I found solace, and an emotional release."

"Actual physical punishment because again you believed you deserved it," Swayne stated more than asked. She knew that experience herself all too well. Leigh nodded.

"It was the only way I knew how to cope with what happened. In a way I was relieved, and I felt so guilty about that. Matt and I were too young, but he ..."

"He let you down," Swayne finished for her. "Wasn't as supportive as you'd hoped." Leigh nodded again. "What did you do?"

"I left. Came back here, to Frankfurt, to find some clarity, and reassess my life, my choices."

"And that clarity included?"

Leigh's growing smirk answered her.

"So you enjoyed the torture back at Huntington then."

"No." Leigh's answer was adamant. "They're two very different situations. The torture *is* abuse. It's designed to break a person's psyche, and okay, there's an element of that in the other, the significant difference is consent. It's the difference between breaking down emotional barriers to understanding yourself, as opposed to inflicting pain for the sake of extracting information. And the application of pain is entirely different," she added with a smile. Swayne continued to shake her head at the very notion of it all.

"Are either Jake, or Karl...?" she began.

"I doubt it. That place freaked them both out."

"They're both in love with you, did you know that?" A frown appeared and disappeared just as quickly from Leigh's face. "Do you love either of them?" Swayne continued. The frown returned, along with a cold look in her eyes.

"It's not an emotion I'm familiar with," Leigh admitted.

"I feel sorry for you," Swayne said.

"Don't," Leigh answered.

"But how can you live your life like this, so cut off, from people, from emotions?"

"Who says I'm cut off? Who says I haven't already done all that, possibly to excess, that what you perceive as restrained is by choice, and I'm content with that choice."

"You're too young to be this jaded."

"Who says I'm jaded?"

"And that shy kid?"

"She's always here, but she's learned, I've learned, to live my life one day at a time, one experience at a time, and not be overwhelmed by anything, be it an event, a situation or an emotion. This lifestyle, and Jürgen, taught me that. Do I like Jake? Do I enjoy being with him? Yes, very much."

"And Karl?"

"I enjoy being with him too, but they're very different men."

"You're not submissive at all, are you," Swayne guessed, and Leigh shook her head with a small smile.

Swayne continued to regard this young woman, at odds with her own set of moral standards and values, and yet still a good person, damaged and hardened by life. Then again, they all were, Swayne surmised, all with different ways of dealing with it. She fuelled her own healing by fighting for, and defending those even more helpless than herself. Jake channelled his into his work, building a reputation for his dogged determination. Karl? She didn't know him that well, but a brief and polite conversation with the man, revealed a sharp mind and wit, and he seemed genuine, not setting off her bullshit detector. That surprised her about him, that a renowned terrorist could also be that charming and attractive. Another victim of this whole tragic affair.

"I'll pray for you," Swayne said, and Leigh heard the pity in her voice. It wasn't patronising. The woman believed Leigh needed saving from this lifestyle.

"What? Five Our Father's and a decade of the rosary?" she shot back, barely managing to keep the cutting edge from her voice.

"Don't mock the power of God, and his ability to heal that pain," Swayne answered. It had been her own salvation, and while she wouldn't normally evangelise, she felt Leigh had lost her way in this world. Leigh's reaction startled her.

"Then don't disrespect my lifestyle, or my choices," Leigh said, keeping her voice even, though it lowered to a dangerous tone. "Just because you cannot comprehend it, it doesn't give you the right to belittle it, to dismiss it as something aberrant, or disrespect it." Swayne took a breath to steady herself. That steely authority showed itself again, only this time directed at her, and she didn't like being on the receiving end of it. Only the sound of traffic below broke the silence.

"We're done here," Leigh told her quietly, dismissing the older woman. While she wouldn't treat anyone in such a fashion, she felt it safer to end the conversation, before it deteriorated into something neither of them wanted.

Swayne felt dismissed, not rudely, but again with that iron authority, the same assuredness and authority Swayne herself normally wielded. And if this young woman was becoming more like her father, Swayne dreaded to think what he'd truly been like.

Chapter 51

A reconciliation process must have ensued in the early hours of the morning, Swayne concluded. With no sign of life when she arose, she checked the only other bedroom in the apartment, and found the three sleeping soundly, Leigh in the middle, and Swayne shuddered to think of the persuasion methods she might have employed. Nor did she think Jake would subject himself to that. But she'd been wrong about Leigh.

She put coffee on to brew, finding a well-stocked larder in the apartment. That it also belonged to Leigh surprised her. Not Leigh directly, but her company which amounted to the same thing. Another facet to the girl, this entrepreneurial side.

She thought on Leigh's words from the previous night, of that restraint, and by choice. While Swayne couldn't bring herself to condone the girl's lifestyle and other tastes, she seemed a grounded individual, reaching a level of understanding in life that most never achieved. She no longer fought the unfairness and injustice of life, she just made the most of it, and accepted it. That she said she took one day at a time also spoke volumes. it was the motto of every recovering addict and alcoholic, everyone knowing and understanding the daily struggle not to slip back into old habits. That Leigh substituted something for drugs was not unusual, just her substitution was not of the run-of-the-mill variety. Still, last night's adventure was the first in over three years, so there was hope for the child.

With the coffee brewed, Swayne sat at the table, and took the opportunity to read through the document that affected so many lives, now that it was intact. Jake inserted the pages Leigh withheld, and he'd rearranged the document. Swayne now understood why Leigh kept them separate. In the wrong hands they were damning, and perfect fodder for blackmail, but she used them to her advantage in dealing with the two men. The child had been correct, they knew perfectly well what they were doing at the time, and seemed to have no hesitation in doing whatever they deemed necessary. It made the betrayals more agonising. That after becoming… Had they become lovers, or just used each other? Their reactions and body language now suggested they had, but it explained the depth of the betrayal Jake felt, thinking his lover at the time attempted to kill him with a bomb. Likewise with Karl, his former lover making it a personal mission to hunt him down and kill him, all the time not knowing who he really was, or the why of it.

Upon their arrival in the apartment, Swayne insisted they revert to English, tired and pissed off at being excluded from the conversation, but she got more than she bargained for, listening into what she referred to as their bickering. Before Leigh's return they'd had a standoff, at one point even pulling their weapons on each other, and only Swayne's intervention stopped one of them from taking a bullet. She took the guns from them, unfamiliar with weapons, and surprised by their weight as she took them to her room. She returned to overhear Karl's admission to grieving for Jaran, continuing to do so right up until the moment he discovered who Jake really was. Swayne suspected more going on between them, and Leigh's outburst confirmed her suspicions.

Swayne also understood why Leigh hadn't brough the documents to Huntington. Lantry was behind it all, and behind Jonathan and his murder. Dear sweet Jonathan, she thought, forcing back tears. She focused on the document, at the twists and turns this sordid story took. And Leigh accurately guessed her father's connection to Jonathan's wife; using her to get to Jonathan. Lantry assigned Lee to watch Jonathan, told him Jonathan was suspected of involvement with illegal arms trading, but that hadn't been true, Lantry set Jonathan up. Lee started to unravel the scheme, realising Jonathan was not the criminal mastermind he was made out to be, and Lee delved deeper than anyone intended, only to find Lantry was using Jonathan to make contact with the necessary people and using Lee to put pressure on Jonathan to get results. Oh, there were notes about Jake, or Jaran, and references to Karl's naïve blunders like blurting everything to Lantry. It got a lot more complicated than that, but that was Swayne's summary.

Swayne let the document drop onto the table top, and wondered how Lantry felt having his nemesis's child under his control. Did he realise she really wasn't? Did he know she plotted against him, the same as her father? That Lee still operated for the greater good, for justice, restored Swayne's faith in the man. Yes, young Leigh had that moral compass, but Swayne knew people were not so easily categorised. Karl was another case in point. Jake called him a terrorist, but Karl wanted to know how well Jake would stick to his moral high ground when he got burned, and left in the cold to fend for himself.

Jake entered, scrubbing his tousled hair, still looking sleepy, interrupting her thoughts.

"Hey," he greeted her, making a beeline for the coffee.

"I see you all kissed and made up," she commented.

"I wouldn't go that far," he said.

"And a three-some."

"It's not what you think," he answered.

"Oh, and what do I think?"

He chuckled at her.

"You're still in shock over Leigh's…. thing, but before you jump to any weird and wonderful conclusions, she didn't tie us up and beat us into submission. We just talked… intensely." He chose his words carefully and economically. That he'd expressed his own curiosity about her predilection to Leigh, didn't need to be known. That she indulged his curiosity during the night, definitely didn't need to be out there. He knew Swayne's feelings on the matter.

"And Karl?"

"He… ah… joined in on the conversation at one point."

"Conversation about what?" Once again her level and manner of questioning reminded him of his grandmother.

"Well, for starters, what happened after we were evicted from Huntington."

"We weren't evicted. I had to get back to Brussels."

"Yeah, with the oh-so convenient call after the renegotiations concluded, and the visa program restarted. We were removed."

"But why?"

"We were in the way, and asking too many questions."

"About what?" she asked, and he cocked his head at her. "Leigh?"

"As well as Jonathan," he said.

"So what did happen to her?"

"How much do you want to know? Or as Leigh would say, do you want the Hollywood blockbuster, or the Reader's Digest version?"

"Give me the blockbuster," she answered. He laughed, and sat up on the worktop thinking of the differences between the two women, Leigh's clinical conciseness and Swayne's all the trimmings.

"She admitted meeting Karl in London, but she says he helped break the code. Then, as you already know, I helped her get back to Ireland, and it turns out the code was correct."

"Why didn't she tell you?"

"Because she went to confront Karl. He'd unwittingly tipped Lantry off that Lee was investigating the situation with Jonathan."

"She would've killed him?"

Jake shrugged and sipped his coffee.

"Who knows. She was pretty pissed with him. Before she returned home though, she took a detour. Of the numbers on the last page, one of them is to Jürgen's tattoo place and she recognised it, so she made contact with him, and he agreed to hold onto the document for her."

"Why would she do that?"

"She'd already disappeared three times, including the time we went to Manchester. Lantry had no control over her anymore. She refused to answer his calls, or in the case of London, didn't even bring her phone with her. She expected trouble when she got back, and wasn't disappointed."

"This Barnett guy."

"Yep, such a charming man. I believe Leigh when she said he hit first. He'd hit her before, the first time I met her in Shannon. He kicked me out of the room when I tried interviewing her, but I got to witness him assault her because she back answered him. She knew Lantry didn't trust her, and that he'd send his enforcer to do the dirty work."

"And back at Huntington?"

"I believe Lantry sanctioned her *'interrogation'*. Brute force was probably the only way he'd get anything out of her."

"Not realising she probably enjoyed it."

He frowned at her.

"She didn't, but her experiences probably gave her the edge to deal with it, to withstand it. With a beating like that, based on the bruising and cuts, I'd have broken down, told them anything they wanted to know."

"And after we left?"

"She got more of the same. He put her on an intense training programme, and I know about those. Lantry put me through a few of them, so I know he subjected her to some behaviour modification techniques, using pain to adjust her behaviour. Those, she probably did perversely enjoy, and maybe that's why she went to that club, to release all the shit that happened in the only way she knew how. Restore the system settings." Swayne knew that last phrase came from Leigh. No one else spoke or referred to events in life in computer terms like she did.

Karl appeared, looking as sleepy as Jake, and a little less dressed than his American counterpart.

"Fraulein," he greeted her. At least she recognised that word. Jake handed him a mug of coffee, and she guessed the conversation must have been extremely intense for Jake to serve him, without pouring the hot contents all over him.

"Okay, back to the blockbuster," she told him, grimacing at the heaped spoonfuls of sugar Karl added to his coffee. "Specifically how you two met." The men glanced at each other.

"Which part?" Jake asked.

"Yours first," she said, then turned to Karl. "We already know most of yours from that document, and the other journals, but if you don't mind filling in the blanks later?"

He nodded and sat opposite her. The noise of running water distracted them for a moment as the shower kicked in.

"I was working on those stolen numbers, when some of them surfaced here in Europe, and I wanted to do field work."

"And you could speak German, that had to help," she interrupted.

"Apparently there was a connection between the numbers and this arms trade thing, but the Deputy Director of Operations in the UK would only work with the US if they sent an agent over, and I fit the bill."

"German speaking, and young enough to fit into an army barracks without drawing attention to yourself," she said, and Jake nodded. "But...," she started and stopped.

"What?"

"You said before, that your assignment was to get close to and eliminate Karl, but you didn't do that. Why not?" she asked. Jake glanced at Karl, and found the older man watching him intently.

"I got conflicting commands," Jake answered. "Lantry wanted him eliminated, but for my own Agency, the numbers were more important. I had to get close, find out what he knew, how he was involved."

"I had nothing to do with those numbers," Karl said. "Not back then. This time, for the European visas, they were supplied by Medlington."

"And if history is repeating itself, he must have been given them by Lantry," Jake concluded. Karl nodded in agreement.

"What would Lantry have to gain?" Swayne asked.

"That's what I'm hoping we'll find in the safe deposit box," Leigh answered, as she entered the room, dressed in her trademark suit, her damp hair curling. Swayne expected her to brazenly parade her naked body, her tattoos and piercings, but was relieved to find the Leigh she knew coming back. Leigh went straight for the coffee, one hand stroking Jake's knee, as she poured a mug with the other.

"You okay?" she asked him, and he gave her a shy boyish smile. Obviously something more than just talking happened last night, Swayne concluded.

"You know which one?" Karl asked, and she nodded.

"You were right about it being a German bank. After I left you, I checked the International Banking Number system." Karl began to rise. "I'm bringing Jake with me." She stopped him, and saw his face harden in anger. "Jürgen recognised you yesterday, and you're wanted in seventeen different countries. How long do you think it would take the BND to find you? Do you have any idea how long it took me to find an apartment like this? I don't need it compromised. It's my base for meeting clients."

Swayne gave her a questioning look.

"Software solution clients," Leigh informed her. Jake eased himself off the worktop.

"I'll grab a quick shower," he said, removing himself from the room. Leigh moved closer to Karl.

"Until we can get this sorted, it's too dangerous for you, especially here." She stroked his face, her thumb tracing along the line of a clenched jaw muscle. "I won't leave you out of this either. As soon as we have whatever dad left, we'll be back."

He seemed mollified by her promise, and nodded. She leaned in closer, and kissed him. For a young woman who declared to be unfamiliar with love, that kiss belied her words, as it lingered on, passionately.

"And put some clothes on," Leigh said, loud enough for Swayne to hear. "She already thinks my clients are men I beat to a messy pulp, I can't have her thinking I'm also running a male brothel."

The wait was agonising, and Karl began to think something had gone wrong. A myriad of scenarios ran through his mind. Had they been captured? Had she lied to him about involving him? Had she dragged Jake back to Jürgen's place? Lee had been into that freaky shit too. How odd that Leigh dabbled in it as well. Honestly, he didn't think predilections like that were hereditary in nature. Had Lee taken her to more than just the tattoo place that time? Had he taken her to *that* place? And if so, was it Karl's fault she fell into Jürgen's clutches?

He'd been held up in Serbia, on the wrong side of the border, unable to get out. He had to contact Lee. Who else could he trust to do the pick-up? He'd no idea Leigh would be dragged along as well. God, what was happening to him? Since she'd re-entered his life, the guilt for past mistakes just kept mounting, and now he had this American woman on his case as well.

Oh, she was well-meaning, and her heart was in the right place, but he found her a nagging and overbearing mothering type. Yes, he replied to her demand for answers about the bombing in Brussels, he regretted the death of the other American Senator, but in his defence he'd been requested to teach Perry a lesson at the time. It was a miscalculation of many variables, resulting in tragic consequences.

And he couldn't escape her. Leigh was right, he couldn't venture out, particularly as Jürgen recognised him, and knew he was somewhere in the city. Chances were German Intelligence were already looking for him. Would her apartment be found? She'd gone to great lengths to make it difficult to associate her name with this place. Why? He'd wondered, but her explanation boiled down to simple economics and market branding, Leigh Harte, the exclusive software developer, wouldn't be connected to the little girl who dabbled in... well, he really didn't want to know. But if her expertise in security systems and secrecy were anything to go by, then he was probably safe enough, except for his inability to escape Swayne.

He heard the door open, and he stuck his head out from her office, the smallest bedroom converted into a base of operations, and the only place where he could hide from that woman. Jake entered alone, shutting the door behind him.

"Where's Leigh?" Karl asked.

"She's not back yet?" Jake countered. Karl shook his head.

"What happened?" he demanded.

"We picked up a surveillance team when we left the bank," Jake explained. "So we decided to split up. I took as many detours as I could before I lost them, but I thought she'd have gotten back before me."

Karl shook his head again.

"Did you get the documents?"

"Yeah, we divided them before we split up," Jake answered, opening the satchel Karl loaned him for the purpose. Karl followed him into the living area, and together they began sifting through the bundles of paper, some bound with string, others loose but snapped elastic bands suggested they'd been held together, before the rubber aged and gave way. Karl found an envelope addressed to Leigh, and he recognised Lee's handwriting. He stared at it, wondering what it could contain, and curiosity at what Lee had to say burned in him.

But it was not addressed to him. Lee had not confided in him, but in his daughter, the one dragged into this world, and dragged into it by Lee, despite his written protestations to the contrary. If he'd designed all this with her in mind, making her the only one likely to work it all out, he must've known her ultimate fate was to become embroiled it in all. He was the one to blame for her being here, now, in the middle of all this.

Lee had been his mentor, his father figure and his best friend, but the years and nostalgia didn't dull or skew the reality of who and what that man really was; a highly intelligent, highly trained agent, who excelled at what he did, manipulating and manoeuvring people, whenever and wherever necessary. He had a softer side, was a gentle and caring father, but would that stop him from manipulating his own child, using her to exact his revenge? Karl loved Lee, very much, for the kindness he'd given him, the stable home and family life he'd provided, but Karl was under no illusions about the man's callous capabilities.

He put the envelope to one side on the table, doing his best to ignore it. Swayne tried to join in, but Jake sent her packing, with a firm tone, before he returned to scanning the documents. He found the ones he wanted to see, the ones relating to the bomb in Germany. Karl knew when he did, the younger man went still and his jaw tightened. Taking that particular batch of papers, he spread them out on the worktop and went over them in meticulous detail, until he straightened and rubbed the back of his neck.

"Well?" Karl asked, putting back a page into its relevant bundle.

"It was meant for you," Jake admitted.

"By whom?"

"Lantry," Jake told him, turning to hand him the document to go with his claim. There'd been no email back then, but Lee got his hands on a copy of the official order. Lantry's signature was at the bottom of it, but Karl read the direction given. Lantry declared him an eminent threat, that he had to be removed at all costs, but with an American operative also being a potential liability, adding that, while not officially sanctioned, there would be no questions or consequences to his termination as well.

"I'm getting a perverse sense of satisfaction in knowing he failed on both counts," Karl said, handing it back.

"That bastard sat by my hospital bed, whispering into my ear whenever I was conscious, telling me over and over again that you did this to me, until all I wanted to do was tear you limb from limb."

"That explains a lot," Karl said. "Not so subtle subliminal programming under medication, no wonder you pursued me with such zeal." Jake pressed the heel of his hands into his eyes, trying to alleviate the mounting tension growing there.

"Leigh was right when she said I needed the journals to be wrong," he admitted. Dropping his hands, he stared at Karl.

"Why?" Karl asked.

"Because it meant... it now means that I've wasted my life chasing after the wrong man, and all that time it was... And then you tell me you never stopped grieving. Have you any idea how that makes me feel?"

"I imagine confused, conflicted... Angry?"

"Or D: all the above. When she said I did whatever I had to do to get close... you're still the only man... I..."

"I know, and aside from that time with her father, you were, well..."

Slight movement registered at their periphery, and they found Leigh leaning against the doorjamb, arms folded, looking amused.

"Ah, I thought you were about to kiss and make up, or make out, whichever. Either's good," she joked, but both men backed away.

"Where the hell did you come from?" Jake demanded, trying to deflect from what almost happened.

"Through the front door," she answered smartly.

"You've a nasty habit of sneaking up on people," he accused her.

"What? As opposed to you two stomping about."

"You managed to lose the surveillance team?" Jake asked.

"Eventually. It took a few taxi switches and tram detours, but yeah." She sounded tired, and held out a backpack.

"This is the rest of it?" Karl asked, and she nodded. "And there's a letter for you," he added.

Chapter 52

No decryption, or code breaking was required. Written in her father's flowing script, the letter was dated the day they died. Karl also found the original envelope used to post it to the bank, and he didn't know who was more nervous about it, him or her, but instead of ripping it open as he would have done, she took her time, perhaps mentally preparing for it.

She left the men to sort through the rest of the documents, and bundled herself back into the oversized coat, disappearing out to the balcony again, with a large serving of white wine, and opened the letter. The glue of the envelope had disintegrated, and she easily prised the seal open, taking out the thick pages. Taking a fortifying sip of wine, she opened the pages out.

> Leigh
>
> If you're reading this and I hope it is you, then well done on breaking the codes. I couldn't be prouder of you at this moment, and you're the only one I could trust to figure this out.
>
> If you're reading this, then you've also become embroiled in this world, the one that I've tried to shield you from. I hope you're strong enough to withstand the demands that this lifestyle takes.
>
> Anyway, sentimentalities aside, you're reading this because I'm dead. Tom has been making far too many visits of late, too many enquiries about our plans. He knows your mother and I are planning a drive today, and both experience and gut instinct tells me something's wrong. Tom's not a subtle man, he wouldn't be asking questions like that, and that's why I suspect an attack. If it turns out I'm jumping at shadows, well, then you wouldn't be reading this letter after all.
>
> As for Karl? Why don't I send this to him instead of you? To be honest I don't expect he will survive. I don't know, if by the time you get to read this, whether you'll remember him or not, but while he's like a

son to me, and he's intelligent with good instincts, I'm afraid his naivety and innocence will ultimately get him killed. He just barely escaped an assassination attempt. He has allowed another agent get close to him. I've only just learned that agent wasn't German but American. I tell you this to point out just how dangerous and devious Lantry is, how he'll use everything and everyone, and he'll use them against you without a moment's hesitation.

I won't explain everything here. If you're clever enough to get this far then all the evidence, the surveillance photos, copies of the orders, well, I know you'll piece it together and work this out.

What you do with it is up to you, but I hope you'll do the right thing, and see justice served. If I die today, believing in that, believing in you, then I'll die a happy man, and a proud father.

Goodbye my sweetheart.

As with the letter that started this all, she allowed tears to fall. She reread it a few times, but as ever, her dad's words were concise. There was no point in trying to infer or extract any double meanings or hidden messages. Feeling the cold, she snuggled into the coat and finished the wine, feeling the sting of icy tears on her cheeks. She returned to the warmth. Jake was missing, but Karl waited up for her.

"You okay?" he asked, allowing her to come to him. She nodded, tired and drained, and handed him the letter. Leaving him to read, she got another glass of wine, pouring one for him.

"Jake?" she asked when he reached the end.

"Asleep," he answered, accepting the proffered drink. "I don't know whether to be pissed at Lee for thinking I wouldn't make it, or be smugly satisfied I exceeded his expectations."

"Go with smug satisfaction," she advised. "Judging by how he thought of you I don't think he'd mind being proven wrong."

"There are times when you're so like him, and then you do something that's uniquely you, and the shy little kid comes back."

"And?"

"As much as I loved your father, don't turn into him."

"I might need your guidance on that." She smiled at him, that shy, self-conscious smile she had when she let her barriers down. He leaned in and kissed her, felt her kissing back with passion. He pulled back.

"And you needn't think you can do that bondage shit with me," he whispered. "Just because Jake let you tie him up and be abused..."

"Jake got the kindergarten version," she said.

"The answer's still no."

"And that's fine, but he did ask. What exactly happened tonight with you two?" she asked, experiencing a twinge of regret as his barrier went back up. She straddled him, facing him. "Whatever it is, you can tell me." She stroked his face, similar to how she'd touched him that morning. He searched her face for any sign of anger or jealousy. All he found was concern, and curiosity.

"I'd never been attracted to a man before, or since. Even with your dad, it was just a role, but with Jaran... I don't know, maybe you're right, that I was vulnerable, but I think he was too. It was his first assignment, and he was only nineteen years old. I was twenty-four before I did a solo run, and even then I pissed myself I was so nervous. Maybe we were just two guys who found comfort in each other at the time."

"And tonight?"

"With Lee's evidence, we finally learned the truth and discovered we had a common enemy, and it wasn't each other."

"And the old feelings came back," she stated, and he nodded. "And that's perfectly alright too," she added, as he pulled her closer.

Chapter 53
Ireland

For a man employed in security and policing, she found it disappointingly easy getting into Tom's house. She hoped for more of a challenge. Not even lo-tech stuff to hinder her breaking into his home, harbouring the ridiculous notion that, as a Garda, it could never happen to him. She took her time wandering from room to room, ensuring she touched nothing, but even where she did, her gloves ensured she left no fingerprints. She found no sense of extravagance, this house as plain as the man himself, and just as devoid of character. If lack of a challenge getting into his house disappointed her, she entertained no illusions about the potential wait in store for his return. His movements were unpredictable. He was not a creature of habit, or a slave to a regular schedule.

She selected a spot in which to sit and wait for him, a concealed chair where she'd at least be comfortable. She sat in the dark, toying with the tip of a syringe, the needle tucked up the sleeve of her coat, containing the means with which to subdue him. In the time spent waiting, she reflected on everything that happened within such a short space of time, less than a year. Funny to think how much her entire life changed. She'd learned a great deal about herself. While there'd always been deep and dark places in her, she only visited them on rare occasions, and under Jürgen's expert guidance. Now, she knew those deep and dark places were not to be avoided, not to be shunned as dangerous. They were to be embraced and accepted, for in there lay surprising strength and power. In under a year, she'd grown physically and emotionally stronger, no longer fighting against those fearful depths, but instead finding a sense of peace. Now she understood how her dad managed the two divergent aspects of his life, and she continued to mull it all over as she waited.

Getting out of Germany proved more difficult than getting in. Karl had his own means, and neither Leigh nor Jake asked questions. If compromised, they couldn't tell what they didn't know. Despite a desire to return to Jürgen's for one last jaunt, Leigh understood that she could never go back. Not even when this current situation was resolved. When this finished, she promised herself, she'd walk away, but agents never retired.

Jake and Swayne got back to Brussels with little fuss, though they gained a surveillance team at the train station in Cologne. Leigh was left to her own devices, and travelled in a similar fashion as Jake and Swayne. Her journey took longer as she zigzagged across Europe, before making it to Paris, and getting the Eurostar to the UK.

Back in the safety of the EU commission, Swayne used her powers of persuasion and position to get talking to the right people. Copies of Lee's evidence made it into the right hands after a decade and a half, and Leigh took a leaf from her father's book, locking the originals away again, somewhere different. Yet Swayne's efforts didn't stop Leigh from being picked up by agents from the Home Office at Folkestone as she tried to pass through immigration. If she expected a rough time, they dashed her expectations. Instead, they treated her with courtesy, questioned her, not interrogated, even asked for her opinion. Swayne's words must have been powerful.

Sanctioned by the Home Office, she now sat with a sense of peace in Tom's house. They didn't need the details of her planned operation, but as it transpired, her father only scratched the surface. His evidence was enough to warrant bringing the situation to a swift conclusion. The full extent of Lantry's activities would never be realised, nor the reasons behind it. Was it for personal gain? To expand his own power base, his efforts to keep terrorism and espionage alive and well? Or was it out of amusement? A trial was out of the question. It would be lengthy and embarrassing for the government, for many governments. No, the final sanction was the only solution, and Leigh wanted in, wanted to follow through and respect her father's final wish. She wanted to see justice done. And if Lantry had to be brought to bear, then so did Tom. She volunteered for this, assured them she could carry it out, and her calmness surprised her.

She heard the door opening, and she took a breath, released it, keeping her mind clear and on the task ahead of her. He didn't turn the lights on, didn't need to in this sparsely furnished place. He bypassed where she sat, heading for the kitchen, and she heard him moving about, getting something to eat, by the sounds of it. She took her time, giddiness and excitement rising. She wanted to take her time, wanted to do this right and wanted to enjoy it. He never knew what hit him as he felt a sting in his neck, and darkness overtook him.

An ache in his arms, and fuzziness, disorientated him more, as he tried to move and shake his head, but his throat tightened. Worse, pressure and pain grew around his groin, and around his feet and legs. And he was cold, so cold. As the day lightened, the drugs wore off, and he realised the full horror of his predicament.

He found himself in a wooded area, bound and naked, his bare feet on the ground but with his knees bent. The rope painfully kept his legs together as his heels rubbed off his ass, while his arms were folded behind him, bound in a similar way. But it was the rope around his neck that caused the most concern. Struggling against it made it tighten, but it also seemed to cause more tightening of the knots of the rope wrapped around his groin.

Movement in the trees drew his attention, and as Leigh approached, several things went through his mind. Had she done this? Why? How? She hunkered down in front of him, and he renewed his struggling, despite the adverse effect, and he gasped for breath.

"This is the art of rope bondage, Tom," she told him. "The more you fight it, the tighter it gets. Now, if that's what gets you off, then go for it, but the knots will tighten themselves around your dick and neck, and will choke you to death." He stopped struggling and glared at her.

"You're a fucking perverted freak, just like your old man," he growled at her, and to his horror she smiled, that same cold, callous smile as Lee's.

"Why, thank you, Tom," she said, toying with him.

"Why?" he asked.

"Because you killed them," she replied. He shook his head.

"No, I had nothing to do with it." He sounded desperate, and he realised he no longer knew her. She was no longer the kid he'd tried knocking sense into all those years ago. If she was turning into him, then what she was capable of? That smile, cold as it was, faded to something even harder.

"We both know that's not entirely true. You told him where to find them." Again, he tried to shake his head, to deny her accusation.

"I... I didn't ... I thought he wanted to warn him,"

Her expression said, in no uncertain terms, that she didn't believe him. She heard movement behind her, but didn't turn to look. She'd been expecting them to arrive, and the look on Tom's face was worth watching.

"I'm sure you remember Karl," she said.

"He's the one," Tom gasped. "He's responsible!" Leigh shook her head. Jake, in the company of Karl, surprised him more. Lantry told him, assured him, the two were arch-enemies, but here they stood, side by side, comrades in arms, and awaiting Leigh.

"Let me introduce my other companion," she said to Tom.

"I already know who he is," he snapped back, his fight and defiance returning.

"I doubt it, Lantry was careful not to tell anyone. This is Jaran Baenleaski." The name registered with Tom, and he looked up at Jake with a renewed expression of horror. It was now coming full circle, but to his surprise Leigh stood, and walked away.

"You can't leave me like this," he called after her, watching as Karl took her outstretched hand to help her step over a fallen tree trunk. The scene was surreal. She half-turned back to Tom at his outcry.

"Oh yes I can Tom. I can already see the headlines, 'Senior Detective dies in compromising auto-erotic perverted wooded sex scene.' Who'll ask questions?" The hardness in which she spoke to him chilled him to the core, almost making her father seem warm. Knowing what the ropes would do, he still renewed his fight against them. The rope at his throat and groin tightened, causing him pain and difficulty in breathing. He blacked out, and she stepped away.

"Will that kill him?" Karl asked, and she shook her head.

"No, it'll just continue to make him black out from lack of air. Despite what I told him, the knots aren't designed to kill," she said.

"Are we going to leave him there?" Jake asked. Again she shook her head, taking her weapon out from inside her coat, silencer already in place. Tom's head snapped back from the force of the bullet before his body fell as far forward as the bondage would allow.

"Now we leave him," she answered, picking up the shell casing from the undergrowth, missing the concern and questioning expressions Karl and Jake exchanged with each other.

Chapter 54
Edinburgh

Karl's phone call to Lantry had the desired effect. Having documentation that proved his innocence enticed Lantry to meet him, and Karl picked a quiet enough place, a coffee shop off a side street in the city. And his price for this evidence? Clearing his name. Not a full reinstatement of his former status. That would never happen. He'd been too much of a bad boy over the years to expect that level of clemency. Lantry claimed he needed to see this so-called evidence for himself, to see what he could do. Karl had no illusions. Lantry would burn him the moment he got his hands on the paperwork Lee left, and Lantry asked about the journals. Karl confirmed they existed, that Lee had entrusted him with three of them, but written in a code that Karl couldn't break. Lantry seemed satisfied with the answers and agreed to the meeting.

Karl arrived early, scoping the place out for where best to sit for this secretive liaison. He sat and waited, ordering a cup of tea that turned out to be decent. He recognised the spotter, the agent sent in ahead of Lantry to find if he, the target, had arrived. It was strange to be on the receiving end of this technique, for a change. The spotter sat down two tables away from him, and typed a text message while ordering. Lantry appeared soon after, looking older than Karl remembered, his facial features more etched.

"You've done well for yourself," Lantry opened with as he sat. "I'm not sure if I should be proud, or disgusted, by the level you've attained." Karl remained quiet at the barb, knowing Lantry attempted to goad him into making a mistake. With his target failing to react he decided on a more direct approach. "You have the documents?"

Karl nodded.

"And my immunity from prosecution?" he asked.

"Ah, you know how the big machine works, that takes time."

"Then I'll hold onto these until the big machine turns."

"I'm doing everything I can, but... well, given your activities..."

"I could promise to be a good boy," Karl offered.

"Then give me the documents, and if they're of value, then you have my word. You'll have my protection until the deal is secured." Karl deliberated a moment before sliding the slim envelope across, but not before noticing the spotter leaving, as did two other customers. That left a dark-haired woman and a bearded waiter on the premises.

Swayne made them a promise, impressing Karl by achieving it, but he'd experienced her relentless methods. While he agreed in principle to the plan, he refused to meet with the relevant authorities. Why would he give himself up like that, after evading capture for so long, without written assurances of his safety and freedom? Until he held that document in his hand, he refused to take the risk. Still, he believed and trusted Swayne when she said she held that document, granting him his immunity. Now he faced their nemesis, as the bait for this. Taking his waiter's apron off, Jake locked the door after the spotter left, having received the order to withdraw, the same order given to the team Lantry had in place to shoot Karl when he left.

Lantry tore open the envelope and extracted the single page, puzzled at first to read the word 'Traitor'. He searched for his spotter, startled and disturbed to find him missing. His eyes fell on the dark hair falling to the ground, as Leigh removed the wig and took aim at his heart, and fired. It would kill him, but would take a few moments for the oxygen to stop flowing to his brain. In that time both Karl and Jake took their own shooting stances. They stood close enough together so Lantry would see them. He would die knowing the three lives he'd ruined, manipulated, distorted and twisted, were now responsible for his death.

Epilogue

Only salespeople, and those who didn't know her, used the front door. In spite of the oppressively hot weather, she dressed in a tee shirt and jeans as the doorbell rang again, longer and more insistent, and found the doorstep occupied by two men. A third waited in the SUV, the engine running idle in the drive, but facing the road, ready for a quick and easy getaway. She looked from one to the other.

"Leigh Harte?" one asked.

"Who wants to know?" she countered. The speaker held up his ID that she made a show of scrutinising.

"Department of Defence," he answered, snapping the ID wallet shut, after what he considered more than adequate time for her to check it.

"And?" She continued to act nonplussed, and nonchalant.

"Have you time to talk?"

"I'm in the middle of something."

"Got something on the stove?"

She heard a hint of condescension in the question.

"No, sex-slave shackled to the bed," she replied.

"Funny," he answered without humour, and she bit her bottom lip to rein a smirk in. He handed over a business card that she stared at, but didn't take.

"We received your file from London, the British Home Office sent it over," the second man said.

"And?"

"We're here to offer you a job."

"In DoD?" she asked, and he nodded. "I'll have to think about it."

"Yeah, we were told you might say that," he answered. After a moment of deliberation, she took the proffered card.

They left, and she watched the SUV disappear onto the main road, heading in the direction of Waterford. She returned upstairs just as he emerged from the bathroom, using the towel to dry his hair, not making any effort to preserve his modesty.

"Who was that?" he asked.

"Department of Defence."

"Why?" he asked, a defensive edge to his voice.

"Job offer," she said, re-entering the bedroom.

"And?" he asked to the closing door, as she shut him out, returning her attention to the other one, immobilised, gagged and shackled to the bed.

Printed in Great Britain
by Amazon